NAVY SEAL
TO THE RESCUE

TAWNY WEBER

MILLS & BOON

All rights reserved including the right of reproduction in whole or in part in any form. This edition is published by arrangement with Harlequin Books S.A.

This is a work of fiction. Names, characters, places, locations and incidents are purely imagined and bear no relationship to any real life individuals, living or dead, or to any actual places, business establishments, locations, events or incidents. Any resemblance is entirely coincidental.

This book is sold subject to the condition that it shall not, by way of trade or otherwise, be lent, resold, hired out or otherwise circulated without the prior consent of the publisher in any form of binding or cover other than that in which it is published and without a similar condition including this condition being imposed on the subsequent purchaser.

St Helens Libraries	
3 8055 25003 8106	
Askews & Holts	17-Jan-2019
AF	£3.99

® and ™ are trademarks owned and used by the trademark owner and/or its licensee. Trademarks marked with ® are registered with the United Kingdom Patent Office and/or the Office for Harmonisation in the Internal Market and in other countries.

First Published in Great Britain 2019
by Mills & Boon, an imprint of HarperCollinsPublishers
1 London Bridge Street, London, SE1 9GF

Navy SEAL to the Rescue © 2019 Tawny Weber

ISBN: 978-0-263-27404-2

0219

MIX
Paper from
responsible sources
FSC™ C007454
www.fsc.org

This book is produced from independently certified FSC™ paper to ensure responsible forest management.

For more information visit: www.harpercollins.co.uk/green

Printed and bound in Spain
by CPI, Barcelona

Tawny Weber is the *New York Times* and *USA TODAY* bestselling author of more than forty books. She writes sassy, emotional romances with a dash of humour and believes that it all comes down to heroes. In fact, she's made her career writing about heroes, most notably her popular navy SEALs series. Tawny credits her ex-military alpha husband for inspiration in her writing, and in her life. The recipient of numerous writing accolades, including the RT Reviewers' Choice Award, she has also hit number one on the Amazon and Barnes & Noble bestseller lists. A homeschooling mum, Tawny enjoys scrapbooking, gardening and spending time with her family and dogs in her Northern California home.

Visit Tawny on the web at www.tawnyweber.com. You can also find her on Facebook, Twitter, Pinterest and Goodreads.

www.Facebook.com/TawnyWeber.RomanceAuthor
www.Twitter.com/TawnyWeber
www.Pinterest.com/TawnyWeber
www.Goodreads.com/author/show/513828.Tawny_Weber

ST HELENS LIBRARIES

3 8055 25003 8106

Also by Tawny Weber

Discover more at millsandboon.co.uk

To the amazing ladies at Mills & Boon Heroes.
Thanks so much for letting me join you!

Chapter 1

Costa Rica, baby.

The small beachside town of Puerto Viejo de Talamanca was filled with character. The laid-back, mellow atmosphere was complemented by thatch-roofed buildings, colorful fabrics and hand-lettered signs.

Midstride down the deserted sidewalk, Lila Adrian stopped to close her eyes and take a deep breath of the rich, ocean-scented air. When she opened her big green eyes again, she was thrilled to see that yes, indeed, it was still gorgeous. What was it about the Caribbean that made everything just a little brighter?

God, she loved her job.

As the brains, brawn and chief headhunter of her own business, At Your Service, she was rocking it. She might be meeting clients in San Francisco one day, in London scouting for an art director the next, visiting a tiny village in Tuscany to woo a former prima ballerina the week after that. And now she was cruising Puerto Viejo for a chef.

Wherever the talent was, she went. And then, with charm, guile and a great deal of wit, she enticed that talent into the job of their dreams. Or into believing the job she wanted them to take was dream-worthy.

It'd all started with a few favors, helping a friend find an elite aromatherapy masseuse for her new spa, connecting a concierge doctor she'd once dated with an upscale hotel chain owned by a friend. But it had been introducing three of her father's fired housekeepers to wealthy families who'd welcomed their services that made her realize she could turn it into a career.

Something she'd been desperate for. Not just to prove herself to family members who claimed she didn't have any marketable skills, but to show herself that she was more than a pretty face. With the strings to her trust fund knotted tight, she'd spent most of At Your Service's first three years living on ramen noodles and depending on the local coffeehouse's free Wi-Fi.

But sheer stubbornness, a ton of charm and taking advantage of the varied connections she'd made over the years had finally done the trick.

That, and her family name.

Something she knew pissed her father off to no end.

Loving that small victory, Lila increased her pace to make her way around a pair of locals pedaling their bicycles, with baskets filled with produce.

Now she was in Costa Rica to add another feather to her cap. She didn't figure it'd take an abundance of charm to convince Alberto Rodriguez, formerly of Miami, Florida, and currently the head chef of the aging Casa de Rico, that he'd like to travel the world as the personal chef to the Martins, a wealthy San Francisco banking family.

Mr. and Mrs. Martin—Joe and Mimi, respectively—

had spent a week reveling in Rodriguez's cuisine on their honeymoon. Food so delicious, they often claimed, that they could still taste it a decade later. Lila had followed up their praise with a little research, which assured her that Rodriguez had a great reputation as a chef who could handle upscale gourmet as well as fusion and regional cuisine. The man was wasted in a one-star restaurant that, from all accounts, was on the verge of bankruptcy. Since research turned up no reasons for him to want to stay, she figured he should be more than ready to make a move.

But just in case, Lila had the charm ready to pour on like syrup.

With that in mind, she pulled her cell phone from the front pocket of her capris and opened the web browser to the hotel's website. She'd already committed the details to memory, but she was a believer in double-checking.

Before she could scroll through the page, the phone rang.

Corinne Douglass. Socialite, diva and the best friend Lila had ever met.

"How'd you know I was holding my phone?" Lila answered with a laugh instead of a greeting.

"You're always holding your phone," her sometimes assistant-slash-roommate answered. "Even if it's not in your hand, you're still holding it in some form or other."

"You have a point. What's up?"

"How's Costa Rica?" Corinne asked instead of answering.

Lila frowned at the sidestep, but looked around anyway.

"Gorgeous. The air is just humid enough to be sultry. The sun shining hot enough to sink into the bones. The people are friendly, the locale colorful and, so far, the job is on track."

"Have you met with the chef yet? Is he interested? Are you coming home soon?"

"Not yet, but I'm on my way to the restaurant now. I'm sure he'll be interested, once he hears the deal. And why?" Suspicion laced the last question, but Lila figured it was well deserved. She might be a card-carrying optimist, but she'd never be mistaken for Pollyanna. "Is something wrong?"

"Nothing, really," Corinne hedged. "Just wondering when you'll be back."

"This shouldn't take more than two or three days," Lila estimated. Which she'd told Corinne when the other woman had dropped her at San Francisco International Airport. "Once again, I have to ask, why?"

"Can't a friend check on a friend?" Corinne dismissed her with a light laugh that Lila knew she used only when she was nervous.

"What's wrong? Did you hear from your dad?" Not only did the two women have a taste for designer heels and sappy chick flicks in common, but they also had wealthy families led by overbearing fathers. The only difference was, Corinne wanted her father's attention while Lila wished hers would forget she existed.

"His secretary," Corinne confirmed. Arthur Douglass rarely deigned to dial a phone himself. "Some things came up. He's delayed."

"So no visit to San Francisco?" "Visit" being friend-code for the man taking an extra half hour to have drinks with his daughter at the airport while his private jet refueled.

"No. I offered to meet him in Milan instead, but he has a full schedule. And, well, you know."

She did know. Her friend couldn't afford the trip or to take time off work at the art gallery. Yet another thing she and Corinne had in common was limited funds. Where they diverged was how they dealt with it. Poor Corinne let it bother her, while Lila, well, she didn't. Much.

"Don't let it get you down," she advised. "I'll be home in a few days and we'll go out, hit the clubs, drink like crazy and dance our worries away."

"Guys?"

"Of course." Lila smiled at the two striding past. Tall, sporting swim trunks and surfboards, they grinned back. "It's always more fun to dance with guys who know the moves."

"I wouldn't know. None of the guys I've danced with had much in the way of moves."

"That's because you're always holding out for guys who remind you of your father," Lila said under her breath.

"Yeah, yeah, you always say that," Corinne shot back. But her laugh faded fast enough to send Lila's smile into her toes.

"What else happened?" she asked.

"Well…"

Lila's stomach clenched when Corinne hesitated. Oh, she knew that hesitation.

"It must be the day for fathers. Did mine leave a message when he called?" she asked quietly. Knowing she was going to need a few moments to get herself together before meeting Rodriguez, Lila dropped onto a vivid pink bench in front of a surf club and waited.

"Three, actually," Corinne said, her words tight with discomfort. "He'd like for you to return his call."

"Like me to?"

"Well, more like he demanded that you call. He's arranged a party at the navy base he expects you to attend. Some sort of celebration for your brother." Corinne cleared her throat, then blew out a breath. "He said something about your duty to play hostess, expectations to the family name and, um, maybe something about snits."

Oh, how she'd like to tell her father just where he could shove his snit. Lila had to grind her teeth tight to keep the words from spewing. But the main drag in a small Costa Rican town was hardly the place to mouth off.

"I'll deal with it later," she promised instead. "Right now, I have me a chef to woo."

With that and a goodbye, she tucked her phone away and turned the corner toward Casa de Rico. Lila grimaced when she stopped in front of the restaurant. Heaps of trash spilled out of the alley beside the building, which probably accounted for the smell. The windows were slicked with the same dingy grime as the once-white exterior, giving the whole place a gray coating of neglect. The hand-lettered sign propped into the window claimed that Casa de Rico was open for business, but the silence pouring from the open door didn't indicate that there were many takers.

She'd take that as a sign of management issues and not the chef, she decided, lips quirking. Which would make convincing Rodriguez to change employers all that much easier.

Still, the beachfront location was ideal. But Lila was pretty sure location and the views were the only things the Casa had going for it. The roof was patched in places, and the railing along the balcony so rusted that it reminded her of a rickety old lady wearing black lace. The landscaping was limited to a few scrubby bushes and, again, that beach view.

Which couldn't be discounted, she had to admit. It was a pretty gorgeous view.

Wanting—needing—to absorb it a little more before she went inside to scope out her target in his natural atmosphere, she stepped around the side of the building and started down the wooden walkway. When she reached the soft sand, she stopped to step out of her kitten-heeled slides.

In the act of slipping off the second shoe, she had to grab on to the bleached wooden railing to keep her balance.

Because the view just got a whole lot more interesting.

A man stepped out of the surf, water sluicing off muscles that made her want to raise her hands in praise.

Hello, gorgeous, was all she could think.

Gorgeous, hot and sexy, all rolled into one very muscular, very intense package.

The guy was ripped. From his broad shoulders to his lean calves, he epitomized manly perfection. She knew she was staring, but she'd been raised to believe that a work of art deserved appreciation.

And oh, boy did she appreciate him.

Enough to offer a big smile as he slowly made his way across the sand to his towel.

Her lips twitched when he glared in return.

She was too amused to take offense.

As a woman who'd garnered plenty of ogling over the years, she supposed she could understand his reaction. And while it wasn't like she'd strolled down and grabbed herself a handful of his undeniably pinchable butt, she'd definitely fantasize about licking those drops of water off his flat belly.

But it was lunchtime, and as yummy as he looked, the guy obviously wasn't on the menu. And she had a job to do.

But her gaze—as unwilling to leave as the rest of her—lingered for a few more seconds. She'd never seen a more visually appealing man. Or, she acknowledged, her eyes flicking over his scowl again, a more discouraging one.

Ah, well, she decided with a philosophical sigh.

At least she'd gotten to enjoy the view.

Sun, surf and sex.

Once upon a time, Travis Hawkins would have called that heaven.

Now?

Now, he was convinced it was hell.

He strode out of the silken warmth of the Caribbean, his feet sinking in the wet sand. Wincing, he adjusted his stride when the sand turned to powder, taking the weight off his throbbing knee.

He noted the sexy little blonde standing on the edge

of the beach. She'd poured her petite curves into a pair of white pants that stopped short of her ankles and a silky red tank that fluttered intriguingly in the light breeze. With her hair clipped up and back, he couldn't tell its length, but he was imagining it was long. Mostly because he had a thing for long blond hair.

Just like he had a thing for confident women. He could tell this one was just that from the way she stood there, dangling her shoes from one hand while the other shaded her eyes. The better to check him out, he supposed. No harm there. He was checking right back.

And what he saw was intriguing.

But he wasn't in the market to be intrigued.

He was in the market to decompress. To make decisions. To figure out the rest of his damned life.

Once upon a time, he'd take the blonde up on the obvious interest on her pixie-like face. He'd have strode on over for a little conversation, a little flirtation. He'd gauge the ground, assess the heat level and if it felt right, he'd have swept her off her sexy little feet and into his bed.

But his sweeping days were over. Hell, all the fun was over. Despite the multiple offers he'd gotten from locals and tourists alike, he wasn't in Puerto Viejo to score.

Travis shifted his weight, carefully balancing on his left foot to ensure he didn't land on his face when he bent over to grab a towel. Pain exploded away, a lightning bolt of misery spearing out from his knee to his hip, down to his toes.

For twelve years, he'd served his country. For ten years, he'd been a SEAL. He'd served with distinction, with honor, with dedication. He'd been welcomed into two different SEAL teams, where he'd played an integral role of dozens of successful missions.

He'd served through pain, sweat, challenge and terror.

He'd freaking loved every minute of it.

He scrubbed the towel over his face, sopping up the moisture pouring off his too-long hair.

One nasty storm, one bad jump from a plane taking a flaming nosedive into the ocean, and his career was over. He was finished.

Freaking finished.

Travis's jaw worked as he glared at the sexy reminder of what he'd lost still looking his way. He deliberately turned away from the blond temptation to stare out at the ocean.

Medical discharge.

Was it ironic or tragic that the ocean he loved, the sea he served, had ended the career he'd revered?

Probably both.

The biggest joke was that he, a man who thrived on contingency plans, had nothing. No backup career, no sideline jobs, not a single idea of what he wanted to do— or more to the point, could do—with the rest of his life once his measly savings ran out.

Once he'd gotten a handle on that, he decided, unable to resist glancing back at the blonde again, he'd be interested in enjoying the finer things in life again.

Because, damn, she really was fine.

Lila told herself she wasn't thinking about the beach hunk as she stepped into the cool restaurant. But she knew he was there, hovering in the back of her mind.

She'd figure out why, later. For now, she looked around the restaurant, assessing her quarry's lair.

The place was empty but for one other couple, and the décor was enough to make her wince. Here they were in the Caribbean, and the owners had fitted this place out to look like an average bar in Anywhere, USA.

A long bar, complete with neon signs and shelves of bottles, covered the back wall. Posters—thumbtacked, not framed—advertised American beer and, for some reason she couldn't figure out, a long-defunct sitcom. Three ceiling fans sent lazy shadows dancing over the dozen tables scattered around the room.

"Hola," a woman from behind the bar greeted her, her black tee stating that Casa de Rico's salsa was the hottest and her name tag reading Dory Parker. "Table for one?"

"Yes, please."

"Have at it," she said, waving one hand to indicate Lila's varied choices before calling for service.

Lila slid behind the table closest to the kitchen with a nice view of the beach. Not the view of the sexy beach hunk, but that was just as well. The man had distraction written all over him.

"Hi," she said as soon as the waitress came over. She was a pretty girl with dark skin and a lip piercing, dressed the same as the bartender except that her shirt proclaimed that their margaritas got you drunker. "I'd love a bottle of water and a menu."

"Got the menu right here," the girl said, handing over a laminated page. "I'll be right back with that water."

Lila glanced at the page only long enough to assure herself that it was the same as the one on their website.

"I've heard that your chef is wonderful," she said as soon as the waitress came back. "Senor Rodriguez, right?"

"Sure, Chef Rodriguez is in the back, cooking up a storm," the waitress said, her vigorous nod sending the bleached dreadlocks bouncing around her round face. "He's good. You'll see. You decide what you want?"

"What's your favorite?" Lila asked, keeping it friendly.

Deciding to take the girl's advice, and since early afternoon lent itself to tapas, Lila ordered a varied selection.

The menu was promising, but she wanted to see for herself if Rodriguez was as good as the Martins remembered. There was no point convincing them if he'd lost his touch.

An hour later—Casa de Rico obviously didn't believe in rushing their diners—Lila had confirmed that Rodriguez was as good as advertised.

What she hadn't figured out was why a chef of his caliber was working in a low-end restaurant like this one. According to her notes, he was in his midfifties, originally from Mexico City, single and childless. He'd worked in various high-end restaurants over the years, with excellent references from all of his previous employers.

It was definitely time to get a few more answers for her files.

"Everything was wonderful," she told the dreadlocked girl when she came to take the last plate. "I'd love to personally thank the chef. Is that possible?"

From the look on her face, it was the first time she'd heard a request like that. But she shrugged and muttered something before heading back to the kitchen.

Since nobody else, including the bartender, was in the room, Lila took a moment to pull out a compact and check her makeup. She refreshed her lipstick, slid one hand over her tidy chignon to make sure no hair had escaped, and decided she'd hit the right note of professionalism. Not always easy when you looked like a blonde Kewpie doll.

"Hola," called out a big voice. It matched the man, who lumbered through a door barely wider than he was and strode across the room. His thick black hair was sprinkled with the same gray that dusted his mustache. Instead of the traditional white chef's attire, he wore blue with a white apron tucked under a gut that proclaimed him a man who loved to eat as much as cook.

"I'm Chef Rodriguez," he greeted, his accent light and musical. "And you must be the woman of excellent taste who enjoyed my food, yes?"

"I am, Chef Rodriguez," she said with a wide smile, rising from her seat to take his hand in hers. "The meal was delicious. I particularly enjoyed the *ceviche tico.*"

"Gracias," he replied, bending so low over her hand that his bushy mustache tickled her knuckles. "It's a pleasure to serve you, senorita."

"Everything was wonderful. Imaginative, delicious and beautifully plated," she told him, laying on the flattery thick and widening her smile in a way she knew highlighted her dimples. Professionalism was still the byword, but with his Old World manners, she figured a smile would go further than a crisp handshake. "And your food is exactly why I'm here in Puerto Viejo."

His dark eyes flashed with curiosity.

"I'm Lila Adrian. We spoke on the phone last week. I'm here on behalf of the Martins."

The friendly smile disappeared, and something that looked like panic burned away the flirtatious ease on his face. He gaze shifted left, skittered right before returning to her face. His smile reemerged, much stiffer and less friendly.

"This is a bad time, senorita. And the wrong place for a discussion such as the one you're inviting."

"Okay," Lila said agreeably, despite her surprise at his extreme reaction. Especially given that during their phone conversation, he'd been the one to suggest she come to the restaurant to negotiate the employment terms.

Over the years, she'd seen plenty of people who didn't want their current bosses to know they were being scouted, but most usually used it as a bargaining tool. For better money out of her client if they left, or better conditions from their boss if they stayed. He'd given a different impression over the phone, but she could play the game.

"That's fine," she said agreeably. "Would you prefer to meet elsewhere? Perhaps Luca's, in the Hotel Azure? I'd be happy to take you to dinner and discuss the Martins' proposal."

They both glanced over as a party of four came into the restaurant with a woman who stationed herself behind the bar. They all appeared harmless enough to Lila, but Rodriguez looked like he'd seen a group of ghosts. His eyes widened so much that the dark circles beneath almost disappeared. He wet his lips before calling out a command that had the waitress scurrying out to seat the newcomers.

"Excuse me," the chef murmured, snagging the tray holding her check and credit card off the table and hurrying to the small station by the bar. His eyes kept bouncing between the new diners, the bartender and Lila as he ran her card.

Curious, Lila watched along with Rodriguez as the newcomers were seated, menus handed out, but none of them glanced their way or yelled boo. But Rodriguez sure looked spooked when he came back with her credit card and receipt. He was so focused on watching the new diners, he almost hit her in the face with the tray.

"Chef?" she finally said, drawing his attention back to her. "Would it be convenient to meet at my hotel?"

"No, no. Nowhere else." Swiping the back of his hand over his sweating upper lip, Rodriguez looked over at the bartender, then at the new diners again, then shook his head. "Here is fine. Here is better. Come back later."

"Okay…"

"The restaurant closes at 1:00 a.m., but the bar is still open. Meet me then."

For the first time, Lila hesitated. Traveling around the world to chase down unique employees for eccentric clients might not be considered the safest career ever heard of. But meeting anyone in a strange town in a foreign country in the middle of the night was pure stupidity.

"How about tomorrow morning instead? Perhaps before the restaurant opens, around 8:00 a.m.?"

His jaw worked, the grinding making his mustache flutter. Finally, Rodriguez gave a jerky nod.

"Make it six. We open early. Go to the office, though. Not the kitchen."

There was something in his voice that sent a shiver up and down her spine. Which was silly. Lila had been traveling—and doing damn near everything else in her life—alone for a decade without any problems.

But spine shivers weren't to be discounted, so she'd take precautions, she decided. And everything would be fine.

"Tomorrow at six, then. Here's my number. Please, call my cell if you need to change anything," she requested, folding the receipt and putting it and her credit card in her bag before handing him an embossed ivory business card.

"Yes, yes, fine." His face creased with worry, he made a shooing motion with his hands. "Go, now. Go."

Okay, then.

Lila went.

Right down to the beach in search of Mr. Muscles, the hottie she'd like to get up close and personal with.

Lila wasn't sure if it was still lingering irritation over word of her father's nagging, or if it was frustration over Rodriguez playing hard to get.

But she suddenly wanted a drink. And having it with a sexy hard body would have made that all better.

But while there were plenty of hard bodies and bare skin lounging on the sand, riding on the surf, the hottie was nowhere to be found.

Figured.

Chapter 2

Stars scattered over the night sky like buckshot against black velvet. Music rolled out of Casa de Rico's doors, blending with the crickets' serenade to the fall of night.

Another day over and done with, and not a damned thing to show for it. He hadn't even come up with a freaking hint of an idea of what to do with the rest of his damned life.

A beer tucked between his thighs, the braided cotton strands of the hammock digging into his flesh, Travis waited for the tension to leave his body. He'd been waiting so long, he considered it a miracle that he still believed it could happen.

Maybe he should have tried a little harder with the blonde on the beach earlier. A bout or three of hot, sweaty sex would have relaxed him a little.

Maybe it was time to give up the beach and head somewhere else. He just couldn't quite work up the enthusiasm to figure out where.

"Yo, Hawk."

"Yo, Manny," Travis returned laconically, lifting a hand to greet the beanpole of a man so dark that he blended with the night. All but the brilliant white of that smile he was always flashing.

"You had phone calls. I took messages."

"Thanks, man," Travis said, taking the scraps of paper he didn't want.

"One is from Paulo. Others are your SEAL friends. I know their names from times they visited, fished here. But nothing from family," Manny said in sad tones, as if not having a family calling to add their nagging to his teammates' was something to mourn.

"No family to be calling," Travis said, tucking the messages into the front pocket of his cutoffs. "Only child, parents gone before I was twenty."

"That's a bummer, man."

It'd been a decade, but the sympathy hit him hard. He'd thought he was long over the loss. But being around people like Manny, with an extended family so big that he had cousins in every other house in town, really brought it home how alone he was. For years, he'd had his SEAL team for family. But while they weren't dead like his parents, they weren't there anymore either.

But all Travis could do was shrug. Nothing else to do, and absolutely nada to say.

"You didn't have to deliver the messages. I would have come by your place tomorrow."

Manny ran a small produce market with his brothers. Not quite a store, not quite a stall, it did brisk business with the locals and tourists alike.

"Now's fine," the skinny man said before lifting a covered plate. "You want fish? I caught it this morning. Glory cooked it nice."

Rich spices escaped the dish, its foil glinting in the moonlight as Manny plopped it onto Travis's bare belly.

Travis grunted. He really didn't want the fish. Just like he hadn't wanted the *gallo pinto* Boon had brought by an hour ago or the *cacao fresco* that Senora Miguel had forced on him at breakfast. But the upside—or downside in his opinion—of crashing at a friend's place was the friend's friends.

"Thanks, to Glory too," he said as he lifted the plate and, bending at the waist, leaned over to set it on the battered crate that served as his table.

"So what you doing for a job now? I'll bet you get bored recreating, right?"

Right. There was no appeal in forced recreating. But Travis only shrugged.

"I know the perfect job for you. You should be a private investigator. Or the police. But joining the police means you follow a bunch of rigid rules, that's no way to get the job done."

Debating whether to point out the plethora of rules he'd lived by in the military, Travis opted to keep silent. He'd learned in his first week in town that Manny and logic weren't real close pals.

"You become a PI and solve all the crimes around here. Like I heard yesterday, that a bunch of *turistas*, they were hit on by two hookers."

Not surprising. Since it was legal, prostitution was a way of life in some parts of Costa Rica.

"The men, they do the grab and feel, but didn't like the merchandise. Happens all the time in my market. Everyone squeeze the melons but not everyone want to buy. But these men? When they don't want a guy, some big bruiser come out and rough them up. Says, 'You touch, you buy.' He put one in the hospital."

Travis frowned. Prostitution might be legal, but pimping wasn't. Neither were prostitution rings, which was what it sounded like Manny was describing.

"My cousin Luis, he says that a bruiser was the one who came around his store last week. He said Luis pay for protection or there will be trouble. Next day, Luis's little girl Lupe got lost."

"She's missing?"

"Was missing until nighttime. The whole family, we went looking, but nobody could find her. She turned up at the market after dark. Said a big man stole her, tied her up and said she had to give a message. If her papa didn't pay, she'd get hurt."

Damn.

Travis grimaced.

Helpless women and children, they'd always been his hot buttons. He was tempted to offer his services. But the reality was that he had no services to offer. Who needed a cripple slowing them down? So Travis forced himself to unclench his jaw and relax instead.

"Sounds like a job for the cops." He leaned back in his hammock again.

"The cops, they are no good here. That's why we need you, Hawk. You can be a PI, you can help with the crimes."

"Thanks for the food," he made himself say.

Manny's face fell, but he didn't push the subject.

"You eat. It's good. Then you go have fun."

Travis grunted, hoping Manny would take that as an affirmative and go.

No such luck.

Instead, the other guy squatted in the sand next to the hammock and grinned.

"You gonna party like a wild thing, yes? Lots to choose from tonight, Hawk. There's a bonfire at the big hotel, a band tuning at Lolo's and the dancing is already kicking over at the Catfish bar."

Not too long ago, he'd have hit all three party spots in a single night. All three and more.

But that was then.

"No, thanks."

"You really should have some fun. Loosen up and have a good time."

"I'm close enough to Lolo's to hear the music," Travis pointed out, gesturing to the bar on the other side of the small dune. "I'll join in if I feel like it."

"You always say that, but you don't look so good." With an assessing look somewhere between doubt and pity, Manny shook his head. "My instructions, they're to watch out for you. You're healing okay. Good food, good rest, it helps. But good spirits, that'd turn the tide."

"My spirits are fine," Travis said somberly.

"Paulo, he's gonna call me tomorrow. What am I supposed to say to him when he asks how you're doing? I'll tell him you won't party, you barely eat, he's gonna be peeved."

Peeved, Travis rolled his eyes, but had to admit—if only to himself—that peeved was the perfect word for Paulo. The chief petty officer didn't get pissed, he never threw fits, he was the perfect gentleman. Some would say a goody-goody, but only if those some hadn't ever watched him eviscerate an enemy combatant.

Still…

"I don't need a babysitter."

"No? Then you need a friend. A lady friend, maybe."

The sexy blonde's face flashed through Travis's mind. She was definitely the kind of friend he'd like to show a good time. For a night, or in her case, two or three.

"I'm fine. I'm gonna eat this good fish, then get some rest."

"You want me to hang out? Visit and keep you company while you eat. Save you cleaning the dish afterward, cuz I'll just take it back to Glory to wash."

"It's a paper plate," Travis pointed out. Then, because he knew the man wasn't going to budge off his damned babysitting duties, Travis made a show of snapping up the plate. He uncovered it, and using his fingers, he snagged a chunk of fish. Spices exploded on his tongue, the flavor reminding his stomach of the good ole days, when he'd liked to eat.

"It's great, man. Tell Glory thanks for me."

"You'll eat it all?"

As much to assure the guy as to get him to leave, Travis tossed back the rest and handed back the plate. "Yum."

It took a few more prods to convince Manny that he was fine, he was full, he was comfortable and yes, he would get some sleep. But finally, the guy took his paper plate and left.

Leaving Travis alone with the sound of partyers in

the distance, and the ocean nearby. As the moon climbed higher in the sky, he watched the waves with eyes that must have been as empty as his soul felt. For what seemed like the hundredth time in the last month, he wondered if recovery at the beach had been a mistake. He'd had friends offer him their cabins in the mountains, a trip to a ranch in Colorado, a condo in Vegas and a high-rise in Manhattan. He could have—should have— crashed at any of them. Instead, here he was watching the one true love of his life.

The ocean, the sea.

For all her fickle whims, all her changeable moods, she was power. She was life.

Some might say that she'd tried to kill him, but Travis figured that just proved she had a dark side.

And watching her from a hammock on a sunset beach was as good a way to heal as any, he supposed.

Lila loved the job she'd created. She really did.

Here she sat in a deeply cushioned lounge chair, her hair loose, a tray on her lap to hold her computer and a frothy drink, complete with pink umbrella at her elbow. Despite the setting sun, the air was warm and the beach quiet as the sun worshippers had gone in for dinner and the partyers hadn't yet gathered.

It really was a great job, she reminded herself as she sucked up more Caribbean Punch through an icy straw.

But, holy cow, where was she going to find a female blacksmith? Specifically one with public speaking skills, an affinity for children and a desire to travel with an educational troupe for a year. Scrolling through the database on her laptop, she scanned for any name that'd spark an idea.

But blacksmiths weren't exactly plentiful in the circles Lila traveled in. So she'd expand them, she decided.

Still, maybe Corinne was right. Matchmaking might be easier. But Lila had less faith in the longevity of love than she did in her ability to track down a buff chick that liked to beat fire and steel.

"Ms. Adrian?"

Her fingers pausing on the keys of her laptop, Lila looked up with a smile. "Yes?"

"Phone for you, ma'am," the young concierge said, holding out a cordless phone on a bamboo tray.

"For me?"

Corinne would use her cell number. So would any clients, friends or prospects trying to reach her.

There was only one person who'd make a point of tracking her down and calling the hotel to ensure she knew she'd been tracked.

Lips pressed tight, Lila gently closed her laptop. She gave herself an extra few seconds to gather her thoughts, to push away the initial rush of emotions that dealing with her father always incited.

Strongest was the heavy weight of regret that she'd never, not once in her life, lived up to her father's expectations. She'd like to blame it on her brother. It wasn't easy to live up to a guy like Lucas. Prep school prince, Annapolis grad, Navy SEAL. Not even leaving the Navy against their father's express wishes had knocked him off his golden pedestal.

Instead of a pedestal, Lila had a gilded cage.

"I'd prefer to take this in my room," she stated. He was probably calling to lecture, would likely round that out with a few unreasonable demands. Whatever her father wanted, she knew she'd rather deal with it in private. "Would you transfer it there, please?"

Lila took her time. She took the stairs. Once in her room, she even took a bottle of water from the small refrigerator. Tequila would be better, but she knew she'd want her wits about her.

She didn't sit on the bed. That'd be too casual, too relaxed. Instead, she pulled out the stiff wooden chair from the small desk and perched on the edge.

One deep breath, and she lifted the phone receiver.

"Hello, Father. How are you?"

"Lila. Your help is required to organize and act as hostess for an event of great import. I'm honoring dignitaries and notable Navy personnel, including your brother."

Pointing out that Lucas wasn't in the Navy anymore would have as much impact as her hello had. So Lila didn't waste her breath.

"It does sound like a worthy event, and honoring our troops—" even the ones who didn't serve in Special Ops, the ones her father pretended didn't exist "—is important. But as commendable as I'm sure it will be, I am not available to hostess or attend."

There. Didn't that sound officious and professional? Two things her father should easily relate to.

But, instead of understanding—or God, forbid, pride—at her work ethic and business success, her words garnered her a lecture.

Duty. Privilege. Expectations. Failure. Disappointment.

Years of practice helped her keep all of the tension, all of the reaction, in her left hand. Clenching, unclenching, clenching her fist. Over and over. *Squeeze the tension, release the stress*, she silently chanted.

When he finally wound down, she gave herself a second to make sure her temper was under control before speaking again.

"I have a business to run and commitments that require my time. A concept you should be familiar with. Isn't that what you always said at every holiday, birthday or potential family occasion?"

So much for control.

"I run a multimillion dollar conglomerate with holdings in twelve countries, producing profits in the billions. You, on the other hand, are playing at running an employment agency for the odd and disenfranchised. Your accrued net earnings for the three years you've been in so-called business are a drop in the bucket compared to just the yearly interest on the trust fund you've rejected with your little act of faux independence."

Everything wasn't about money, Lila wanted to shout. Some things were worth more than dollars and cents. Like independence. Or pride. Or respect. She'd happily walk away from her trust fund if he'd give her any one of those.

But there was no point in telling him any of that. He never listened.

"As I understand it, you're in Costa Rica to procure a chef for Joe Martin. That's no longer necessary."

"What'd you do?" she asked, her words a furious whisper. "What did you do?"

"My secretary will find them five comparable chefs to choose from, freeing you to come home."

"The Martins are my clients, and it's my responsibility to fulfill their request," she snapped.

"That's inconsequential. I've arranged for a helicopter to transport you to the San José airport where a private plane is scheduled to depart in the morning," he continued, his tone of absolute confidence the only thing Lila had ever wished she'd inherited. "The itinerary is in your email inbox. I expect you to be here in two days."

While Lila was choking on her stunned fury, he hung up.

She wanted to call him back and scream.

She wanted to throw the phone through the window.

She wanted to cry.

She shoved her hands through her hair, tugging on it until the urge passed.

Then she got up to pace off her fury.

Her entire damned life, he'd done this. Ordered, demanded or manipulated. She'd tried reason, she'd tried threats, she'd even run away from home. She'd tried to cut herself off from the family, even going so far as to use her late mother's maiden name in her teens. It hadn't made any difference.

Nothing got through to the man.

All she could do was focus on her life, and her business. Which meant figuring out what he'd done and undo it, Lila told herself. It still took a couple more paces of the room to calm down enough to listen to herself, though.

When she did, she figured she'd better call Joe Martin and ensure she still had a client. Otherwise she was going to have to rewrite her company's tag line to guarantee 95 percent satisfaction instead of 100.

Lila opened her laptop to pull up his phone number and saw her email notification flashing.

Flight details.

Her jaw set, her finger shaking, Lila deleted the email without replying. And contacted her client, instead.

"Mr. Martin, hello. This is Lila Adrian."

Thirty minutes later, she'd smoothed over the trouble her father had caused and promised complete satisfaction in the form of Chef Rodriguez. No substitutes, no replacements, just him.

When she hung up, she knew she was tiptoeing a shaky line, making that kind of promise. But years of watching her father had given her plenty of insights into how the rich and influential operated. She'd built her business on those insights. She might not like the man a whole lot, but she couldn't deny that his business skills were legendary.

Legends weren't built on empty promises.

But neither were they built on fear, she told herself as she headed back to the Casa de Rico. She couldn't wait until morning to talk with Rodriguez. Not with a man like Wayne Adrian making travel plans, whether she liked it or not. She wouldn't put it past her father to send someone to the hotel to ensure she made that flight. She wasn't going to comply, but it wouldn't hurt to nail down the details with the chef tonight.

Snatches of noise rolled out of the buildings, the beat of a steel drum and thrum of guitars playing backup to the sound of Lila's heels tapping down the sidewalk as she wove her way through the partying crowds.

People poured out of bars, gathered around restaurants and a happy couple danced in front of the hardware store. She'd had no idea that Puerto Viejo was such a party town. But safe enough, she supposed as she returned friendly greetings, refused two cleverly worded propositions and sidestepped a would-be pickpocket with an apologetic grin.

She hadn't quite worked out her pitch, but she knew it'd be smarter to talk with Rodriguez tonight.

Maybe.

Two steps inside the restaurant and she could barely move. It obviously did a better dinner service than lunch, because it had wall-to-wall bodies.

Still, she gave the bartender a friendly look when she finally wiggled her way to the counter.

"Hi, there. Bar or restaurant?" the woman asked, giggling as a passing customer patted her on the butt.

Lila angled her head to peer around the column and check out the crowds. The small bar was three people deep, with bodies spilling into the restaurant.

"I'd love to chat to Chef Rodriguez instead." Lila tried a wide-eyed, innocent smile when the woman arched one brow. "I'm working on an article and was in earlier. I had the ceviche. It was great. I was hoping to ask him about a few follow-up questions."

The woman gave her a narrow-eyed look, but finally shrugged.

"Sure. Go on back."

Fighting her way through the crowd, Lila took a deep, grateful breath once through the kitchen doors.

A dozen faces turned to stare at her in surprise. But none was the one she was looking for.

"Chef Rodriguez?"

She got a series of shrugs, a couple of scowls and one frown from the dishwasher, who jerked his chin toward a door leading to a narrow hallway.

"Try his office."

"Thanks."

Remembering the chef's earlier reluctance to talk, Lila closed the door behind her. The grumble of voices hit her when she was halfway down the hall. Men. They were speaking Spanish, but it was a dialect she wasn't familiar with. But the rage in their tone came through loud and clear.

Biting her lip, Lila paused. She took one step back toward the kitchen, then spotted a door leading outside. Probably better to go out the side, she supposed, ignoring the frustration tightening her jaw. She wanted to talk with Rodriguez tonight, to get her offer in first.

The voices rose. She recognized enough to know that one man was pleading, another cursing. She'd just talk with the chef in the morning, as planned, she decided, nervously sidling over to the door.

Before she could turn the knob, there was a whine and a pop. Lila jumped, barely choking back her scream at the loud crash, the sight of papers winging through the air.

Another pop, and the partially closed door burst open, slamming into the wall. Before it could ricochet back again, a body flew out, landing in the hallway with a sickening thud. Something splattered, spraying the walls, spewing across the floor.

Blood?

Was that blood?

Hers drained out of her head, leaving her dizzy and blinking against the tiny black dots dancing in front of her eyes.

Chef Rodriguez, she realized with a silent scream, recognizing the body that splattered blood over the floor. A very dead Chef Rodriguez.

Oh, God.

Oh, God.

Oh, God.

Lila's whole body shook. She swiped at the doorknob, but it wouldn't turn. She swiped again, trying to get a good hold on the metal with her sweat-slicked hand.

Get out, get out, get out, she mentally chanted, her breath coming in ragged gasps. *Get out before they see you*.

She heard footsteps.

The sound of something hitting the wall.

They were coming.

She let out a squeal of panicked relief when the door opened. She tried to run, but her knees were as useful as Jell-O, so she hung on to the doorjamb to keep from falling on her face.

"Hey!"

Lila heard the office door ricochet off the wall again, the horrible squelching sound of someone sliding in blood, a big body hitting the wall.

They'd seen her.

Lila considered herself to be a smart woman. A world traveler trained in self-defense. A woman who followed and respected the law.

She knew she should scream. Call for help, yell for the police. There were at least fifty people twenty feet away. Someone would help her. Someone would save her.

"Hey. You."

Lila didn't even wait a heartbeat. She didn't scream. She didn't head for the kitchen.

Nope.

She ran like hell.

Ripped out of a dream, Travis jerked awake, instantly coming to full alert.

Where was he? What'd happened?

Hammock.

The beach.

In Costa Rica.

Shit.

He rubbed his hands over his face, cleaning the fatigue away before glancing at the sky. From the angle of the moon, the position of the stars, he estimated that he'd slept for about three hours.

Three uninterrupted, peaceful hours.

Not bad, he decided as he swung his legs out of the hammock and, balancing carefully, got to his feet. He doubted he'd get any more tonight, but three was good enough.

He'd go back to Paulo's house—a hut, really—and chill. He was a man skilled in keeping his mind occupied and hands busy. A talent that came in handy before a battle. And, apparently, while mulling what the hell to do with the rest of his life.

Because the life of a beach bum was getting old.

Grinning a little because, yeah, those had been a great three hours of sleep, Travis headed for his temporary home.

But before he had taken ten steps toward the hut, he had his hands full of a hysterical blonde. Her hair flew around him in silken ropes. He felt rather than heard the loud crack as his knee gave out, but the woman continued to grab at him, her fingers clutching his back like he was a lifeline.

Despite her violent shaking and gasping sobs, he knew the only thing keeping him from planting his face in the sand was the woman grabbing at him.

If that wasn't annoying, he didn't know what was.

Travis gritted his teeth against the pain and grabbed her right back. He damned well wasn't letting go until he had his footing. After a few seconds, her continual squirming and wriggling had a different effect on his body than vicious, shooting pain.

Whoa. Now that was a sensation he hadn't enjoyed in a long time. Too long, he figured, if a panicked woman hell-bent on knocking him on his ass was a turn on.

"Nice to meet you and all," he said, reaching around to grasp her wrists and unleash himself from her hold. "But I think that's enough for now."

"No. No, no, no," she gasped, her words breathy with terror. "You've got to help me."

"As soon as you let me go."

But instead of releasing her hold, she tried to burrow deeper.

"Lady, you grab me much harder, you're going to be inside my skin."

He managed to break her arm's lock on his waist, but before he could unwrap himself, she jumped in his arms, shoving him off balance again.

Travis didn't bother to censor his curses as he struggled to find his balance.

"What the hell is your problem?" he finally snapped, getting a firm grip on her shoulders and pushing her to arm's length. She shook harder, her hair flying as she looked behind her then back at him.

It was the sexy blonde from earlier that afternoon, he realized. The one he'd flirted with. If this was her follow-up, it was seriously twisted.

And, based on his body's reaction, it kinda worked.

"They're after me. Bad men. They saw me. Police. We need the police."

Seriously? Adjusting his weight onto his left leg, Travis rolled his eyes.

"Get a grip," he told her.

"Dead," she gasped, almost sobbing the words. "They killed him. He's dead."

"What?" Dead? His senses hitting high alert, Travis looked over her shoulder, tracking the path she'd run. He could see the furrow of her steps in the sand and the lights of Casa de Rico beyond. There was a handful of people on the beach, but they all looked to be alive. "Who do you think is dead?"

"He's dead. They shot him. Oh, God, there was blood

everywhere." Swallowing so hard he heard the click in her throat, the woman had to take a couple of deep breaths before she could finish. "They killed Rodriguez. The chef at Casa de Rico."

Her thick lashes were spiked with tears over eyes of a misty, sea green that might be pretty when they didn't have that glassy sheen.

Someone down the beach shouted. She gave a short scream and jumped, turning so fast that her hair slapped him in the face.

"Is that them? They're going to come after me. Oh, God. I need to get out of here. I have to get away."

Her voice was so thick with panic, he could barely make out her words. He reached out to grab her when her body sagged, not surprised to feel her shaking like an earthquake. She screamed again as soon as he touched her.

"Calm the hell down," Travis snapped. Then, seeing no other option that didn't make him a complete jerk, he grabbed her arm.

"What are you doing?"

"Taking you somewhere safe."

Chapter 3

Safe.

Safe was good.

The sand seeping between her feet and sassy wedge sandals, Lila stumbled in his wake. She was glad he was holding her arm, since her knees were gooey now that the adrenaline was gone.

She blindly went along with no idea where he was taking her. Gorgeous body and a little flirting aside, she couldn't figure out what it was about this rude man that made her feel safe, but she'd take it over the faceless guys with guns.

The image of the chef hitting the floor flashed through her mind again, the sound of his body crashing to the floor, the red spray across the walls.

She wanted to ask him to slow down, but Lila's breath jammed in her throat, choking on the words before she could utter them. She blinked hard and tried to focus.

That's when she realized that they'd left the beach, heading into the tall trees of the rain forest.

Where was he taking her?

Was it really safe?

Was he?

Get a grip, Lila told herself. And she needed to get it fast, before she ended up like the stupid blonde in every horror movie who went into the basement to check a noise.

"Let's call the cops," she said, trying to pull free of his grip on her arm. "I want the police."

She dug her cell phone out of the pocket of her capris with her spare hand.

"Smarter to use a landline where we're going to call the local station. But if you want, go ahead and make the call yourself."

His easy disregard calmed a few of her nerves. Not all of them, but enough that she was able to get a better look at where they were going.

Not a neighborhood, per se. But a tidy row of thatched-roof houses, bordering a low hill leading into the forest. A pair of elderly men sat smoking in front of one house, both lifting their hands to her escort in a friendly greeting. Since neither said a word about his dragging her along by the arm, she had to wonder if this was some weird courtship ritual of his.

A weary looking woman swayed in the open doorway of one house, patting the back of the crying babe in her arms.

"Colic again?" Lila's rescuer called out.

"Again and again," the woman returned in a sing-song voice. "We'll be hurting too much to sleep for a little while yet."

"I keep telling you, a shot of Jim Beam will take care of the problem."

"Is the whiskey for him? Or is it for me?" the woman asked with a laugh.

"Whatever works."

It was his easy humor as much as the crying baby that reassured Lila enough to have her tucking the phone back in her pocket. Either way, she'd wait for a little privacy to call the police. Privacy and, she decided with a deep, calming breath, a few minutes to get herself under control.

The man might be gruff and overwhelming, but she was pretty sure he was safe. Or, safe enough, she amended, watching the way his muscles flowed as he strode a step ahead of her. He had a slight limp, like he was favoring his right leg. She frowned, squinting at the scars crossing, bisecting and wrapping around his knee. She wasn't an expert, but that looked fresh, to say nothing of painful.

"Slow down," she insisted. When he frowned, she made a show of pointing to her feet. "I'm wearing heels. So unless the bad guys are actually chasing us, let's keep it to a reasonable pace."

He didn't bother to hide the roll of his eyes, but he did slow his pace. Enough, she was glad to see, that he wasn't limping as badly.

From the front, the house looked smaller than the others, barely bigger than her apartment in San Francisco. But it had impressive hardware on the door and windows, and, if she wasn't mistaken, a state-of-the-art alarm system.

"Worried about break-ins?" she asked as he reached

for the doorknob. As soon as he twisted it, she realized she had her answer. It wasn't even locked.

"Not my place." He pushed open the door and gestured her inside. He gave her an impatient look when she hesitated. "It belongs to a friend. He's not here a lot, so he keeps it secured."

Okay. Lila wet her lips. As she hesitated, a loud crash came from the path they'd come from, followed by a couple of gruff shouts. Lila rushed through the door so fast, she almost tripped over his feet.

"In a hurry?"

"It's been a crappy night, okay?" she snapped, hurrying over to peek out the front window. The same old men still sat, smoking. The same woman still swayed, singing. But nobody else was out there. She pressed her hand against her stomach, trying to calm the sharp jabs of fear.

"It's been something, all right," he agreed under his breath, pulling the door shut behind him.

"Lock it. Please. Lock the door."

His eyes skimmed over her face, and even though she could feel his exasperation, he silently turned the lock.

"Feel better?"

"No."

She looked around with a frown. The bulk of the square footage seemed to be in this main room, with a pair of doors on the end leading to what she assumed was the bed and bath. The furniture was simple. A long black couch and a huge black recliner stood in the center of the room, both so big she was surprised they fit in the room.

A table and two chairs were shoved in a corner next to a refrigerator that looked older than the house itself.

Something about cataloging the room calmed her. Enough so that she started to feel her legs again and her hands started to tremble. She didn't want to close her mind; she wasn't ready to see the scene in her head again. But she figured she had a handle on the babbling enough to make a coherent report.

"We should call the police now."

"You sure? Maybe you want to wait a few more minutes. Think it all over again."

Lila turned to stare.

The man was gorgeous. Even in the sad light put out by one rickety looking lamp, he was a work of art. From his sculpted jaw that needed a shave to his eyes, as dark as his midnight-black hair, he had the looks. The body, too, she remembered. She didn't let herself ogle it for the same reason she wouldn't let her mind reenact the murder. Because she wasn't sure she could handle it.

But she couldn't deny the man had it all going on.

All that, and he was still an idiot.

"You think I went running willy-nilly down the beach on the verge of hysterics, then grabbed on to you, all just for entertainment?" She barreled on before he could say anything to go with the amusement in his eyes. "You think I threw myself into your arms, that I made up the whole story about seeing something that horrible? Why? Just to get your attention?"

"I didn't say that."

"You don't believe me," she said with a scowl. "So why did you bring me here?"

"To give you time to calm down before you did something stupid, hurt yourself or hurt someone else."

"Aren't you the hero," she muttered, turning her back on him and pulling out her cell phone.

"What're you doing?"

What did he think she was doing?

"I'm calling the police," she said, shooting a defiant look over her shoulder before pressing the keys. One. One. One.

Before she hit the seven, a hand reached over her shoulder to take the phone.

"You sure you want to call the cops?" he asked, his voice a slow rumble vibrating against her back. Irritation made it easy to ignore the sensations coiling in her belly, but Lila figured it was smarter to step away regardless. No point in letting her body get stupid ideas.

"Look, buddy," she snapped, turning to face him rather than leave all that temptation hulking at her back. Mistake, she realized as soon as she stared up into his dark eyes. Big mistake. But she was good at ignoring mistakes, she reminded herself before taking a deep breath.

"I don't know how things are handled in your world. But in mine, murder means we call the cops. So get out of my way and let me do that, then you can get back to your beer and your beach and whatever the hell else actually matters to you."

Lila wished that her voice wasn't shaking almost as hard as her hands, but a person could only take so much.

"You need to calm down," the man said, obviously impervious to her nasty tone and cutting words.

"You don't believe me?" she accused, slapping her hand on his bare chest to keep him from walking away. "Why? Why would I make something like that up?"

His eyes locked on hers for a long heartbeat, then dropped to her hand. Her fingers tingling, Lila dropped it to her side. His gaze met hers again and he shrugged. A slow shrug that was just as indifferent as the rest of his attitude.

Years of being ignored, of having her simplest wants and needs and thoughts dismissed as inconsequential exploded in Lila's head.

She used both hands this time, not to stop him from walking away, but to shove him back a step. Ignoring the look of amused surprise on his face, she gave him another shove. There was something about having a man's full attention that filled her with a feeling she barely recognized as power.

God, it felt good.

"Call the damned police. Call them now," she ordered, her voice vibrating with fury. "They'll figure out what happened. They'll find Rodriguez."

"You're sure?"

She slapped her cell phone against his chest.

Ignoring it, he gave her one last, long look, then stepped over to grab the receiver of an ancient rotary dial phone and made the call.

He spoke Spanish in the local dialect, his words flowing too fast for her to make out more than every third. Her eyes widened when she realized he was actually talking to the chief of police.

"*Sí*. Rodriguez," he confirmed. "Casa de Rico."

Lila held her breath, waiting for the rest of the conversation, but the only thing she heard from then on was grunts on her pseudo rescuer's part until he said goodbye.

"They'll meet us there."

"Someone else probably called it in by now," she mused, her fingers clenching and unclenching as she thought it through. "There's no way nobody noticed the chef on duty missing and didn't go looking for him."

"No calls from that location or in the vicinity."

"How do you know?"

"I asked."

Oh.

"Let's go then," she said, heading for the door. "We want to be there when they get there."

"Give me a minute."

A part of her wanted to unleash that fury again, to yell and demand and see him respond. But he was already doing what she wanted, she realized. So letting loose her anger wouldn't be a show of power. It'd just be showing her bitch face.

So Lila stayed silent while he stepped out of the room.

She glanced out the window, noting that the baby must have fallen asleep because the swaying woman was indoors now. The forest was a tangle of shadows in the dark, but she could still make out the path to the beach. She squinted, wondering if she could see the ocean from here. Maybe in the daytime.

But she could see well enough that she'd notice anyone coming their way. Cops. Killers. She stared until her eyes watered, but nothing moved.

She was so focused on watching out the window that she almost screamed at the sound behind her.

It was the beach bum, still shirtless but wearing jeans and heavy black boots instead of cutoffs and bare feet. He strode over to a drawer and pulled out a gun. A black, lethal looking weapon that had her breath knotted in her throat so tight she could barely breathe. He pulled out the magazine, checked it, then shoved it back in place before tucking the weapon into the back waistband of his jeans. He snagged a T-shirt off a pile on the chair. Pulling it over his head, he strode to the door and threw it open.

Without a word about the gun.

Why that should make her nervous after everything else that'd happened, she couldn't say.

"I'll walk you back to your hotel."

"I'm going to the restaurant," she snapped. "You remember, the scene of the crime."

"Of course you are." He gestured toward the open door. "After you."

"Do you have to be such a jerk?" she asked as they headed through the tree-covered path.

"Do you have to be such a drama queen?"

"When I see a man murdered right in front of me, yes. I think I'm entitled to wear the drama crown."

His lips twitched.

"Yeah, I suppose you are. If you did."

It took her a couple of seconds to puzzle that out.

"You honestly don't believe me? Why would I lie? What purpose is there in making something like that up?"

It wasn't until he'd joined her on the path, his steps

just a little hesitant, his gait just a little off, that Lila realized she'd thrown herself into his arms, gone with him into a strange place, leaned on him for emotional support and was dragging him back to a murder scene.

And she didn't even know his name.

"Who are you?"

What difference did it make? When Travis shot the blonde a questioning look, she amended, "I mean, what's your name?"

"Hawkins."

"That's it? Just Hawkins?"

He didn't figure they were going to be exchanging mail. Or, despite the appeal of her pretty little body and sea witch eyes, good-mornings over sex-tangled sheets. So, yeah, he shrugged. That was it.

"I'm Lila."

"Okay."

She stared. Blinked. And stared again.

"Seriously?" she muttered under her breath. "Just, okay? Could you be any ruder?"

"I'm sure I can if I put a little effort into it."

He didn't know if that puff of sound she made was a laugh, but it made him grin.

"Just walk me back to the restaurant and help interpret with the police," she told him. "Then I promise, I'll leave you alone with your beer and your beach."

"Anything you say. Lila." He put a little extra agree-ableness into his tone. The kind he used with irritating officers who were superior in rank only.

"Just for that, I want an apology before you drop your butt back in that hammock."

Travis shot her an impressed glance. The woman must be better versed in Smart-Ass than the last admiral he'd answered to.

"Or?"

She stopped on the path that led from the beach to the restaurant and gave him a long study. Then her smile flashed, sassy and challenging.

"Or I'll keep bugging you until you do."

Damned effective threat, he silently acknowledged as she continued with surer steps toward the boardwalk, then up toward the side door of the bar.

Smarter than the front entrance, he supposed. The fewer people who saw her, the less flak she'd get later. He knew enough about the local *policía to* know they weren't going to be too thrilled at being hauled out of their comfy chairs on a bogus call.

"Get your apology ready," she said, giving him a snotty look over her shoulder as she grabbed the doorknob. Travis didn't bother to tell her to forget about it. The doors around here automatically locked on both sides.

She gave it a twist and tugged it open just an inch.

"Quiet," she whispered. "They might still be in there."

Huh. Travis frowned at the door, then touched the Glock nestled at the small of his back. He silently followed her inside, first looking toward the door to the kitchen, then toward the office.

"The door wasn't closed before. And the body? It was lying there in the doorway. Where is it?" she asked, her words so quiet they barely floated on the air. Her gaze slid to his just long enough for him to see the sick dance of nerves in her eyes, then with a sharp breath, she started for the office.

He liked the way she didn't back down, despite her fear. But Travis still laid his hand on her arm, halting her steps. He drew in a long breath through his nose, noting the faint scent of solvent.

"Wait."

She stopped and bit her lip, looking at the door, then back at him, then at the door again.

Nobody stormed out with guns blazing, but Travis still had a nasty tingle dancing down his spine.

He didn't know if they really were standing in a murder scene or not. But his senses told him that something definitely wasn't right here.

Maybe she felt it, too. Or maybe she simply realized that safer was smarter. But Lila gave him another considering look, then took two steps back and to the side to place his body between her and the door.

"Why aren't the police here yet?" she whispered.

"They probably don't see this as a priority." He didn't bother to keep his voice down.

"Murder isn't a priority?"

"We take murder quite seriously, senorita."

As one, Travis and Lila looked back. A short man stood—posed, was more like it—in the doorway to the kitchen, giving them both enough time to take in his leather pants, waxed mustache and slicked-back hair. Standing behind him was a man so nondescript, Travis was surprised he didn't simply fade into the background. A handy skill for a cop, he supposed.

Lila gave a relieved sigh, but Travis didn't figure it was either cop's looks that had her tension lowering even as his rose. It was more likely the shiny silver badge hanging from the waistband of the man in the lead. The shorter man murmured something they couldn't hear, but whatever it was sent the other scurrying away.

"Montoya." Travis grimaced when it was just the three of them.

For a brief second, he considered shifting positions with Lila. The fact they stood at an alleged murder scene where possible killers had been carried less potential threat than the man walking toward them.

"Senor Hawkins. Why would you be involved in this, might I ask?"

"I asked him to come with me," Lila said, walking forward with her hand outstretched. "I'm Lila Adrian, and I witnessed a murder."

"Mmm-hmm." Dismissing her in a single glance, Montoya studied Travis out of dark, beady eyes. "And you, Senor Hawkins? Did you witness this, as well?"

Travis debated. He'd had run-ins with Montoya before. The man had a serious hate-on for members of the US military, considered them all cocky hotshots who should stay in their own country and off his beach. Still, the whole helping a damsel in distress thing was simple enough. But he suspected that the minute he said he hadn't seen jack, Montoya would toss him out the door, intimidate Lila into recanting anything that'd disturb his comfy existence and maybe grab a drink before heading back to his carefully structured office.

Then Travis could head back to his own carefully unstructured hammock and comfy nonexistence. Which was, after all, priority number one.

He glanced at Lila, noting the way her brow furrowed and the frustration in her eyes at Montoya's dismissal. He could practically see the smart-ass remarks balanced on the tip of her tongue; she was just waiting for a chance to jump in Montoya's face. Which was all the excuse he'd need to toss her in a cell and make his point to the town council about the trouble with tourists.

Travis sighed. Looked like his hammock was going to have to wait.

"I'm here with the lady," he told Montoya. "You want the details of what happened, ask her. She can fill you in."

Okay...

Lila's stomach clenched. Her nerves, already frayed near to breaking with the events of the evening, jangled dangerously. She didn't know what had caused the tension between the cop and the beach bum, but it felt significant. Was that a good thing or a bad thing?

Lila looked from one man to the other and back again. She couldn't read either's expression, but there was enough malice in their words to make her throat dry.

"Senorita?" After a long stare at her companion, the policeman gave her a questioning look. "Why do you claim to have seen a murder?"

"What?" Why? *Claim?*

Nerves forgotten, Lila scowled. Her fists clenched

at her sides. Before she could snap at him to kiss her butt, the beach bum—Hawkins, she had to remember his name was Hawkins—touched her. Just a single finger to the small of her back for barely a second. But it was enough to warn her to reel it in.

So she gritted her teeth and tried to do that.

"Earlier this evening, I saw a man killed in the doorway. That doorway." She pointed her still clenched fist toward the office. "Someone shot Chef Rodriguez."

"How do you know Chef Rodriguez?"

"What difference does that make? I saw him fall to the floor covered in blood, right there in that doorway."

The policeman held her gaze for a long, uncomfortable moment before he stepped around her and Hawkins and walked casually toward the office. Lila cringed, seeing in her head the body fall again, the blood splatter.

Wait.

Her eyes tracked the cop's steps, not so much to note his progress as to check the walls. The floor. Where was the blood?

Where was the body?

"This is the office where you thought you saw a man fall, senorita?"

The policeman threw open the door and gestured inside. Unwilling to move any closer, Lila craned her neck instead and tried to see the body. But the floor was bare of a body. Nowhere to be seen was a hurricane of scattered papers or broken furniture.

Lila rubbed a hand over her trembling lips.

"There is no dead body. No blood. No evidence of any wrongdoing," the cop enunciated in careful English. "Perhaps you are used to attention in your country, senorita. But we frown upon such fabrications here in Puerto Viejo."

He gave the office one last look around, then swaggered over to shift his intimidating stare between Lila and her companion.

"I'm not making it up," she breathed, shaking her head. Not sure why, since he hadn't believed her either, Lila shot Hawkins a beseeching look. "I wouldn't lie about something like that."

"Why don't you check on Rodriguez? Make sure he's not floating facedown somewhere." The suggestion was made to the cop, but Hawkin's eyes didn't leave Lila's.

"Perhaps you should remember that we have no use for hotshots such as yourself here in Puerto Viejo, senor." His beady eyes shifted between the two of them again before Montoya smiled.

Lila wanted to ask what the hell that meant. She clenched her fists, ready to demand to speak with the chief of police, the mayor. Whoever the hell was in charge.

But between his flat gaze and those small, sharp teeth, the cop reminded her of a shark. The kind of shark that'd chew her up and spit her out without so much as blinking.

So she kept her mouth shut.

"I will overlook your games this once, senorita. But only this once." With that, and another sneering sort of smile, the policeman strode down the hall and out the door.

Leaving Lila with no dead body, a raging headache and a gun-carrying grouch.

Chapter 4

Lila could only stare in shock as the dapper little cop strode away, his steps as rigid as his attitude.

He thought she'd made it up.

He thought she was lying.

The sexy beach bum with the lousy attitude thought that, too.

Years of being disregarded, of being dismissed or shunted off to the side as unimportant, exploded in her head. She wanted to scream. More, she wanted to grab something—the stapler off the desk, the rolling chair, the computer—and throw it to get him to pay attention to her.

She'd taken only one step, the red haze of fury blurring her vision, when someone laid a hand on her shoulder. Just one hand, but the simple touch calmed her.

Even as the frustration ebbed in her gut, her gaze shifted to meet Hawkins's. In those dark eyes, she saw the same irritation that she felt. Then again, he'd seemed irritated since she met him, so maybe that was simply his go-to expression.

Regardless, Lila took comfort in his steady gaze.

"I did not imagine it, and I'm not making it up." Her knees shook, but she forced herself to take three steps toward the office so she could point through the doorway. "I saw Chef Rodriguez killed. Right there."

"Okay." It wasn't agreement, it wasn't doubt. Lila knew the word was simply acknowledging what she thought she saw. It was enough to steel her spine, though.

So she wet her lips and took a hesitant step toward the office. Hawkins followed, so the next one was easier. Still, when she reached the door, even with Hawkins at her shoulder, she had to force herself to shift her gaze. To look around the office. To check the floor.

The policeman had said the room was clean.

He hadn't lied.

Rodriguez was nowhere to be seen. The room was tidy, the floor bare.

She pressed her fingers to her lips to stop their trembling.

"Lila."

The voice came as if from far away, its rumble soothing some of the tension in her belly. It didn't explain the room, though.

"But…"

Her head doing a long, slow spin, Lila took two deep breaths, then stepped all the way into the office.

It was one thing that the body was gone. But where was the blood? The mess?

"They shot him. He fell. There." She pointed at the doorway. At the bleached pine planks underfoot. "Blood. It was all over the floor. It smeared on the wall."

But the floor was spotless. The wall clean.

Lila rubbed her knuckles over the pain throbbing in her forehead, trying to hold back a moan.

"I didn't imagine it." She turned to face the beach bum, her voice insistent. "I wouldn't make something like that up."

"I didn't say you did."

"That policeman, Montoya, he thinks I made it up." Hawkins shrugged.

"He does have a point. There's no body here."

"I didn't make this up."

"Besides a body hitting the floor, what do you think you saw? Who shot him? What'd they look like? Sound like?"

"I only saw a hand. A man's hand, holding the gun as it shot the chef." Lila rubbed two fingers over her temple, trying to remember more. "He wore a long-sleeved jacket. Dark. The voices were low. Two men, at least, two, but they spoke too quietly for me to make out what they were saying."

"That's not a lot to go on." His words as casual as his stance, the beach bum crossed his legs at the ankle, propped one shoulder against the door frame and shoved his hands into the front pockets of his jeans. The black tee gripped his shoulders like a tight hug, molded that broad chest.

Despite the confusion, beyond the misery in her gut, Lila couldn't stop her gaze from taking in the perfect example of male beauty standing there. She'd admired it on the beach earlier today, but now all that perfection was a little irritating. Or maybe it was the look on his face: arrogant amusement and a hint of condescending impatience.

"A lot or not, Montoya still should have done more," she stated, her frown sliding into a scowl.

"Like what?"

"I don't know." She threw her arms in the air. "Something. Anything. He's a policeman. He should do police work, shouldn't he?"

"The cops didn't see anything."

"The police are wrong." Lila shot him a sideways glance that was as close as she could get to a sneer. "And you're wrong, too."

"I'm wrong. The police are wrong. Everyone's wrong but you. Sweetheart, you take the cake."

She wanted to tell him where to shove the cake, but she managed to smile instead.

"I didn't imagine seeing a man killed."

"Okay."

That agreeably sarcastic tone was different, and the single word wasn't what she was used to hearing. But the subtext? Oh, Lila knew every word. She was an expert on arrogance and well-versed in patronizing disdain.

Her fists clenched so tight her hands shook. She knew it was pointless. There was no reasoning with that subtext. Nothing she said would matter. But she still couldn't keep herself from snapping.

"How can you guys blow this off? What kind of men just dismiss murder? Just shrug off a man being shot and killed? Somebody took Chef Rodriguez's life and you just stand there, giving me that *I'm so perfect* sneer. What the hell is your problem?"

"If I'm perfect, I doubt I'd have any problems."

"I didn't say you were perfect," she corrected meticulously, ignoring the tickle in her belly that argued that if looks were anything to go by, he had perfection down pat. "I said *you* think that you're perfect. And some might say that you think incorrectly."

"Is that any way to talk to the man who gave up his quiet evening to ride to your rescue?"

"You were swinging in a hammock."

"Yet another example of my perfection. With no preparation or warning, I was able to effect a clean op, mount a rescue and end the mission without incident." He grinned. "Besides, I was swinging pretty damned quietly."

"Who the hell are you?" she snapped, squeezing the fingers of her left hand, releasing, and squeezing again.

"Me?" He shrugged, the movement making the muscles of his chest and shoulder ripple. "Just a guy on vacation."

"No. That policeman called you a hotshot. What he'd said about you thinking you can handle things better than the cops, what'd that mean?"

"Civilians sometimes get pissy when dealing with guys with Special Ops training."

Special Ops training?

"What branch?" she choked out.

"SEALs," he said, giving her a curious look.

Lila could only shake her head.

No freaking way.

Mr. Tall, Sexy and Gorgeous was a SEAL? A Navy SEAL?

With her luck, he'd served on the same team as her brother. Probably the same squad. He'd have met her father, been honored by one of Adrian the elder's kiss-ass dinner parties. Even, God help her, golfed at the club.

Tears—as much from fury and frustration as from self-pity—burned her eyes.

The events of the day won, she decided.

She couldn't take any more.

Her legs were wonky. Too wonky to hold her up any longer. Uncaring that it was the same spot she'd seen a body fall, she dropped to the floor and wrapped her arms around her torso, hoping the pressure would hold in the pain.

Seriously?

She was going to fall apart now?

Right here, on the floor where she thought she'd witnessed a murder?

Striding over to the tiny refrigerator in the corner, Travis shook his head. He'd never understand women. She'd thrown herself at him, all but climbing inside his skin.

Not that he had much problem with that, he decided in retrospect. She'd fit damned nice, and all that hair of hers was a silky temptation.

He yanked open the wobbly door of the stained appliance and grabbed a water. Twisting off the cap, he walked back and held it out, waiting in silence.

Lila shifted so her head was resting against the wall instead of on her drawn-up knees. The movement threw her face into sharp relief, the flickering overhead light angling down, accenting that full mouth, with its slight overbite. The curve of her cheekbones and the deep hollows beneath. She'd closed her eyes so her thick lashes fanned out over those cheeks, giving her a look of vulnerability that tugged at his gut.

Then she pulled in one long, deep breath that made her blouse slide temptingly across her full breasts.

And he got a tug a little south of his gut.

Then she did it again.

And Travis realized that yes, indeed, bum knee or not, he was alive and well.

By her third breath, he had to suck in one of his own.

He wasn't the kind of guy who liked to see people fall apart—especially women. But it was pure pleasure to watch her pull herself together.

Still, enough was enough.

"You got a grip on yourself yet?"

"What?" When those lashes fluttered open, her eyes were fogged with confusion and pain.

"Just checking. Are you finished with that meltdown?"

"Meltdown?" she snapped, pushing to her feet. She slammed her hands on her hips while her face curved in fury. She had a wicked glare, one he figured would cut a lesser man to the quick. But his ego was made of steel.

So he just grinned.

"Yeah. You were crying and babbling and seeing things. In my book, that reads like a meltdown."

"I saw a man killed," she said, each word clipped and precise. "I heard the bullet, the sound of it piercing his flesh. I watched his body fly backward, bleeding and ripped. I heard men cussing before one of them aimed that same gun at me."

She stepped forward and poked a sharp finger into his chest.

"So if I had a meltdown according to your stupid book, then I figure I'm due."

Damn.

Travis couldn't stop smiling.

Well, what d'ya know, he realized with surprise, downing the water she'd ignored. As the icy liquid poured down his throat, he gave thanks.

Because, oh, yeah. He still had a libido.

"Okay," he said after debating the merits of keeping her riled up versus being a gentleman. "Anyone who saw that sort of thing would have a right to melt on down."

"Anyone?"

"You, in this case." Not interested in arguing the point, he shrugged. "How much time passed between your supposed escape and mowing into me?"

"I don't know," Lila said, sounding a little frantic as she shook her head. "A few minutes, I suppose."

"Factoring in the five or so minutes it took you to reach me on the beach, then to calm down and make sense—"

"You mean for you to quit bitching about being knocked over and listen to me."

"And the five minutes it took us to walk to my place. I called the cops, we met them here within ten minutes, give or take," Travis continued, ignoring her. "Less than a half hour, all told."

"So?"

"So if an as yet unknown number of men killed a harmless chef, and saw you witnessing the murder first, don't you think they'd have pursued when you ran? But, instead, you figure they cleaned up all evidence, scrubbed the place clean of blood and guts, tidying the office while they were at it. Then they hauled the body out of a busy restaurant, on a busy beach, without anyone noticing?" He waited a beat, letting that sink in, then added, "And all of that in less than thirty minutes?"

"How would I know?" She threw her hands in the air. "All I know is what I saw."

With that, she headed out the door.

"Where are you going?"

"The cops don't believe me. You don't believe me." She shot him a nasty look. "So what difference does it make?"

"I believe you are upset." He glanced through the grimy window. "And I believe it's a little late to be storming around town alone."

"Oh, sure," she said with a sneer. "Being a hero isn't enough for you. You just have to play gentleman, too."

Ignoring her attitude shift from lady of the manor to peasant, Travis gestured for her to precede him out the door. Despite his service as a SEAL, Travis had never wanted to play hero. But he couldn't ignore the need to do something to fix this mess for her, to do whatever he could to make her feel better.

"C'mon," he said, walking over and offering his hand.

She looked at it, then those mermaid eyes rose to his face before dropping to his hand again.

"What?"

"Let's go."

Brows furrowed, she looked around the office and gave a small shudder before tucking her hand in his. Her fingers were slender, making Travis want to be extra careful not to crush those delicate bones as he pulled her to her feet.

Upright, she swayed a little, so he left his hand in hers. Just because he didn't want to have to scoop her off the floor, he told himself.

Her gaze, foggy with confusion and frustration, skimmed from the floor to the wall, then shifted away.

"Where are we going?" she asked, her words faint as they moved through the doorway.

He shoved the side door open, gesturing with his free hand for her to go first, then pulled her down the beach. They'd take the ocean route, give her time to decompress.

And him time to think.

"Your hotel should work."

"Look, buddy. You're hot and all, but there's no way in hell I'm going to sleep with you after all this."

God, what a woman. His lips twitched. He loved that her mind just went there.

"Not for that, but thanks for thinking about it. We're going to figure out what the hell happened here tonight."

"What do you mean?"

When he didn't respond, she dug her feet into the sand. It wasn't much in the way of an anchor, given that she hardly weighed a thing and couldn't get much of a grip in those fancy heels of hers. But Travis stopped anyway.

"What?"

"What do you mean by that?" Lila asked again. "The figuring out what the hell happened part."

"Just what I said. You think you saw some guy murdered. I don't know if you did, but I'll accept that you saw something. Now we've got to figure out the particulars."

"Wait here," he told her.

A lifetime of her father's arrogance had her chin lifting and an automatic refusal on her lips. But given that the alternative to obeying was to open the door to her room herself, she kept her mouth shut. And yes, maybe took a couple of steps back toward the stairs.

Just in case she had to make a run for it.

But Hawkins, the mighty SEAL, used her key to unlock the door and shoved it open. She held her breath when he disappeared inside. But a few moments later, he was back in the doorway, gesturing for her to come on in.

"The room's clean," he said when she joined him.

"Of course it is. It's a good hotel and I'm hardly a slob." She caught his eye roll. "What?"

"I meant clean, as in there's nothing dangerous in here."

Oh.

"Thanks," she murmured. Still, she left the door open. Just in case. "I appreciate you walking me back, but you don't have to stay."

"I didn't plan on it." His smile flashed, fast and wicked. "Just making sure you're okay before I go."

"I'm fine." Teetering between embarrassment over the night's events and frustration that her rescuer was a damned SEAL, Lila gestured coldly toward the door. "Feel free to go."

Before he took a step, there was a thump on the open door. Lila jumped so high, she almost lost her shoes. A scream lodged in her throat. All Lila saw was a shadow and a flash of silver.

Hawkins pivoted, cussed and grabbed his gun, gestured for her to get behind him.

With her heart locked too tight in her throat for the sound to escape, she closed the two feet between them in a single jump to angle herself behind Hawkins. Thank God the man was so tall and broad. He was as good as a wall.

A hint of guilt seeped through the terror pounding through her. Enough guilt that Lila forced herself to shift just enough to see around him.

"Senorita Adrian?"

Oh. The rush of adrenaline left so fast, Lila had to grab Hawkins's arm to keep from falling when her knees went soggy.

"Are you okay?" The girl from earlier who'd brought Lila the phone was there with a tray, a tidy stack of pink messages and a bright smile.

"Fine." Lila thumped her fist on her chest to make sure her heart was still beating the right tempo. She stepped into the open and gave the girl a shaky smile. "Just fine."

"*Bueno*, senorita. I have your nightcap, Ms. Adrian. And a few messages."

"Is it alcoholic?" Lila asked, almost desperate for a drink at this point.

"Hot spiced tea and cinnamon cookies," the girl said with a smile, lifting the lid. "It does go well with tequila if you'd like me to have some sent up."

With a flirtatious smile, the sloe-eyed brunette gave Hawkins a once-over as she stepped around him, then offered Lila an arch look.

"Would you like a second serving? I can have it delivered very quickly."

"No. No, thank you," Lila added, trying to soften her tone from frantic anger to genial gratitude. "This is fine."

It took a few more minutes of chitchatty friendliness to scoot the girl out the door. Mostly because the brunette was more interested in the beach bum than in leaving.

Finally, Lila got her out and, this time, closed the door. She barely resisted snapping the lock. Instead, she strode back to the small table with its covered tray and yanked off the dome.

At first sniff, she wished she'd opted for the tequila. Still, maybe flowers and spices would settle her nerves enough to figure out what to do next. So she lifted the etched orange mug. Then, remembering her manners, she turned to face her reluctant guest and lifted the cup.

"Would you like some?"

"Hell, no. That's going to taste gross," the beach bum declared, casually leaning against the wall and crossing his feet at the ankles.

Did the man never stand upright, Lila wondered, taking a defiant swallow.

She almost gagged.

It tasted like flowers sprinkled with nutmeg. Which, she decided after a second sip, was pretty gross.

"You should have sent for the tequila."

"Why are you still here?" Irritated, she shot him a dirty look. Did the guy always have to be right?

"Just doing the gentlemanly thing and making sure you're okay after your traumatic experience."

"I'm surprised."

"That I can be a gentleman?"

"That you think I had an actual traumatic experience," she corrected, exchanging the tea for a cookie. It was actually pretty good, she decided after a tentative nibble.

"I don't doubt your experience."

"Just my perception?"

"Look, whatever you saw, just put it out of your head. Get some sleep," Hawkins suggested, straightening from the wall and putting one hand on the doorknob.

"Every time I close my eyes, I see him hit the floor." She tugged her fingers through her hair, needing any relief she could get from the tension dragging at her brain. "I see the blood splattering everywhere. Hear Rodriguez's body as he hit the floor."

"Maybe try erasing those images. Replace them with something else," he suggested, his eyes focused on her hair as Lila finger combed it in an attempt to relieve the pressure on her scalp.

"You think it's that easy?"

"I didn't say easy."

There was something in his eyes that reminded Lila that SEALs worked damned hard to earn those hero badges. They saw ugly things, did ugly things. Which meant he probably knew what he was talking about.

Did Lucas get that same look when he thought about his time as a SEAL? Would she even recognize it if she saw it firsthand? She was pretty sure she had a better handle on the expressions on this stranger's face than she did her own brother's. Did this guy, Hawkins, know Lucas? Had they served together?

She didn't want to ask.

Her stomach clenched.

She didn't want to know.

She just wanted this to all be over.

So she strode to the door.

"I'll be fine," she said as confidently as she could, twisting the knob and throwing it open.

Obviously used to following orders, he straightened and walked over, stopping inches from her.

Lila held her breath.

The look in his eyes was still intense, but wasn't filled with horrors. Or worry.

She was pretty sure that look in those dark depths was desire. Her fingers gripped the doorknob so tight her knuckles hurt when he reached out to give her a hesitant pat on the shoulder. She trembled a little at his touch, not sure if it was comfort or answering desire spinning through her system.

It didn't matter, she realized. She couldn't do justice to either.

"Call down to the front desk, get that tequila if the night gets rough."

"Thank you," she said quietly, her eyes locked on his.

His gaze dropped to her lips for a single heartbeat. Lila's mouth went dry. Then he met her gaze again and gave the briefest of smiles.

"Take care."

That was it.

Just "take care," and he was gone.

She shut the door most of the way, angling herself behind it. And watched through the crack as he strode down the hallway. His jeans were on the baggy side, so the view wasn't as sweet as it had been when he'd strode out of the water in cotton trunks that afternoon. But given that he had some really long legs and slender hips beneath incredible shoulders, she realized it was just as well.

Seeing the curve of his butt would probably be the last straw for the night. She'd call him back, ask him to tuck her in, maybe share that tequila he kept talking about.

And that would be bad, she told herself.

The guy might be an uptight jerk, but the man was seriously hot. Hot, sexy and, maybe deep, deep down, kinda sweet.

And he was a Navy SEAL.

Lila sighed.

Didn't it just figure.

Chapter 5

Over the course of his recovery and during his self-enforced seclusion here in Puerto Viejo, Travis had made a point of avoiding hard alcohol. A beer here and there wasn't a big deal. But he'd seen too many strong men fall into a bottle during hard times, never to climb out again long enough to discover if the times had gotten any better or not.

But as he walked away from pretty blonde Lila's hotel room, he rubbed his hand over the back of his neck and debated making tonight the exception.

He'd been too focused on busting his ass to be the best SEAL possible to follow the expected Navy tradition of heavy drinking and wild partying. Of course, now that he'd jacked up his knee, he had plenty of time for bellying up to the bar.

But as he approached the beachside drinking hole, he kept hobbling on.

"Hey, there. Yo, it's Hawkins, right? Hold up. I want a word."

"Take as many as you like," Travis said, not slowing his pace. He wasn't surprised to see the cop who'd backed Montoya at the bar sidle up to him.

"I want those words with you, senor. Let's step in here." The cop slapped one hand on Travis's arm and jerked his chin toward the little side street between the market—with its windows boarded up for the night—and Lolo's bar, sparsely populated since everyone was partying on the beach.

"You want to talk, do it while we walk."

The guy's plain face screwed up into an expression of outrage.

"Do you know who I am? You do realize I'm an officer of the law, yes?"

"Yep."

He didn't know the guy's name or rank. But he'd met plenty of cops like this one. They could be found in any small town in any country in the world. They used the little bit of power bigger cops allowed them to puff themselves up and annoy the hell out of everyone.

"If you know who I am, then you know I work for Montoya. With my help, Montoya runs this town."

It wasn't the words that made Travis stop and stare. It wasn't even the implicit threat. It was pure curiosity.

"What does any of that have to do with me?" he asked, leaning against a bench made from a couple of planks slid through the holes of cinder blocks.

"Perhaps nothing." The cop planted his feet in the dusty grass in front of the bench as if his skinny frame and holstered gun would stop Travis from making any unexpected moves.

Figuring it would probably be less a pain in the ass to

make nice now than show the guy how wrong he was, Travis shifted the weight off his bad knee and gave the cop a smile.

When his eyes went wide and the cop took a stumbling step backward, Travis toned down the teeth and tried a friendlier tone.

"I didn't get your name."

"Uh, Agente Garcia. I'm the special liaison with the Policía Turística," Garcia said, pride giving his quiet voice an edge. "We're on special assignment, you know. To ensure the safety of tourists and visitors to our fine country."

Travis rubbed one finger over his chin and wondered if Garcia realized he'd left out those pesky local citizens from the list he was sworn to serve and protect.

"We know who you are, of course. Senor Hawkins, yes? You're a military man, good friend with Senor Constantine and living in his home while he's serving his duty to your government. You are here to rest and recreate." Garcia offered an ingratiating smile that stopped just a step or two below ass-kissing. "You're not here to get involved in silly local issues."

Now Travis didn't care if it made Garcia nervous. He had to smile.

"You all think murder is silly around here?"

"No, no." Garcia looked almost animated when he shook his head. "Real murder, that's bad. We take action when someone is truly killed."

Okay.

Travis watched a pair of drunk women walking,

wearing more fabric in their shoes than they had covering their butts.

"Did you guys run down Rodriguez?" he asked, his eyes, like Garcia's, on the swaying hips as the drunks fell on each other in groping giggles.

"Montoya, he'll take care of it," Garcia assured him, his skinny head tilting when the women almost giggled their way horizontal. "In the meantime, the captain, he was just wondering if you were thinking about making trouble. He likes a peaceful town, you know. But that lady, Senorita Adrian, she's got trouble written all over her. He doesn't much like that."

"And being civic minded, Montoya sent you to give me a warning that the blonde is trouble?"

"You could say that."

"Was that the extent of the warning?"

"*¿Qué?*"

"Did Montoya have anything else to add to the warning? You know, like probable outcomes if I don't stay away from the blonde troublemaker. You know, the follow-up threats that go with the warning."

"Would we threaten a man as powerful as you, Senor Hawkins?" Garcia asked, lifting both hands with fingers spread wide. "That would be very careless on our part. No, no. We are a small police force with limited resources. I believe that the captain is simply concerned that those resources be used correctly."

"She wasn't making it up just to get attention," he told the cop. "Whatever Lila Adrian actually saw, she's not budging from her story."

"She's mistaken."

Travis was good at reading people, but he couldn't get a read on this guy. His tone was nervous, but looking at his face was like trying to see someone through smoke.

"You said Montoya was running down Rodriguez?"

"I'm sure Captain Montoya has spoken with him."

And Travis was sure he hadn't.

What he wasn't sure of was whether Montoya hadn't done so out of disinterest, out of laziness or out of complicity.

Bells chimed a warning in the back of his head, but Travis easily silenced them. He was here to recover from his injuries and figure out his life. Not to get involved with local politics or blondes.

He didn't care how irritating he found the former or how hot he thought the latter.

"No worries," he said with a shrug.

"Senor?"

"Tell Montoya not to get his panties in a twist. I'm not here to make trouble." Aching from the quick march from his place to the restaurant, then the restaurant to the hotel and now back again, Travis shifted his weight again. "Besides, I doubt I'll ever see the blonde again."

"There are plenty of other pretty *turistas*. And you are a hot catch, senor," Garcia said, his slap to the shoulder having the same impact as a mosquito bite. Quick, irritating, then forgotten. "I'm sure you'll find someone else to enjoy."

Yeah.

Whatever.

Travis didn't say goodbye.

He just left.

He didn't bother returning to the hut. No point.

Being inside that little civilian house at night was a little rough lately. Like trying to sleep in a box while the sides were falling in. It wasn't claustrophobia. He'd spent years on a submarine, which was only slightly less roomy than a sardine can.

He knew what the problem was. He'd been told enough times by plenty of people he respected. Flashbacks and dreams, the feeling of being trapped by circumstances. They were all symbolic for the rest of his life. If he ever figured out what to do with that life, the dreams, the suffocating stress, they'd all go away. The problem was, he wasn't having any luck figuring out what to do.

Scrubbing his hand over his head, Travis headed for the beach and his hammock. And the hoped for oblivion of the night.

He threw himself into the comfortable mesh and searched for peace in the stars above and the sea beyond. But like most nights, that peace was nowhere to be found.

But tonight instead of being kept awake by the pain in his leg and the litany of questions over his future, it was the memory of Lila's face.

He'd thought the woman was hot the first time he'd seen her. And once he'd seen her with her hair down, hot had progressed to incendiary.

Because, damn, he had a thing for long hair on a woman. Lila's was a sweet combination of silver and gold, the colors twining together like ropes. He wasn't an expert, but he'd guess those were expensive highlights.

Everything about her screamed costly. Or wealthy. No, he decided after contemplating that for a half minute. The woman was definitely expensive.

She'd cost him plenty tonight, not just by being a pain in the ass.

And the cost hadn't just been in those strained relations with the local cops. That he actually didn't give a rip about. Montoya was an ass. Garcia, too. But asses or not, he didn't figure they'd be dogging him much now that they knew he wasn't going to play.

No, her cost was more along the lines of peace of mind.

Given that his mind hadn't touched peace in about eight months, one could say that was a worthy exchange. At least he'd be distracted from his problems by a sexy blonde. She had a sweet little body and a sharp tongue. His favorite combination.

Travis sighed.

Because as sure as he was that he'd finally found a woman intriguing enough to distract him from the hell that was his current situation, he was just as sure that she was a whole mess of trouble.

Once, he'd specialized in trouble.

Now he was just no good at it.

And no amount of sexy could negate that.

Lila needed comfort. She debated whether to call room service for that tequila. There was nothing like a nice, stiff drink or a huge hunk of chocolate cake for comfort. Or given this night from hell, she figured she deserved both.

But as she reached for the phone on the desk, she saw the blinking red light and let her hand drop to her side. She'd make do with crappy tea and dry cookies.

And maybe a few painkillers.

Or if she checked those messages, a few dozen.

Lila kicked her shoes off with enough force that one hit the closet door and the other slammed into a wall. She left them there for three long seconds before she couldn't stand it. With quick steps, she snagged the one that'd ricocheted off the wall, then strode over to the closet for the other before setting them neatly, side by side, inside.

Then she got back to pacing, her steps fast and rigid as she made her way from the bathroom to the window, from the door to the wall and back again. Four points, over and over again.

All the while, she debated.

Did she follow her father's orders and take that helicopter in the morning? she wondered when she reached the window.

She really had seen a man killed. Hadn't she? She turned at the bathroom and headed for the door. A man she was here specifically to see, whose body had disappeared?

She came up against the wall and made another turn to stare out the window. She stared out at the sliver of beach visible from here. Was Hawkins out there somewhere? She'd bet he was glad to be done with her.

She dropped her head against the glass, letting it cool her overheated forehead as she gave a soft laugh.

The poor guy.

She just had totally screwed up his night.

Not as much as poor Chef Rodriguez's was screwed up, though, she reminded herself, forcing her feet to start moving again.

That poor man was dead, dammit. She knew he was. What had he been scared of? Because that'd been fear she'd seen on his face when they'd talked. She should have asked. She should have pushed. Maybe she could have saved him? Helped him? Something?

And what did Hawkins do when she told him she'd found a dead guy? He'd all but called her a liar. Sure, he'd stuck by her, but that didn't negate the fact that he didn't believe her.

She'd watched a man get shot, saw him fall in a splatter of blood. How could he have survived that? Was it possible that he'd gotten up off that floor? Could he still be alive?

Maybe she was wrong.

Maybe she hadn't seen what she thought.

She ran a trembling hand through her hair.

The cops didn't think she had.

Neither did Hawkins. Mr. Perfect SEAL, with his elite training. He probably had a bunch of degrees and a chest full of medals and a file full of commendations. Which made him, what? A total know-it-all with a hero complex.

Oh, she knew the type. She'd grown up in the shadow of them. Oh-so-perfect and filled with righteousness.

No wonder the police hadn't believed her. Why would they if Hawkins didn't?

And then there was the lack of evidence. No body.

No sigh of foul play. No creeps who looked capable of murder chasing after her.

Her father would say she was just trying to get attention.

She gave a low growl.

Here she was, in a totally different country, and she felt as if her controlling father and her perfect brother were right here, looming over her shoulder. Leaking their judgment and righteousness and domination all over her in big, oozing drips.

She clenched her teeth to hold back the scream.

At least Hawkins hadn't oozed.

Instead, he'd been all manly and helpful. He hadn't believed her, yet he'd called the police. He hadn't wanted to deal with her, but he'd not only gone back to the restaurant, but he'd walked her to her room.

What did that make him?

A hero *and* a gentleman?

A very sexy man?

Okay. Maybe he was a little sexy, she thought, shoving both hands through her hair so it lifted off the back of her neck, then releasing so it fluttered over her shoulder blades.

Or a lot sexy, she admitted with a hefty sigh.

Not just his looks, although those were a few degrees hotter than hot. Maybe it was that body. There was a lot of it and all of it was prime.

Which didn't matter in the least.

There was no reason for her to waste time thinking about that beach bum. She was sure he'd stopped thinking about her before he'd hit the hotel exit.

Which meant that giving him even one more thought was stupid. Especially with everything else she had to worry about.

Lila dropped into the desk chair with a huff and shoved her fingers through her hair again, this time, gripping them tight close to the scalp. Elbows propped on the desk, she stared at the blinking red light until her eyes watered.

She knew who it was.

She knew what he wanted.

She was going to ignore it.

No way in hell she was going add to her rotten night by listening to a cacophony of orders by yet another man who didn't give her credit for having a brain.

Besides, she knew what the messages would say. Bottom line, her father expected her to be on that helicopter in the morning.

The helicopter that would provide her with a free ride out of town. Away from dead bodies and sexy beach bums and obnoxious cops. All it'd cost her was a week of party planning, a night of playing hostess and a ton of pride. And sure, maybe she'd have a few sleepless nights and guilt-ridden nightmares. But she'd be through with this mess.

Before she gave in to years of giving in to the temptation, she jumped up and hurried across the room to grab her scarf out of the closet, then tossed it over the phone to hide the blinking light.

Her cell phone rang, mocking her determination.

And, she realized as she grabbed it, her assertion of

her own brainpower. Her stomach unclenched when the screen didn't show temptation.

"Hi, Corinne."

"Hey. How'd the meeting go?"

"Oh, so bad."

"Oh, please. How bad could it be? You're the queen of closing the deal. You've probably got three new clients while you're signing up that chef."

Lila knew that tone. It was Corinne's kiss-ass tone. Which meant that she had something to do with at least half of those blinking lights. Usually, she'd placate and soothe and cheer. But this had been one hell of a night.

"The hottest guy on earth thinks I'm a drama queen pain in the butt. The local police think I make up crimes for attention. And my reason for being here was shot in front of me tonight."

"Oh."

Lila listened to glass hitting glass, looked at her tepid flower water and rubbed two fingers between her eyes. God, this night sucked. With that in mind, she filled Corinne in on the details.

"Chef Rodriguez is dead?"

"Well, I saw someone shoot him. I saw blood. He hit the floor. So yeah, he's dead."

"Are you going to tell your father? You should call him. He has contacts. He can help."

She'd rather set her hair on fire.

"Not even my father can bring a man back from the dead," she pointed out before adding, "and since that's beyond his power, there's no reason for him to hear anything about this. Right, Corinne?"

"Okay." Somehow, Corinne managed to fill that single word with so much doubt that it practically oozed through the phone. "Then you're coming home? Or are you heading for San Diego?"

"Home. I need to arrange a ride to San José, change my flight and be home the day after tomorrow."

With that in mind, she flipped open her laptop to pull up her flight info. Hearing the clicking over the line, she knew Corinne was doing the same, so she tried to click faster. But as usual, Corinne hit the info first.

"Since the hotel doesn't have transport, you'll need to pay for a ride." She reeled off the choices and costs before Lila found the website. "There's a hefty penalty for changing your flight. But it's still cheaper than continuing to pay for a hotel room."

Lila's head hurt enough that she was willing to risk the tea. It took two tries before she could swallow it, but once she did, she said, "I'll take it from here."

"Wouldn't it be easier to take the free ride with its plush seats and free drinks and actual in-fight meal and a cozy blanket that didn't come wrapped in plastic?"

"You are an airline snob," Lila pointed out.

"Or a smart woman who knows that building a long-term, successful business takes more than determination. It takes planning. It takes foresight. It takes connections, Lila. You really should stop pissing off yours."

Nope. Not going to happen. When it came to her doing what her father wanted, she'd rather be covered in honey and dipped in ants.

"I'll handle my own travel arrangements."

"Sure. If that's what you want." Even her words

pouted. "But I thought you were kinda, well, you know, financially challenged."

"Are you implying that I'm broke?"

"Aren't you?"

Lila toggled over to her bank account and pulled a face. She'd argue poor rather than broke, but Corinne had a point. After buying a new computer system and recent travel costs, Lila didn't have a lot of money to waste.

"This trip was supposed to be funded by the Martins' finder's fee. My commission on hiring Rodriguez would have covered my travel expenses. My hotel fee. And, yes, my rent and business expenses for the next three months."

"And you're sure you won't take your father's help?"

"I'm sure."

"Are you sure that cook is really dead?"

"Someone shot him." Lila dropped her head to the desk and let it bounce a couple of times. "He looked dead."

"But the police said he wasn't, didn't they?"

"The police didn't find a body, so they made no actual determination."

"So he might be alive?"

"I don't see how. He was shot multiple times and there was so much blood. He hit the floor and he didn't get up." This time Lila knocked back the tea without hesitation, letting the vile spice coat her throat. It didn't do anything to wash away the images burned in her brain. "The man was dead, Corinne. He was dead."

"But are you sure it was the cook?"

"Chef," Lila absently corrected, shoving away from

the desk to pace off the pictures in her head. "Rodriguez is a chef. Was a chef. I don't know."

"But if he's not dead, then you can still hire him and make the Martins happy. Mrs. Martin is preggo, which means if they're happy with their dinners, they're going to hit you up to find them the perfect nanny next."

"Darlene Porter would be perfect for them. She speaks three languages, lived in Europe for two years as an au pair and once she got over obsessing about juice cleanses, she hit the right note on healthy eating that'd really appeal to them."

She was already seated and making notes on her pitch when she remembered that the only way she'd make her commission was if she satisfied the Martins. To satisfy them she needed a living chef. Rodriguez, to be specific.

"I'm pretty sure he's dead," she said under her breath.

"Pretty sure isn't totally sure," Corinne pointed out encouragingly.

What if the cop was right? What if she'd imagined the whole thing? It wasn't like she'd actually seen his face straight on. But the body had been sporting the same bushy mustache and impressive gut as the chef. And he'd been wearing the same clothes she'd seen on the man earlier in the day. Same hairstyle, same thick part in the same color of hair. And yes, he'd been in the chef's office where everyone she'd asked had said Rodriguez was working.

But maybe it hadn't been him.

Lila tapped her pen against her notepad in a couple rounds of rat-a-tat before sighing.

"You know, maybe I should visit the restaurant

again." She opened the database on her laptop and started scrolling. "But I have his home address here. The police didn't seem interested in following up, but I can check on him myself."

"Um, maybe not by yourself. If the chef really is dead, someone killed him."

"The cops think I made it up."

"What about the sexy guy? Will he go with you?"

"He thinks I made it up."

"He stuck with you all evening, then walked you back to your hotel."

"He's a gentleman." With maybe the nicest butt she'd ever seen. Which was beside the point.

"But you were hot for him."

"I wouldn't say hot." Extremely warm, with a few icy sparks due to his lousy attitude and a strong cold front due to his being a damned SEAL.

"You trusted the guy enough to grab on to him when you were scared," Corinne pointed out. "You should take him with you."

"Trust is a stretch. I'd have jumped into the arms of any big, strong man who looked like he could handle a couple of gun-toting killers."

"Lila, the guy stuck with you through all that. I'm sure he'd do the right thing again for an hour or so tomorrow, too."

Of course he would.

"He's a SEAL."

"Oh." Glass clinked again. "Look, text me before you go to the restaurant. Make sure there are other people there when you go in. And absolutely, positively do not go to his house alone."

Before Lila could protest, Corinne added, "A guy was killed. It's not paranoid to consider that a dangerous situation."

"I'll be careful," Lila promised grimly, her knees giving a quick tremble in remembered terror. "I'm only staying long enough to find out whether Alberto Rodriguez is dead or alive. If he's alive, I'll give him my pitch, I'll convince him to take the job, then I'll get the first flight home."

"And if he's dead?"

Lila threw her hand in the air. She'd already reported it to the police. To a SEAL. What was left?

"I'll get someone to listen," she vowed.

"Lila, this whole thing makes me nervous. You should come home tomorrow. Your dad made arrangements already. Use those. Come back to California. You'll save in travel costs, make nice with your dad, get back home safely, get your dad's support. You do that event your dad wants, make some new connections, find us a handful of needy new clients. It's a win-win."

Lila pushed aside the dregs of crappy tea and looked around the hotel room with its brilliant colors and tired art. She glanced out the window at the gorgeous moonlit ocean and shadowy figures, any one of which might be a murderous killer.

"Okay. Maybe," she acknowledged, sinking into the bed as her faith in herself sank as low as her energy. "I'll call you tomorrow."

She clicked off, tossed the phone aside and rubbed her

hands over her face. She wished she could wipe away the aching confusion. When that didn't work, she shoved to her feet and, snagging her robe from the closet, headed for a hot bubble bath.

She'd soak away her worries, then she'd go to sleep. She'd decide on the rest on the morning.

But by morning, all Lila had was a headache brought on by a lack of sleep and the million questions and doubts ricocheting around in her mind.

She was 100 percent sure that she didn't want anything to do with her father.

She was 90 percent sure she'd witnessed a murder.

She was 85 percent sure the man she'd seen killed was Rodriguez.

What she wasn't sure of was what the hell to do.

Since she didn't, she finished packing and tucked her key card in her pocket before leaving her room to see if the local drugstore was open yet. She needed something for this headache, something for the nausea in her belly and, maybe, a bowl of fruit.

"Buenos días, senorita," the pretty girl at the front desk greeted with a smile bright enough to add to Lila's headache. "You have messages."

Of course she did. Lila took the pink slips of paper the girl held out without a word. She knew who they were from, what they said, and couldn't quite summon the energy to be annoyed. Instead, she tucked away the reminder to try again later along with the messages.

"Can I get aspirin?"

"I'm sorry, senorita. We can't dispense medications."

"Where's the nearest pharmacy or drugstore?" she asked, looking around the quaint lobby.

Walking a lot faster than the easy stroll she'd enjoyed the previous evening, she followed the simple directions to the edge of the beach.

Instead of containing partying people, this morning's crowd was sparse. The handful of people on the street looked like they were heading for work, a handful biking with baskets filled with fruits and vegetables. She peered at each of them, trying to see if she saw murder on any of the faces.

She was pretty sure murderers were more the night prowling sort than the veggie carting kind. But how could she be sure?

She couldn't.

She hadn't seen the shooters' faces. She'd seen half of a man holding a gun, and heard two male voices. That wasn't enough to pick them out from the crowd.

Still, the knots were so tight in her stomach that she figured she'd better get nausea medicine along with the aspirin.

For now, she just needed to forget about it. Enjoy the view, she told herself, glancing past the sandy dunes at the white-tipped waters beyond. The fishermen were out, she noted, seeing their boats dotting the horizon. Anchored next to a rickety looking dock of dry, rotted wood was a cabin cruiser that looked too battered to brave the crashing waves.

She felt a little like that boat.

Rough.

Unstable.

And seasick.

Or maybe it was the nerves bouncing around in her belly making her woozy.

She hurried around a pair of dogs into the tiny convenience store with its poster-plastered windows and local candy display. Five minutes later, a small paper bag in one hand and her head now throbbing so hard she could feel every beat of her heart, Lila headed back to the hotel. And yes—her shoulders drooped—to her father's pilot.

Independence was all well and good, and something she'd spent years chasing. But even knowing the cost of giving it up, Lila didn't see any other choice.

She wasn't going back to that restaurant by herself. She didn't care if Chef Rodriguez jumped out of a cake he'd baked himself and yelled surprise. She'd relived that body hitting the floor a dozen times in her dreams.

Her father had said he'd have the helicopter here at eight, so it'd be here at eight. She was already packed, so maybe she had time for breakfast and a whole handful of meds.

She glanced at her watch, then someone jostled her shoulder. A beefy hand grabbed at her as if to steady her steps. Before Lila could snap that she was fine, before she could do more than turn her head, the same hand slapped over her mouth, another wrapping around her waist to drag her toward the beach.

She jammed her heel into the guy's leg. When it got her a curse and slowed him a little, she kicked a few more times. He yanked her into the deep doorway next to a bike shop to get a stronger grip on her.

She squirmed, wrenching her arm this way and that,

trying to yank it free enough so she could reach into her purse. There was pepper spray in there. She never traveled without it. She just had to get her hands on it. One finger on the canister, and she'd be able to blast this hulking man right in the damned face.

Or she could scream. Screaming was good. Even at six in the morning on a deserted beach, there had to be someone out there who'd hear her. But now that he'd readjusted his grip, he continued dragging her to the beach. Through the tall tufts of grass, she could see a dock, and glinting in the morning sun, a boat.

Lila fought harder.

He managed a few dozen feet before she was able to wiggle her jaw enough that his hand slid higher. As soon as his finger hit the seam of her lips, she bit, hard, grunting her triumph at the taste of blood.

But while her abductor uncovered her mouth to shake off the pain, he didn't release her.

So all Lila could do was scream.

And hope someone—anyone—would hear.

Chapter 6

Travis didn't know what had woken him from a dead sleep, but his eyes flew open. Heart racing, he jackknifed into a sitting position, forgetting that he had crashed in the hammock. It went swinging like a carnival ride as he looked around, trying to get his bearings.

The beach.

Yeah. He was on the beach.

He squinted at the sun as it rose over the ocean and deemed it about six in the morning. The beach was empty but for a few bodies curled up here and there in singles and pairs. Leftovers from the previous night's bonfire, he supposed.

So what had woken him?

Another nightmare?

He had only a vague handle on his last dream, but he was pretty sure it'd included bare skin and hot pleasure instead of vicious pain.

So that probably wasn't it.

He tried to puzzle it out, but all he could come up with were images of silken hair, sweet curves and a spike made to jab into his temple.

Then there was a scream.

Another scream, he realized, shoving gracelessly to his feet.

That's what'd woken him.

Lila was in trouble.

He was sure of it.

Oh, God.

Lila squirmed, trying to loosen the rope wrapped around her wrists. Her flesh burned as she twisted her hands from one side to the other, but the coils held tight.

Her earlier headache was now pounding hard enough to make her eyeballs throb, so she gave up twisting long enough to close them and let her head fall back against the wall.

Over the murmer of two men's voices fading into the distance, she could just imagine her father's response, his litany of *I told you so*'s as familiar as her own name. He'd pay a ransom. She knew he'd pay. She should have a little gratitude, and dammit, she was digging deep trying to find some.

But as much as she wanted to be rescued, as terrified as she was about whatever was going on, over what these men might do to her, she knew that if her father ransomed her, she'd never stop paying.

He was a man who expected a high return on his investments.

Maybe she could stay here.

She squinted her eyes open just enough to look around the cabin. Styrofoam showed through the fake-wood laminated walls dotted with the same black mold sweeping over the green Astroturf-style carpet. The dead fish scent was almost strong enough to overpower the aroma of musty mold.

She didn't want to stay here.

She wanted to go home.

Since the only sound she heard was the ocean, she forced her eyes open all the way and looked around.

She had to swallow three times to get air past the terror bubbling up in her throat. Once she'd found air, she managed to focus on the space.

No thugs in sight.

Nothing that looked like weapons of torture.

Maybe they kept the torture devices in another cabin.

Fingers clenching and unclenching behind her back, she multiplied sevens in her mind until her heart rate slowed enough to stop choking her.

Think, she told herself, letting her almost clear head fall back against the wall. Then, remembering what was on the walls, she yanked it upright again as fast as she could. Barely resisting the urge to scream, she shook it hard to try and get rid of anything that might've crawled into her hair.

She had to get out of here.

Now. God.

How?

She twisted again, this time her entire body instead of just her hands. When twisting didn't work, she squirmed, wriggled and damn near contorted herself into a pretzel. But the ropes didn't budge an inch.

She clenched her teeth tight to keep the scream from exploding from her throat. Her vision went black, white spots dancing in front of her eyes until she forced herself to breathe again.

Breathe and think.

Okay.

Maybe she should scream. Someone might be close enough to hear her. They'd come looking, stage a rescue and get her the hell out of here.

Then again, if the goons were on this boat, screaming would bring them running. And despite snapping her teeth on one goon's hand, she hadn't managed to get a solid look at any faces.

She didn't know if she'd been grabbed over the chef's possible murder, or if she was here in some crappy kidnapping quest.

And she was pretty sure that she wanted to get out of here before she found out.

Travis wasn't up on the voices of every female resident or tourist in Puerto Viejo, so he couldn't scientifically explain why he was sure those shrieks he'd heard were from Lila. In any case, he rolled out of the hammock, slammed his feet into shoes and hit the sand at a hard run.

The scream had come from the edge of the boardwalk. He scanned faces as he ran for anyone who looked like they might have seen or heard a thing. It took less than ten minutes to confirm that it was the curvy blonde who had been grabbed. That it was only one guy, whose description ranged from a short blond man with a beard to a huge bruiser with a scar.

His knee was throbbing by the time he'd finished

asking around. Since the direction the guy had hauled the blonde was as vague as the guy's description, Travis ran the most likelies and loped painfully toward the beach. The gamble paid off when he saw the deep furrows in the sand.

Since the ruts ended at the grayed wood dock, Travis took a second to review his options. He could get the cops. All it'd take was a whistle to get someone's attention. He could let the cops make the call. But their competence was iffy, and after the crap with Garcia last night, and every encounter he'd had with Montoya, he simply didn't trust them.

So he was on his own.

Outside his teammates, that was the way he preferred it.

So he assessed the situation.

It was possible Lila's captor had a boat waiting, but Travis hadn't heard a motor. He didn't see a wake. So the likeliest possibility was that the guy had dragged her to one of the boats on this dock.

Process of elimination ruled out the ski boat, Manny's dad's fishing boat and the oarless rowboat, leaving a cabin cruiser he hadn't seen before.

Target sighted.

Chances were high that Lila's captor was armed. But unless there were a dozen of them with automatic weapons, Travis figured he would have to handle it barehanded.

He kicked off his shoes and walked silently into the water. An easy swim around the perimeter gave him a view through three of the four portholes and assured him that the cabins were empty. Which meant Lila was in that last cabin. Whether or not she was alone was the question. He did a through recon of the top deck to assure himself that it was clear.

Travis grabbed on to the side of the boat, then hesitated.

And took a deep breath.

He'd been involved in a hell of a lot of rescue missions. He'd gone behind enemy lines to reclaim his men. He'd once rescued a freaking kitten from a palm tree— and how the hell that tiny ball of fluff had scampered thirty feet up was a puzzle.

Bottom line, he was an expert at scooping the needy out of messes.

So the fact that he had what might be nerves skittering down his spine over doing what came naturally was an irritation. But he had to actually stop and take another slow breath. He regulated his heartbeat, then silently flipped over the side of the boat.

Travis kept low, angling across the trash-ridden deck to the ladder that led below. He waited for the silence to shift. When it didn't, he slid down the rails, gripping tight to hold his weight so his feet made no impact when he set down.

He had the layout of the boat firmly in mind and knew which cabins he'd scoped were empty. Whoever had grabbed Lila appeared to be gone. But training was training, so he checked each one before pulling out his pocketknife to pick the lock of the last door.

Hand on the knob, Travis listened carefully before

twisting it open. He slid inside, silently pulling the door shut behind him and looked around the dimly lit cabin.

His jaw clenched at the sight of Lila tied to an exposed pipe. She was holding it together really well, but her fear was obvious. She was trembling hard enough that her feet bounced on the floor, her breath catching with each inhalation while she gnawed on her bottom lip.

He wanted to plow his fist into the face of the son of a bitch who'd grabbed her. He wanted to make him suffer for every second of fear she'd felt.

And he'd do just that, he silently vowed.

First, he'd get her out of here. He'd stash her somewhere safe. He'd figure out what the hell was behind her abduction, and who the hell had grabbed her.

Then he'd kick their asses.

But he had to start with the rescue part.

Immediately, he decided, watching her throw her head back.

"Hello," Travis said quietly, figuring he'd better head her off before she let loose the scream he saw building up there.

Blond hair tumbled around her flushed face, her mermaid eyes sparking fury as she glared. Her cheeks were flushed, her mouth poised to lose it. He had the feeling that if she weren't tied up, she'd fly across the room and try to kick his ass.

Then, as if suddenly realizing who was dripping seawater in the doorway, her mouth snapped shut and her eyes widened. She released her breath and her shoulders seemed to sag in relief.

Damn, she looked good.

"What the—"

"Quiet," he warned, keeping his voice down. The boat was empty, but sounds carried on the water and he didn't know when her captor would return.

At his admonishment, her mouth snapped shut. He watched with interest as she yanked herself in line. She took two deep breaths, which did some interesting things for her T-shirt, then pressed her lips together. She fluttered her lashes, narrowed her eyes, then shifted those full lips into a sexy smile.

"What took you so long? Aren't Super SEALs supposed to move faster?"

He couldn't figure out why, but her mouthy lack of appreciation made him want to grin. Instead, he gave her a hard-eyed scowl and arched one brow.

"You want out of here or not?"

She caught her breath, then let it go.

"Yeah. I want out of here."

"Then stop squirming so I can free you." The *shut up* he wanted to add to that was unspoken, but from the fury in her eyes, she obviously heard it all the same.

Damn, that was sexy.

He used his pocketknife to make quick work of the ropes around her ankles, then moved behind her. The rich, flowery scent of her hair wrapped around him tighter than the ropes around her wrists. He figured swimming to the rescue had earned him a little pleasure, so he breathed deep as he worked the blade through the three layers of hemp.

Untying her probably wasn't as sexy as tying her up

would be under different circumstances. But it sure put images of that scenario in his head.

Nice.

As soon as he'd cut the ropes, he rubbed his hands over her wrists to get the blood moving again. Her skin was like silk, her bones delicate. His hands moved slower, his thumb sliding along her flesh, easing the welts. She was still trembling.

Fury dug into his gut.

He knew the first step in this mission was to get Lila to safety. Which meant getting her off this boat and away.

But he wanted to beat the hell out of whomever had done this to her. He wanted to set her in the corner and wait until the son of a bitch came back, then beat him into a bloody stain on this mold infested carpet.

It wasn't training that had him shoving his personal impulses aside. It was the tiny tremors he felt in her wrists that beat time with her pulse.

Lila was the priority.

He'd beat the hell out of the guy later.

He jumped to his feet before he changed his mind. His knee pinged in an explosion of pain that shot from ankle to hip like shards of fired lightning.

Dammit.

He sucked in air, waiting for his vision to clear.

He gritted his teeth.

So much for freaking Super SEAL.

That part of his life was over.

Blown to hell, along with his goddamn knee.

"Um, Hawkins?" Lila kept her voice down, whether

because she was afraid of alerting her captor or because she realized he was in excruciating pain, he wasn't sure.

"What?" he snapped, damned if he'd take her pity.

"Can you help me up?"

Oh, yeah.

With a long, slow breath, Travis yanked control back where it belonged: firmly under his thumb.

"Rotate your ankles, make sure the blood is flowing before you stand. I don't want to have to carry you out of here."

"Such a gentleman," she murmured under her breath, stretching her legs out so her toes pointed, then arched before she circled each foot.

While she did, Travis tried to figure out why watching her work on her circulation was sexy. It wasn't the moves, so it had to be the woman.

"How many men did you see?" he asked, as much for distraction as because he wanted to know.

"One grabbed me, but I heard him talking to another one."

Two, minimum. Easy enough on his own. But he wasn't on his own.

"Let's get out of here."

Making sure to keep his weight on his left leg, he bent down and wrapped his hands around her waist. The move got him a face full of her hair and a lung full of what seemed like the smoky scent of flowers at midnight. Why the hell was that so sexy?

Gripping her waist tighter, he lifted her into a standing position and held on until he was sure she could stand on her own.

"There you go," he murmured, setting his jaw. Since the scent of her hair was getting to him, he placed his hands on her shoulders, pushed her forward a few inches. "Now we need to get out of here."

Before he did something stupid.

Really stupid.

Lila wished Hawkins hadn't let go of her.

She might start shaking again or something. Her heart was still bouncing and her knees did feel a little wonky. And his hands were big and warm. And surprisingly tender.

Or she was in a state of shock from being grabbed, tied up and tossed in a smelly room.

A smelly room he was rescuing her from.

"You ready?"

"To leave this dump?" Lila turned to give him a sardonic look. "Lead the way."

When he jerked his head toward the door, she figured it was a signal to head for the door. Despite the minute or so of circling her ankles, those first two steps were iffy. Her legs twitched and tingled enough to make her want to scream. It felt like a million spiders were electrocuting each other in her limbs.

Before she could do more than whimper, Hawkins wrapped one arm around her waist and half carried her to the door. Torn between embarrassment and a desperate desire to get the hell out of this pit, Lila grabbed the doorknob. Travis grabbed her hand before she could twist and yank.

"Have a little caution," he said, his voice low.

His hand still over hers, he twisted slowly but instead of opening the door, he laid his ear against it. Listening for that horrible man, she realized, shivering as dread curled in her belly.

Without thinking, she angled herself behind Hawkins, wrapping her free arm through his and holding tight. She didn't know what he was listening for, and couldn't hear a thing over her pounding heart.

That guy who'd grabbed her was huge. What if he was out there?

It was hard to swallow since her mouth was so dry, but after a couple of tries, she managed it.

Hawkins opened the door a centimeter at a time. Before he hit two inches, she squeezed his arm.

"Stop," she whispered urgently.

Shutting the door as silently as he'd opened it, Hawkins shifted just enough to give her a questioning scowl.

She didn't care if he looked angry. Her safety was in his hands. She had a right to feel safe, dammit.

"What's your whole name? First name," she corrected, shaking her head to rid herself of the confused thoughts racing through her brain. "Full name, and your rank."

His scowl sharpened as he lifted one brow.

"I beg your pardon?"

"Would you or would you not qualify this as a dangerous situation?"

His stare was hot enough to burn away the last remnants of sleep from her legs, but Lila didn't budge.

"There is minimal possibility of danger, but it never hurts to be prepared."

Lila pursed her lips and blew out a long breath. She knew doublespeak when she heard it. After all, she'd been hearing it most of her life.

"So if that guy and his friends are out there, it could get ugly. And while I'm sure you can handle anything that comes up, I believe that I deserve to know the full name of the man who's going to protect me."

He simply sighed before shifting his shoulders just enough to give the impression that he'd come to attention.

"Travis Hawkins, formerly Chief Petty Officer Hawkins of SEAL Team 7 under the command of Captain Jerry Traeger."

Lila felt like returning to the pipe and tying herself back up. Her brother served on the same team. As far as she knew, so had hundreds of others. But this was her life, so this sexy beach bum of a Super SEAL was probably BFFs with her sibling.

"Problem?" he asked. "Need to know my mother's maiden name or my BUD/S scores?"

Maybe. But she was too afraid the kidnapper might come back to take the time to ask.

"I'll ignore your sarcasm and you can save my life. Go ahead," she told him, giving a shooing motion of her hand. "Let's do this."

"Stay behind me."

As if she needed to be told that? Lila rolled her eyes, grabbed on to the waistband of his still-damp jeans and took a deep breath.

"Let's do this," she said again.

She followed him out the door, doing her best to keep her steps as silent as his. She couldn't do it, but she figured it was better to focus on that than wonder what they were going to face.

The boat might be filled with more creeps. The bruiser who'd grabbed her had bruised her with his big fat hand; he'd hurt her arms and legs tying her up so tightly. And he'd scared the hell out of her.

The idea of more like him scared her even more. Especially since she didn't know what they'd planned to do with her. Whatever it was, she was sure she wouldn't have liked it.

Nope. Focus on the steps. Watch where each foot goes to avoid the scattered trash. Toes first and ease to the heel.

She focused on her feet, following Hawkins from room to room. Cabins, she corrected after the third one. They were on a boat.

"It's clear," he said, his words so quiet she saw them more than heard them. When he tilted his head to the ladder, Lila stepped aside so she could follow his lead. She watched him grab the rails and pull himself onto the deck without his feet touching a single rung, and almost laughed. She wasn't following that lead. Numb or not, she needed her feet.

"It's the same crappy boat I saw earlier," she said, looking around when she'd reached the top of the ladder. The deck was covered with crumpled trash, crushed beer cans, splintered planks and a nasty stench. It looked like the scene of a frat party on spring break.

Having experience with frat parties, she tiptoed over to a bench to peer behind it. She angled her upper body to the right to check the helm in case anyone was hiding behind the wheel.

She inched over to the hold, bit her bottom lip and, cringing, started to lift the lid.

"What the hell are you doing?"

"Checking for creeps." *Duh.*

"The boat's clear. Let's get out of here before your creeps return." He pointed the fingers of both hands toward land.

"Are we swimming for shore?" she asked quietly. And, not that she didn't trust his skills, but she couldn't stop looking around in case the creeps were hiding nearby. "I can swim fast."

"You can swim. Or you can join me when I take that boat," he said, jerking his chin toward the dingy. "Either way, let's get the hell out of here before they come back."

"Boat. Definitely boat." She gave him her brightest smile and fluttered her lashes. "My hair takes forever to dry."

Since she was pretty sure that twitch on his lips was a smile, she grinned all the way down the ladder and into the boat.

While he settled onto the bench opposite her and took up the oars, Lila felt all of her adrenaline sink into her toes as she watched Hawkins row. His biceps bulged, then stretched with each stroke, the movement doing amazing things for his tight cotton tee. Was the fabric as soft as it looked? Were those muscles as hard?

She forced herself to look away, focusing on the water

instead of the hotness, and blew out a long breath. The man had rescued her from a horrible situation; the least she could do to show her appreciation was to not objectify him.

She knew what it was like to be seen as no more than a pretty face. Her own father basically saw her as a windup doll to be pulled out for hostessing duties, fundraisers and photo ops.

So it was rude, downright obnoxious, to reduce the man to a bunch of muscles.

Then she considered her day.

She'd been kidnapped by a monster goon, held in a moldy cabin, was rescued by a Super SEAL and had, somehow, survived it all.

She leaned back, resting her elbows on the back of the boat and let her eyes roam the muscled breadth of Hawkins's shoulders, slide over the mile-wide temptation of his chest, then rest on those mouthwatering biceps.

Hawkins was hot.

So damned hot.

And while she was pretty sure it wasn't even noon, she was pretty sure today had been the most horrible one of her life.

So if anyone deserved a treat, she did.

Chapter 7

It wasn't a major op and he might be a team of one, but Travis was pretty sure he'd rocked it.

Then again, he was pretty sure a Boy Scout—with or without his handy-dandy compass—could have tracked down the victim, rescued her from a dangerous situation on par with a flat tire on the freeway.

Still, he estimated that the time from scream to rescue was twenty minutes, five of which were on account of her babbling. Lila was unharmed, they'd left nothing behind and nobody had spotted them. It was good to know that not all of his skills were rusty.

At least, his rescue skills, he corrected, glancing over at Lila. His decision-making skills might be on the fritz. Because now that Travis had her installed in his place, he wasn't quite sure what to do with her.

She'd gone quiet in the boat, but she'd had a look in her eyes that touched off a flicker of heat in his belly and made him wonder if, once they'd found privacy, she'd suggest they strip naked for a round of sexual gymnastics.

But she hadn't jumped him. Instead, as soon as they'd

gotten here, she'd thrown herself on the couch like a fainting belle, complete with one arm thrown over her forehead.

Leaving him to grab a beer and toast a done job, if not a job well done. And debate whether he was relieved, or disappointed, that she wasn't interested in acting on that heat bouncing between them.

Relieved, he finally decided, drinking the beer.

That was a very sexy woman on his couch. But she was a very sexy woman that he'd just rescued. Which meant he shouldn't be focusing on the tempting curve of her breasts, thrown into sharp relief by the angle of her arm. His gaze traveled the length of her torso. Her waist was so small, he figured he could span it with both hands. By the time his eyes reached her hips, his mind was filled with all sorts of ideas, most of which needed a lot less clothing.

Damn, for a pain in the butt, the woman was seriously hot.

So, yeah. She had to go before she caused more trouble.

The kind that was a lot harder to get out of than abduction or murder.

He chugged half of his beer while he walked over to the couch.

"Are you ready to get out of here?"

"And go where?" Lila asked, her words muffled by her arm.

"To the police station, for starters. Then I'll drop you at your hotel room where you can do this damsel in distress thing in private."

"That'd be a no. A definite no on the first. And I am in distress, dammit. I was stuck in that smelly cabin for God knows how long. Don't I deserve a few minutes of damsel drama?"

Since she wasn't looking, Travis didn't bother to hide his grin.

"Well, get over yourself. You need to call the cops."

"That would be the same police department that called me a liar last night?" she said, dropping her arm to her side to give him a wide-eyed, incredulous look.

She had a point.

"They aren't the only cops in Puerto Viejo."

Her sigh was a work of art, but it did get her into a sitting position. She shoved both hands through her hair so it fell like a blond curtain over her shoulders, then tilted her chin to one side.

"And you think the other police in this town are going to believe me?"

He considered that, then shook his head.

"Probably not."

"Then why bother?"

"Maybe because you were abducted, which is illegal."

"So is murder."

"But unlike the missing dead guy, you're here to press charges."

"Against who?" She pushed to her feet and threw her hands in the air. "It isn't like either of us saw my abductor. And maybe, just maybe, that boat is registered or whatever to whoever is behind it, but what do you want to bet it's not? Or given the way my luck is going, that it's just gone."

She hurried over to the window with a hard stare, as if she could see all the way to the water and beyond the dunes to where the boat had been anchored. It was gone now, which meant the goons knew she was gone, too.

"I don't suppose you got any information about that boat? The vessel's name? Registration number?" She shot him a doubtful look over her shoulder. "Anything?"

Of course he'd looked. Travis debated taking offense, but since the vessel's name had been scratched off the hull and the registration painted over, he didn't figure it was worth the energy. Instead, he downed another swig of his beer and shrugged.

"You were the one searching the deck. Didn't you find anything significant?"

"I was looking for bad guys, not clues. Besides, you're the Super SEAL," she reminded him, turning around and giving him a look that made it clear that she didn't think much of that designation. "Isn't reconnaissance a part of your job description?"

"I was on rescue, not recon."

"Likely excuse," she said, and dismissed it with a flick of her wrist. "The bottom line is that we have nothing to take to the police that'll ensure they cooperate. They already believe I make crimes up for attention, remember?"

"Your call." He shrugged. "But your abduction might give credence to your murder claim. Something to keep in mind."

"If you want the police involved so badly, maybe you should have brought them with you to the boat, then," she suggested with a smile so sweet he was surprised her teeth didn't fall out.

"I was too busy chasing after your screams to stop and call the cops," he pointed out. "Rescuing you was the priority. And rescue you, I did. A little gratitude wouldn't hurt."

He'd expected a little more sass. So he was surprised when the corners of her mouth drooped and her eyes filled with regret.

"Sorry. I have a headache."

"Take some aspirin."

"I lost my aspirin when that horrible man grabbed me. My aspirin, my wallet and my phone." For the first time since he'd met her, she looked pissed. "My passport was in there, dammit. All my credit cards. Everything. That's going to make getting back home quite the adventure."

Intrigued, Travis watched Lila pace her way from the window to the couch and back again. He'd never thought much about it, but if he had, he'd probably have figured a lone woman in a foreign country who'd just been kidnapped would be a little more freaked out or panicked. Instead, Lila just looked irritated.

"What do you do?" he asked. "For a living, I mean."

"I'm a headhunter. I match wealthy clients with specially skilled employees. Chefs, nannies, concierges and the like." She reeled it off in a matter-of-fact tone that told him she'd explained it plenty of times.

"That's a job?"

"No. It's a career," she snapped. "A career that not only requires the right kind of connections and a talent for understanding what people really want, but also intelligence, and organizational skills and freaking determination. Maybe I'm not out there fighting off the country's enemies, but I make a difference in people's lives. Do you have a problem with that?"

There was an awful lot of bitterness in that tone, but for the first time since he'd rescued her, she looked like she was going to cry. So Travis let it go and gave her an easy smile.

"Actually, the way you keep cool and roll with the punches, I figured you might do something a little more kick ass. Cop, military, security. That kind of thing. Still, ass kicker or matchmaker, it doesn't much matter to me what you do, as long as you're good with it."

He tilted his head to the side and gave her a quick once-over, then smiled.

"So? Are you any good?"

Lila didn't know if he was referring to her job skills or something else, but either way, she wanted to wipe that smirk off his face.

So she angled her hips to one side, thrust out her chest and threw back her shoulders to make the most of her assets. She tossed her hair back and gave him a sultry look through her lashes.

"I'm better than good. I'm amazing. One hundred percent satisfaction, guaranteed." She ran her tongue over her bottom lip and arched one brow. "Not that you'll ever find out. Believe me, I'm way out of your league, Super SEAL."

"Now that's just mean," he said with a deep, appreciative laugh that made her want to smile. "And after I swam out, rescued you and everything."

"Sorry," she murmured, her words more frustrated than shamefaced. "Like I said, I have a headache."

One that was growing steadily worse as she tried to figure out what to do next. Leaving without a passport was going to be rough enough. But without her phone? Her credit cards?

But they did. Whoever *they* were.

Just thinking about it all was enough to make her want to scream.

Hoping to hold off on that, she dropped to the couch again and rubbed her forehead with the heels of both hands.

"I don't suppose you have anything for a headache?" she asked, now rubbing her temples.

He shook his head. "I'm not a fan of drugs. Of any kind."

She almost asked what he took for his sore leg, but she managed to bite back the question at the last second.

"You said this is your friend's place. Doesn't he and/or she have anything? Aspirin? Morphine? A good, sharp ax?"

"It's a he, and he handles pain the same way I do."

Oh, God. Lila wanted to groan. Not only Super SEAL, but Super SEAL from Martyr Land.

"So, what? Neither of you never experiences pain? Pain you want to get rid of, I mean."

She realized her mistake the second the words left her mouth. Thankfully, Hawkins kept his response to an ironic smile.

"You know what I mean," she muttered.

"There are plenty of other options. Stretching, breath work, meditation."

"Unfortunately, I'm a yoga beginner."

"What's yoga?"

Lila opened her mouth, then snapped it shut. She couldn't tell if he was joking or not.

"Any chance you'd be willing to run to the market, then?" she asked instead.

He rolled his eyes, but at least her pathetic expression had him chugging the last of his beer before tossing the bottle into a bin.

"You're proving to be a pain in the ass," Hawkins told her as he moved around behind her. Before Lila could twist around to see what he was doing, his hands gripped her shoulders.

She almost jumped to her feet, but before she could, his thumbs dug into the rigid knots and, with a quick twist loosened the tension, making her moan.

Okay. She could wait before making him stop. A few minutes, an hour, two or three days.

With each stroke, he rubbed away tension and soothed the pain riddling her body. He worked his way over her shoulders and along the sides of her throat before his fingers danced down her shoulder blades. He seemed to know exactly where to touch for the most impact.

"Oh, man," she groaned quietly. "You're so good."

"That's what they all say."

She'd put money on that.

When his fingers shifted from digging to soothing,

her body shifted into meltdown mode. Without the pain to distract her, all she had left was lust.

Totally inappropriate, she told herself. She'd never been the type for easy, no-strings-attached sex. Every physical relationship she'd even been involved in had come after weeks of dating and days of angsting over the possible repercussions.

So no matter how good Hawkins made her feel, no matter how stirred up his touch made her, it didn't matter.

She wasn't easy.

And the man himself was impossible.

Still, he did have amazing hands.

Such amazing hands.

Hawkins's fingers found every pain point, digging gently, releasing tension, soothing aches.

Hands that skimmed down her waist now, then back up her sides so his long fingers skimmed over her bra, just along the cups. Her breath caught as desire danced through her system, heating her belly and hardening her nipples.

For the first time in her life, Lila wanted to throw reason and responsibility aside and give in to the needs spinning through her system. She wanted to shift, just slightly to one side, so his hand could cup her breast.

He'd be incredible.

The best she'd ever had.

He'd make her forget everything.

In his hands, under his body, she'd forget all about her abduction and seeing a man murdered. She'd lose herself in passion, experience new realms of pleasure.

It would be incredible.

"You okay?"

Oh, God.

The man was simply trying to help her—again—and she was lusting after him. Again.

She was glad he was behind her when the heat in her belly climbed high enough to wash over her cheeks. She blew out a long breath, gave herself one more second to enjoy the sexual haze, then forced herself to twitch her shoulders.

"I'm fine," she said quietly. "That's a lot better. Thanks."

Lila didn't look at him. She couldn't do anything about the heat that probably still colored her face, but she knew enough to keep her lust-filled eyes averted as she hurried over to the front window.

For the first few seconds, she focused on trying to get her body's reaction under control. When that didn't work, she shifted to listening, trying to guess what he was doing behind her. But that made her imagine all the sexy things she wished he was doing behind her, so Lila forced herself to count the trees instead.

By the time she reached seventeen, she was ready to scream.

"Do you think they'll come here?" It was the first question that came to mind, and as soon as she asked it, she wished she'd just gone with silence and kept counting.

"Probably."

She was so surprised, she actually turned around to stare at him.

"You do?"

"Yeah." She tried to ignore the way his T-shirt shifted

over those mile-wide shoulders when he shrugged. "The highest probability is that whoever grabbed you is involved in the shooting. Which means they most likely know I was with you last night. When they realize you've escaped, they'll check your hotel first, then target me."

Lila wasn't sure which surprised her more.

The fact that he admitted that they were in possible probable, even—danger.

Or that he was smiling about it.

"And you think that's a good thing?"

"Yeah. Why not?" At her incredulous stare, he dropped onto the couch and gave another shrug. "Look, whatever is going on, you're in trouble. Since you've dragged me out of my hammock and into the middle of your problems, I'd prefer to get it settled as quickly as possible."

"So you can get back into your hammock?"

"Exactly." He pointed a finger at her in agreement. "The sooner they come after you again, the better."

Lila wondered if she should be offended at his easy welcome of murderers having another go at her. He had a good point, though. She'd dragged him into this, so the sooner it was done, the sooner he could go back to being a beach bum.

"I can just leave town," she said, ignoring the hoops she'd have to jump through to get out of here without a passport.

"Without answers? You'd leave without knowing what happened to Rodriguez or who's behind it? Doesn't seem like the kind of thing you'd do."

"How would you know what kind of thing I'd do?" He didn't know her well enough to have a clue what she'd do. She could easily follow that up by sharing multiple examples of all of the things she'd bailed on, from the boarding school she'd run away from to the two engagements she'd ended to the various careers she'd tried before founding At Your Service.

"I'm a good reader of people. Good enough to figure you'll be here when I get back."

Lila frowned, watching him kick off his boat shoes and pad, barefoot, toward the back of the small house.

"What are you doing?"

"You might have avoided an early-morning swim, but I didn't. I'm going to hit the shower." He tossed his T-shirt onto the pile of laundry in the corner on his way to the bathroom. "Wait here. Keep watch. Come get me if you see anyone heading this way."

Just like that?

Lila stared at his back until he disappeared behind the closed door.

He acknowledged that they were in danger, then trusted her to handle it? Even if it was just keeping watch, it was more than she'd figure a man like him would believe she could take care of.

It wasn't like she was an idiot. Plenty of people trusted her. Corinne showed it on a regular basis, getting into mess after mess and expecting Lila to fix it. The clients Lila worked with in At Your Service trusted her to make their perfect match.

But Travis—the man had almost brought her to a climax simply rubbing her back, so they were going to be on a first-name basis, in her mind, at least—Travis was trusting her with his life.

It was a little mind-boggling.

Travis was a man.

A totally alpha, take-charge-and-control-everything man.

He was a SEAL.

Her last boyfriend hadn't trusted her to choose the right wine with dinner. Her brother, also a SEAL, didn't trust her enough to know anything more about his naval service than his rank. Her own father didn't trust her to capably handle her own life.

But Travis was trusting her to keep watch for murdering kidnappers.

Lila leaned against the windowsill and watched the trees wave lightly in the breeze, and tried to figure out why that scared her.

Before she could find an answer, he was back. Probably that navy training, she thought, watching him stride back into the room. Fully dressed, which was a minor shame she wasn't even going to think about.

"Nothing to report?"

"The lady with the fussy baby went somewhere."

"Maria. She works as a maid at one of the hotels." He strode over to the refrigerator, and this time when he held out a bottle of water in question, she nodded. "Her husband's a fisherman. He was out on the water long before your little adventure."

"And the baby? Is he at work somewhere, too?"

Hawkins's lips twitched, but otherwise he seemed to take her question much more seriously than her smart-ass tone merited.

"Maria's aunt lives with them, so she's likely taking

care of him now. But I'm sure he'll be up and working soon. People around here stay pretty busy."

Lila twisted the cap of the water off, then twisted it back on without taking a drink.

"Are you going to call the police again?"

He took his time answering, chugging down half of his water while he considered. Then he gave another one of those shrugs.

"You were right. Probably no point in bothering."

"Why?" She knew her reasons why she didn't trust the police. But she wanted his take.

He didn't bother with an immediate answer.

Instead, he gave her a long, considering look. Her heart jumped when he walked over. She told herself it was because he was so tall, he totally loomed over her.

Then he reached out and took the bottle of untouched water from her and took a long drink. As she watched him swallow, she had to admit that at least half of her bouncing heart rate was due to lust.

"Why don't you tell me what you think?" he suggested after he'd recapped her water and handed it back to her.

Lila took a moment to wet her lips and set aside those thoughts she didn't particularly want to share—especially the ones that featured him, naked.

"They didn't believe me last night, so there's no reason to think they'd believe me today." She waited, but he gave no indication if he agreed. "Is that why you don't want to call them?"

"I didn't say I didn't want to. I said there was no point. You nailed part of it. Montoya runs the *policía* and he's big on tourism. More specifically, on the benefits tourism brings."

"And murder has a way of dampening tourism?"

"About as much as a pretty woman being grabbed in broad daylight does."

He thought she was pretty? Lila told herself to ignore the flutter in her belly at his words. Like the shoulder massage, she was sure it didn't mean anything to him.

"So what are we going to do?" she asked, half-hoping he'd suggest taking her to the nearest airport and finding a way to get her the hell out of here.

"Do?" He shot her a wicked grin. "We're going to kick some ass, of course."

Chapter 8

"Senorita Adrian?" The desk clerk stared in surprise. "How nice to see you again. We thought you'd checked out."

"I'm sorry?" Lila frowned at the big-eyed brunette. "Why would you think that? When I saw you a couple of hours ago, I told you I was getting aspirin."

"I'm sorry, senorita, but our records show that you checked out." The woman's easy smile faded as worry creased her brow. "I was working the desk myself when your friend came by. He had the proper documents. He said you were leaving. He paid your bill and asked that your bags be brought down. Since they were already packed, we did so."

"What documents gives someone the right to do that?" Lila scowled. "You gave my possessions to a stranger? What the hell kind of establishment is this?"

Her voice rose higher with each word, stopping just a few decibels below hysteria. Wasn't it enough that she'd been abducted? Now her possessions had been commandeered, too?

She drew in a long breath to tell the clerk just exactly

what she thought of this damned hotel. Before she could utter a word, Travis gripped her shoulder. His warning touch warmed her skin, tamped down her fury enough for Lila to take a calming breath.

"Why don't you fill us in on who this man was, and what documentation he had?" Travis suggested in a friendly tone.

All it took was a sideways glance to see he had a flirtatious smile aimed at the woman. Lila's frown turned into a scowl. He never bothered to flirt with her. Then again, he was usually trying to get rid of her, not trying to get information out of her.

Still, there was no call to get flirty.

They both knew it must have been the kidnapper. Maybe he thought she'd hidden something that'd link him to the murder. Lila cringed, thinking of that hamhanded goon pawing through her laptop and undies.

"He was quite the gentleman," the desk clerk told Travis, her tone warming into a gossipy cadence. "Well-dressed in a nice suit and he spoke with an American accent. He said he was Senorita Adrian's executive assistant. He showed me his business card, his passport and a photo of Senorita Adrian. He had all of her information. Passport number, address and driver's license number. Everything."

"My photo?" Lila's brow furrowed. Most of that had been in her bag. But her photo? Had she been right before? Was the abduction because of her father instead of the murder she'd witnessed— ransom instead of intimidation?

Maybe she should mention that to Travis, tell him

that there were other possibilities at play. But that would mean explaining her family. Her father.

Shuddering, Lila wrapped one hand around the other, gripping and releasing her fingers until the nerves receded enough that she could breathe again.

"The photo, can you describe it?"

"It was clearly the senorita," the desk clerk told Travis with a sharp nod. "A casual pose taken on the beach. White sand with the ocean in the background. The senorita, she was alone in the photo, wearing a pretty dress and sandals."

"Was it a local beach?"

"Perhaps, perhaps not." The woman frowned as if trying to remember, then shrugged. "I don't know. But the manager, it was with his approval that I checked out the senorita."

"He let you give my possessions to a complete stranger, simply because the guy had my picture?"

"Oh, no. He let the gentleman pay for the bill, and ordered us to gather your belongings and hold them in the security room. The suitcases, they were already packed, so Senor Tomás, the manager, he felt the man was telling the truth. Still, Senor Tomás would not release them to this man."

"Did the guy ask for her luggage?"

"He didn't, no. He said she'd contact the hotel to arrange to have it shipped to her home in San Francisco. He even prepaid the costs of storage and shipping."

"That's was mighty thorough of him." Travis slanted Lila a look and asked under his breath, "San Francisco?"

More confused than ever, she just nodded. Yes, she

lived in San Francisco. This all sounded like the kind of thing her father would order done, and she couldn't think of a single reason for kidnapping murderers to care about her luggage.

Still, she should mention the possibility.

He'd look at her differently once she explained. Everyone did, as soon as they found out who her father was. Or, in the rare event that they hadn't heard of him, when they found out how much money her family was worth they got weird. Greedy or grabby or gossipy. Sometimes all three.

Travis was a Super SEAL beach bum, which meant he probably wasn't living life for the money.

Probably.

She squeezed her hands again, frustration spinning through her. Whether or not he was interested in money, he'd still look at her differently. She could already hear him adding spoiled brat to the drama queen designation he'd tagged her with.

Lila blinked back tears she didn't understand.

"I want my stuff," she heard herself say. She wasn't sure what she was going to do with it—head to the airport or get a room at a different hotel using charm and a smile instead of cash. But whatever she did, she wanted her things. "I'd like you to release my luggage to me right now."

As soon as she said that, she remembered that she didn't have her purse, nor any identification.

God, this day was sucking. Lila rubbed two fingers over her temple in hopes of preventing that nasty headache from returning while she figured out what to do. But

apparently eager to make up for their questionable early
checkout choice, the desk clerk gave a smile and nodded.

"This way, please," she said, and gestured for them
to follow her around the counter and down a short hallway to a locked room. "Would you care to go through
the suitcases to ensure everything is as it should be?"

Three large suitcases, a makeup case and her computer bag were all stacked neatly in the corner of what,
from the rolling racks, Lila assumed was the bell captain's room. A quick look showed the locks still in place,
each suitcase's zippers meeting in the corners the way
Lila always closed them. It didn't look like anyone had
gone through them, but given her luck so far this week,
she figured she should check anyway.

"I'd prefer to go through my things in private."

The desk clerk nodded and, with a quick look to ensure that there was no other luggage in the room, offered, "Feel free to use this room. I'll be at the front
desk if you need me."

Lila waited until she'd left, closing the door behind
her, before huffing out a long breath.

"My suitcase key was stolen this morning, along with
my wallet and aspirin."

"No worries," Travis said with a shrug. "I can break
those locks."

He stared at the pile of suitcases with a frown.

"What?" Lila asked after a handful of seconds, looking from his face to her pile of luggage and back again.
"Is this where you make some snotty comment about
how much stuff I brought?"

"How long have you been in Puerto Viejo?"

"I arrived yesterday. And before you ask, I'd planned to leave right after I'd gotten Chef Rodriguez to agree to come work for my clients. I'd figured tomorrow or the next day at the latest."

"Four bags, four days. Sounds about right." He bent over to check out one of the locks, then shot her a look. "Impressive security. Is your underwear lined with gold?"

Color stained her cheeks. Not over Travis thinking about her underwear. That she kind of liked. But she was too embarrassed to explain that the locks were a gift from a paranoid parent with control issues. No point in letting a man she'd like to show her underwear to know she had daddy issues.

"Is that your way of saying you can't open the locks?" she asked instead.

"I can open anything. The question is, what are your plans once I do?" With complete disregard for the possibility of gold-lined panties, Travis sat on the suitcase and gestured. "If you want to stick around, we need to get you situated somewhere safe. If you want to get out of here, you need to get to the US Embassy in San José so you can start unraveling red tape."

Or she could call her father and let him take care of everything. He'd contact the pilot who'd likely paid the hotel bill and have him stand as security. A few pulled strings and she'd have ID, a passport, cash and credit cards.

Lila bit her lip.

It was so tempting to take the easy route.

"I don't want to run away," she said quietly, staring at her hands for a long moment before meeting his eyes. "I wouldn't like myself if I did."

"Choosing the option to leave doesn't fall under the self-help category," he said impatiently. "Think it through. You came here to hire a cook for a new job. That cook is most likely dead. You stay here trying to confirm that death, you're in danger."

He was right.

There was no reason for her to stay. But her stomach clenched at the idea of leaving. She didn't know why, though.

She shifted her gaze, staring at Travis.

Maybe he was why.

He had a long, deep streak of grumpiness and the most incredible body of any man she'd ever seen. If his back rub was anything to go by, he knew exactly how to use it.

He had a career she hated. But he'd protected her; he'd saved her. He made her smile, made her feel safe and made her feel strong.

He turned her on; he pissed her off.

Often both at the same time.

Which was nearly as confusing as the riotous feelings she had for him. Feelings she barely recognized.

None of which were reasons to stick around, she told herself.

"I really should go," she decided, searching those dark eyes for something. Anything. "As long as I'm here, I'm putting you in danger, too."

"If that's your only reason for leaving, get over it. C'mon," Travis said, looping her makeup tote's handle over one suitcase's pull, then grabbing the biggest bag's handle. "Can you take care of the last bag and your laptop case?"

Get over it? Just like that? The man might have the sweetest set of shoulders she'd ever seen and magic hands when it came to massage. But he had a jerk personality.

Instead of answering, Lila hooked the leather strap over her shoulder and snapped open the pull of the smallest case. She'd talk to the front desk, find out how to get to a bank, the embassy, the airport. Without ID, none of it was going to be easy.

With that in mind, she followed Travis out of the cupboard of a room and around the front desk. He waited while she settled things with the desk clerk, not looking surprised when he instructed the woman to keep Lila's departure to herself.

Together, she and Travis crossed the lobby toward the door. Before they reached it, Montoya strode inside. The three of them stopped at the same time, the cop casting an interested look between the two of them while Lila gave the tiniest of groans.

"Hey, there, Montoya," Travis greeted easily. "How's it going?"

"Senor Hawkins, what a surprise." Montoya's snake-like gaze shifted from Travis to Lila, his expression considering. "Senorita, I was coming to talk with you. A few moments of your time, *por favor.*"

"Actually—"

"In here, please," he interrupted, gesturing to the mostly empty dining room before she could finish her excuse. "Unless you'd prefer the police station?"

"I am hungry," Lila declared, flipping her suitcase so the wheels faced the dining room. She twitched her shoulder to ensure the laptop bag didn't slide and, chin high, strode toward the possibility of breakfast.

"Feel free to wait in the lobby, senor. There's no need to accompany Senorita Adrian."

Lila's stomach rattled. Before nerves could dig their claws in, though, Travis wrapped his arm around her shoulder.

"That's cool. I'll stick with Lila."

He led her into the dining room at an easy pace.

There were no diners, and the glass tables were being set by the pair of servers. One woman wrote the day's specials on a chalkboard, while another checked the glassware for spots. Rich scents poured out of the double doors leading to the kitchen, making Lila's stomach grumble.

But Montoya cleared the room with a single gesture before she could ask for a menu.

"Be seated," Montoya said, pointing at a corner table that hadn't been set yet. Instead of hurrying over and grabbing a chair, Travis strolled at half-pace, pulling Lila's suitcases behind. He stacked them tidily against the wall, then gestured for Lila to bring hers over, too.

A little afraid of Montoya's impatient glare, Lila hurried over, yanking her suitcase behind. The wheels twisted in the wrong direction so it thumped over the carpet, almost making her trip. Before she could heft it higher, Travis took it and added it to the tidy stack next to the table. Gesturing, he pulled out a chair and waited for her to be seated before taking the one next to her. They both looked across at the cop.

"Are you quite comfortable?" Montoya asked once

they'd settled. So much sarcasm coated his words that Lila was surprised it wasn't dripping from his mustache.

"We'd probably be more comfortable with something to eat. Any chance of getting a late breakfast?" Travis asked, looking around the dining room as if expecting a waiter to hop on over.

"I am hungry." Lila's conciliatory smile faded at the cop's dead-eyed expression. "But I can eat later."

"Indeed." Montoya made a show of pulling out a small notebook from his shirt pocket. He uncapped a pen, then gave them both an expectant look.

Lila waited, but he didn't say a word.

He just stared.

Ooh, intimidation tactics. Her gaze met Travis's, her lips twitching when he rolled his eyes.

But after fifteen seconds of silence, she shifted in her chair and, unable to look at the policeman any longer, watched her fingers instead.

After thirty, she was ready to confess anything and everything, from the lies she'd told her father to the time she'd stolen a lipstick from her bitchy college roommate. Or the drunk-on-daiquiris one-night stand she had with a stripper after that same roommate's bachelorette party.

At the one-minute mark, she opened her mouth to spill it all and beg Montoya to tell her what he wanted. Before she could make a sound, Travis gripped her knee under the table. The warmth of his hand on hers sent tingles through her system, desire drowning out intimidation.

"Seriously, dude. If you plan on keeping us here long, we could use a menu," Travis said, his words straddling that line between friendly and firm. "And don't bother to threaten us with a visit to the station house again. We both know if you had cause, you'd have hauled us off there already."

Montoya tapped the pen against his notepad for a few moments, then inclined his head. "Indeed."

That word was going to get annoying after a few more dead-eyed utterings, Lila decided.

"What was it you wanted, Captain Montoya?"

"You were seen at the apartment of Alberto Rodriguez this morning at five forty. I would like to know why."

Lila blinked. For a man so well informed, you'd think he'd have all of the details of the shooting, right down to the color of the murderer's socks.

"You went by Rodriguez's place this morning?" Travis snapped, giving her a serious WTF stare. "Are you crazy? You see a guy get shot dead, so the first thing you do is go to his apartment? Did you stop to consider for even a second that guys with guns might be hanging around there, waiting to grab you and throw you on a freaking boat?"

Spine stiffening as if covered in steel, Lila thrust out her chin and gave him the same look she gave every domineering ass she knew. An unwavering stare, one brow arched high and an ice-cold smile.

"No. Despite any possible mistakes I might have made trusting you, I am not crazy. And while I did witness a murder—" now she included Montoya in her chilly stare "—I did not go to his apartment."

"You were seen."

Lila planted her forearms on the table and leaned forward.

"The convenience store where I went to get aspirin is right next door to his apartment," she said, biting off each syllable. "Which means I did nothing reckless or crazy. The only thing I can be accused of is having a headache."

Travis's narrow-eyed stare didn't shift; neither did the cop's. Despite Lila's lifetime of experience with intimidation attempts, it wasn't working this time. Because she had a big, bad SEAL by her side. So she simply folded her hands together on the table and widened her smile.

"What exactly is it that you're accusing me of, Captain? Please, be specific so I can give all the details to my attorneys." She named her father's firm, not because she expected Montoya to recognize it, but simply because it sounded officious and arrogant.

She wasn't surprised when Montoya broke under her smile. He didn't drop his gaze, but he did tap his pen on the notepad a few times before saying, "You are accused of nothing, senorita. You are simply a witness, yes?"

"A witness to a crime you don't believe happened?" Travis asked as he leaned back in his chair to rest one ankle on the opposite knee. Since the just-short-of-a-smirk look on his face was likely to piss the cop off, Lila leaned forward to get Montoya's attention again.

"Look, Captain, why would I lie about witnessing a murder? And if I did, if I'd lied, would some creepy jerk have grabbed me this morning, tied me up and tossed me in a boat?"

Well, that got a blink out of him. Montoya pursed his lips and flipped to a clean notebook page.

"You claim that you were abducted this morning?"
Lila gritted her teeth.

There was that word again: *claim.*

"Given that I personally untied her from the boat she'd been hidden in, if I were you, I'd use a different word than *claim*," Travis advised.

"Senorita Adrian is lucky to have you here to play hero, Senor Hawkins. Again."

"Yeah. Just think, if I wasn't here, she'd have to rely on the local police." Travis didn't bother smiling this time. He simply stared Montoya down until the policeman looked away.

"Mr. Hawkins has been a lot more helpful than the police," she pointed out, leaning forward to get Montoya's attention. She knew what Travis had said about reporting the abduction, but she had to try. "He helped me last night and saved me this morning."

"Indeed?" His black eyes shifted from Lila to Travis and back again before Montoya flipped his notepad to a fresh page. "Please, give me the details."

Lila filled him in.

She described the events of the morning, from the minute she'd left the hotel to the moment she'd returned. She skimmed over the terror, skipped her paranoid kidnapping for ransom theory and completely left out the back rub—and its stirring effect.

"I see." Not taking notes now, Montoya just tapped a staccato beat on his notepad. "And yet you didn't plan to file a police report of these alleged crimes?"

Alleged?

Lila tried to remember if she'd ever wanted to smack

anyone as hard as she did this cop, but her mind was blank. Which she figured was the reason why she didn't snap at Travis when he leaned in to take control of the conversation out of her hands.

"Why don't you stop with assuming what Lila was or was not going to do, and do your job instead? Better yet, consider this your official report." Travis gestured with one hand toward Lila. "Go ahead, do your job."

Lila held her breath, waiting for Montoya to explode. Sure, he had cold eyes and the demeanor of an icebox, but that had to have pissed him off.

But instead of snapping, he simply inclined his head to one side, wet the tip of his pen with his tongue before placing it on a fresh page and said, "Let's go over it all again, shall we?"

Just like that? Lila blinked a couple of times, then went over it all again.

"And that's when you ordered us into this restaurant, where we can smell the delicious scents of food but are not being allowed to order a single thing to eat," she finished, shrugging as if none of it had mattered.

"Don't forget the guy who checked you out of the hotel," Travis said, watching Montoya like a suspicious hawk.

Lila bit her lip.

Since she was pretty sure her father was behind that little stunt, she wished Travis had left that part out. For the first time since Montoya had blown her off, she hoped he continued to dismiss facts as fiction.

Seeing the look on his face, pure disbelief, she almost sighed with relief.

"Yes, Senor Tomás mentioned that your bill was paid

in full and your bags stored at the request of a gentleman he didn't recognize. He said that at that time, he discovered that they were packed with the locks intact."

"Does the hotel manager report to you?" Travis asked, giving the policeman a menacing scowl.

Ignoring it, Montoya flipped back through his notebook as if checking his snitch list before giving Lila another one of those tell-all-or-else looks.

"So what is your plan, might I ask? To run away after stirring trouble and starting false rumors?"

Weren't all rumors false? Lila resisted the urge to ask. One smart-ass at the table was enough, and Travis had already claimed that role.

"Since my original plans were changed by a bullet, my new plan was to leave this morning. I had flight arrangements," she said in the superior tone she'd learned from the mean girls at boarding school. "A flight I've now missed, thanks to that grabby jerk who tied me up on a boat. You know. The one you don't believe exists."

"There are no flights out of Puerto Viejo."

"I flew into San José," she pointed out. "I'd planned to fly out the same way."

He gave her that dead-eyed stare for a solid thirty seconds.

"And how were you getting to the airport?"

Lila wet her lips. For the first time, she wished Travis were somewhere else. The only thing more embarrassing than a twenty-four-year-old woman being told what to do by her father was admitting how much money her family had. Especially when she obviously didn't measure up.

Before she could decide to confess that her father had sent a helicopter for her or lie, Travis shook his head.

"Let me get this straight. Lila is a witness and a victim, yet you're talking like she's done something wrong." Travis pushed to his feet, bracing one hand on the table as he straightened. "Your job is to find the man who grabbed her, the one who stole her purse. And to figure out what happened to Rodriguez. So why don't you get to doing that? Because unless you have actual questions instead of insinuations, I'd say we're finished here."

Oh.

Lila had to force herself to breathe through the burst of lust shimmering in her belly.

Who knew a forceful man coming to her defense could be so damned sexy?

Montoya looked as if he wanted to argue, but after another look at Travis's face, he folded up his notepad and stood, as well.

"I believe it's in everyone's best interest that you remain in Puerto Viejo. Where will I be able to reach you, Senorita Adrian? For future questions, that is." His eyes shifted to Travis for just a moment. "Or in case your items are recovered, of course."

In other words, don't leave town. She started to give him her cell number, then remembered that it'd been stolen. Along with her ID, her credit cards and her passport. Frustration burned hot and wet in her eyes as Lila tried to figure out what to do.

"You've got my number," Travis said, gesturing to Lila to get to her feet. "She'll be with me."

Chapter 9

Travis didn't know what was going on in Lila's head, but he could see the wheels grinding away. She'd been ready to bolt before Montoya had put the brakes on her.

He didn't mind that.

With her gone, he'd be alone again.

Just the way he wanted it.

But she was hiding something. That, he did mind.

He'd seen it in her eyes in that closet where they'd stored her luggage. He didn't know what it had to do with the mess she was in, but since he was in it with her, he planned to find out.

He was a skilled interrogator; he could easily get it out of her. But she'd had one hell of a twenty-four hours. He'd get her securely back to his place, feed her something and let her chill for a while.

Then he'd interrogate her.

"What a jerk," Lila babbled, totally unaware of what she was in for. "Can you believe that man? That's twice now that he basically called me a liar."

Travis set aside his plans to watch her rant, amused

at the way she stomped along the sidewalk in cadence with her bitching.

She'd changed out of the snug jeans and purple tee she'd worn earlier, claiming the clothes had *abduction ick* all over them, whatever that was. After he'd busted the locks on her suitcases, she'd used one of the hotel rooms—compliments of a slightly abashed manager—to shower off the boat smell and change her clothes.

Now she looked a little dressier, if not any less frazzled.

Her sundress was a breezy material that floated around her curves in swirl of greens and blues hinting toward purple. Her hair floated around her shoulders, soft curls bouncing and adding to the mermaid effect. He wasn't sure how she was keeping up with his long strides in those purple stilts of hers, but she was doing just fine.

"Look, it's not worth getting yourself twisted over," he advised when she finally stopped for breath. With a jerk of his chin, he indicated they step off the sidewalk and onto the dirt path that led to his house.

"You don't think a policeman claiming that I made everything up is a reason to twist?" She shoved wind-tossed hair out of her face and gave him a narrow look. "This is it, isn't it?"

"The part where I say I told you so?" He grinned. "Yeah, this is it."

"He's not going to do anything, is he?"

"Nope."

"So why did he waste our time like that? Was it some obnoxious power play? He kept us in that dining room for over an hour, without a single thing to eat. Isn't that against the Geneva Convention or something?"

"Only if we're prisoners of war," Travis said, laughing. Then, afraid she was serious, he gave her a closer look. Thankfully, there was a twinkle in those pretty green eyes.

Then he frowned.

"It was a waste of time, wasn't it?"

"I think it was an intimidation thing. You know, to make me so uncomfortable that I..." She shrugged. "I don't know, something. What's his endgame? I'm already leaving town."

"Actually, you're not," he pointed out, gesturing with the suitcases he was now carrying since dragging them through the dirt seemed rude. And, more importantly, slow.

"I will be. As soon as I replace my documents and get some money, I'm out of here," she insisted, her voice a little less animated now as she tried to be casual about peering into the trees and around corners. "And for all he knew, hauling me off like that just to be an intimidating jerk would have made me miss a flight."

"Did you have one booked?"

"No. Well, not really. Maybe."

"Standby?"

"Yes," she said so enthusiastically, he was surprised she didn't jump out of those sexy shoes. "That's it. Standby."

Travis didn't bother to hide his eye roll. It was beyond him why Montoya didn't believe her. The woman was such a lousy liar, it was obvious that her criminal claims were the truth.

But if he pointed that out, she might stop bouncing.

And given what she'd done to his morning, he figured he'd earned the right to enjoy the view.

Because the woman had one hell of a bounce. Her hips swayed, her breasts jiggled and her skin glinted like marble veined with sunlight.

"Do you have food at your place? I didn't get breakfast. Or lunch. And I really am starving," she said, pressing her hand against her stomach in a way that emphasized her curves even more. "If you have any ingredients, I can cook. Or I can take you out to eat. I had a little money stashed in my luggage. Not a lot. Not, like, hotel room money. But enough for lunch."

She gave him a smile and a shrug.

"I don't want you to think I'm taking advantage or anything. You know, since you're letting me stay with you instead of staying at the hotel until I can get money wired. If I have it sent in your name, my lost ID won't be an issue, right? I'm sorry to be so much trouble. I still think that if I talked to the hotel, they'd let me keep staying there."

The woman really had an issue asking for help. She hadn't liked the idea of staying with him at first. In fact, he was pretty sure she didn't like it now.

As if hearing his thoughts, she cleared her throat.

"I appreciate your offer. I really do. But I really should be making arrangements to get home."

"You're broke, you're currently undocumented. Yes, you can have money wired to me in your stead. I'm fine with that. But it doesn't change the fact that you're a person of interest in a series of local crimes. And that the local top cop is annoyed with you, and you have at least one person looking to grab you for as yet unknown reasons."

Instead of asking if she needed him to keep listing reasons why it was a stupid idea to leave right now, he just slanted her a sideways look. By her abashed frown, he figured he'd made his point.

"I'll stay, then. Thank you," she said, her tone belying the grateful words. "But if I can use your phone, I can make some calls and start arrangements to replace my passport and get what I need."

Did she really think it'd be that easy? Travis didn't consider being in the military the same as working for the government, but he was sure the red tape was just as thick, tight and tangled.

She'd just have to find that out for herself, though.

"Sweetheart, you get yourself legal and I'll put you on a plane myself."

"You don't have to sound so grumpy about it. I said thank you," she muttered under her breath. "And I offered to do my share."

What if he wanted to take advantage of her? Travis wondered. For all her habit of talking his ear off, the woman was pure temptation. Still, she was an assignment. Not officially, not militarily. But still, an assignment.

As long as he thought of her that way, he'd keep his hands to himself.

"I've got no problem with you pulling your weight until you're gone," he finally said as they followed the last bend on the path to his bungalow. "But until you're gone, I want you where I can see you. It's a hell of a pain in the butt to have to come after you every time you get in trouble."

"You're as bad as Montoya," she said, shaking her head in disgust. "He thinks I'm making up trouble, and you think I'm out searching for it."

"After you got your aspirin, you were going to go by Rodriguez's apartment, weren't you?" He pointed at the stubborn look on her face. "Admit it."

"I figured it couldn't hurt," she explained, turning to face him. "Look at it from a business perspective. This trip has been one expense after another. If I didn't sign Chef Rodriguez, I'd not only lose my commission, it'd damage my reputation. I was just going to go by the restaurant, then his apartment."

"Look at it from a safety perspective. Going by a dead guy's apartment where his murderers might be hanging out is dangerous. How's your business going to do if you're hurt, killed or otherwise messed up?"

"You think I'm an idiot, don't you?"

"No. I think you are trouble, which is entirely different. Still, you're entertaining," he said as they reached the bungalow and dragged her suitcases up the steps.

"Well, goody for me."

He glanced over just in time to see her amused eye roll. Why that sent him over the edge, he'd never know. But over he went.

Without thought, without even being aware he did it, he grabbed her arm. One swift tug pulled her up against his body, her soft curves pressing into him as Lila gasped.

He took her mouth before she could voice the questions he saw in her eyes. Damn it, she tasted as good as she looked. Better, even, he realized as his tongue dipped further into the sweet warmth between her lips. He watched those mermaid eyes glaze over as he took the kiss deeper. He felt himself blur as he lost his way in the hot delights of her kiss. Their lips slid as tongues tangled, teeth scraped and their breath shortened.

Hot, was all he could think. She was so damned hot.

A hot assignment, that little voice whispered, finally getting through the desire fogging his brain. She was off limits.

Even thinking that, knowing that, it took him another long, delicious second to pull his mouth from hers.

He watched as Lila slowly opened her eyes. Blinked. Then frowned. Despite the passion still clouding her gaze, he knew she had plenty to say. She always did. But he didn't want to hear it.

"Forget it," he ordered.

"I beg your pardon?"

"That was a mistake. Forget it happened."

Every bit of passion disappeared from her eyes, anger taking its place.

Travis ignored it. Forced himself to ignore her.

Scowling, he shoved open the door. One look inside had him throwing out his arm to keep Lila from crossing the doorway.

"Son of a bitch."

The place was trashed.

Nothing like a little mayhem to put things in perspective.

Lila grabbed on to his arm and peered around his

shoulder. He felt her dismayed moan as much as heard it. He absently patted her trembling hand, then without thinking, meshed his fingers with hers.

"Son of a bitch," he said again, this time under his breath. Whoever had tossed the place had done a damned good job. He started to walk into the bungalow, but Lila wouldn't let go. "Come inside. I need to check it out."

"No." She dug in her heels, but given that they were resting on flimsy little sticks, she didn't get much traction in trying to hold him back. He simply pulled her over the threshold with him as he stepped into the mess.

"You need to call the—"

He glanced over when she snapped off the rest of that sentence.

"Yeah," he agreed, appreciating how fast she'd figured it out. "I figure this is the result of Montoya's— what did you call it?—obnoxious power play?"

Too shocked to resist, Lila let him pull her into the living room, where she dropped onto the couch. One arm wrapped around her suitcase, she gave him a horrified look.

"The police are involved?"

Travis waved one hand around the room, letting the destruction answer for him.

"Are you sure? I mean, you said whoever grabbed me would probably come here," she said, her eyes darting around the room. She edged a little farther behind the suitcase. It wasn't big enough to hide behind, so she must plan on using it for a weapon. If it weighed anything like the ones he'd carted in, it just might work.

"Look, I know you don't want to think that the cops are dirty. But there are dirty cops everywhere."

"Just my luck they happen to be here."

"The question is, what are they into? And what was Rodriguez doing that got him killed?" As he asked, Travis strode through the small house, doing a safety check for booby traps or hidden goons. He cleared the living room and kitchen quickly, but when he moved toward the bathroom, Lila jumped to her feet.

He rolled his eyes, wondering where she thought she was going to run and hide. She tucked her laptop case into an undamaged corner of the couch, and bent down to grab one of the wooden legs broken off the shattered coffee table.

Hefting it high on her shoulder, she took a deep breath and gave Travis a nod.

He had to take a second. First to process her gutsiness, then to admire how good it looked on her.

Then, after giving her an approving look, he angled himself to one side so as to present less of a target, and gestured that she do the same. As soon as she did, he threw open the bathroom door with the precise force to slam it against the wall, but not enough for it to fly closed again.

Given the size of the room—four by five, max—it didn't take him long to give it a thorough inspection. Once finished, he glanced over his shoulder to see Lila there, watching with that table leg still ready to swing.

For a pain in the butt, she was pretty damned cute.

Stepping out of the bathroom, he set his back against the wall and reached for the other doorknob. Given the size, the bedroom was a more realistic hiding place, so this time he gestured for her to move closer to the exit and off to one side.

He twisted the knob slowly, the movement barely visible. If anyone was inside, the conversations and the slam of the bathroom door would have warned them the bungalow was now occupied.

But even a single second of surprise could be an advantage.

Once unlatched, he pushed fast and went low. But it didn't take more than a glance to assure himself that the room, like the rest of the bungalow, was empty.

He cleared it anyway.

"Travis?"

"It's fine," he responded to Lila's tentative call. He ducked into the closet and, kneeling carefully, tapping three fingers along the baseboard twice, opened the secret compartment Paul had told him about. From the array of weapons and communication devices, he chose a SIG pistol and encoded tablet the size of his palm. Then he closed it up again and, pushing off the wall to keep pressure from his knee, straightened. For good measure, he tossed some of the laundry the goons had tossed around on the floor in front of the compartment.

He stepped back into the living room just as Lila heaved a sigh of relief and dropped onto the couch.

"They did all this and left behind a gun," she exclaimed, her butt barely scraping the cushion before she jumped to her feet again. "What are you going to do with that?"

"Defending us in case they come back," Travis said,

tucking the SIG into his waistband at the small of his back. He waited, wondering if she'd protest the weapon or be smart and be grateful.

As always, she did neither. Instead, she frowned.

"Why didn't you pull that thing out earlier? It would have been a lot better defense than my stick."

"I didn't have it earlier. But I do now," he said, looking around the mess.

Adrenaline surged through his system, his body poised to act. His every instinct said to kick some ass. He wanted answers. He wanted to know exactly what was going on, who was behind it. And make them pay.

"Are you going after them, the *them* that did this, that grabbed me?"

He wanted to.

But his first duty was to protect. As much as he wanted to get revenge for what'd been done to Lila, what'd been done to Paulo's property, he had to put right the damage and keep Lila safe.

"First things first. We coordinate the battle. The overall mission is to identify and neutralize the assailants, mitigate any damage inflicted and—" he looked around the trashed remains of what'd once been his refuge "—extract payment."

Lila gave him a long look, irritation clear on the surface but something else—that something he'd seen earlier—lurking beneath. But all she said was, "I beg your pardon?"

Civilians, he sighed.

"We're going to figure out who's behind all of this, find out why they're doing it and stop them once and for all."

"How?"

"I'm working on that. While I do, let's get this mess cleaned up."

Figuring she'd understand that easily enough, Travis righted the recliner he'd spent a night or two sleeping in. Bent metal hinges meant the footpad wouldn't close, but he could fix that later. He gathered the pieces of a broken table, then got a good look at Paulo's pride and joy, the eighty-inch plasma TV. Now decorated with an impressive spiderweb of cracks.

Damn.

Irritated despite himself, he glanced at Lila, still standing there, doing nothing but staring.

"C'mon," he ordered. "Clean house."

"Clean house? Just hang out here, where the bad guys know we'll be, and tidy up?" Her eyes wide with dismay, Lila looked like she was biting back the urge to scream.

Considering that he was going to have to pay out of pocket to replace every freaking thing in this place, Travis could sympathize.

Still…

"Don't start overreacting," he advised.

"Overreacting? What, exactly, qualifies as overreacting?" She threw her hands high in the air. "They broke dishes. Food is everywhere. The couch cushions are shredded. How can I not react?"

"Is it going to do any good? Will having a meltdown clean this up? No? Then save your energy." He strode into the kitchen to toss her a roll of garbage bags. "If you want to help, throw the mess in here."

"All your stuff is ruined," she said as she bent down

to scoop broken crockery into a bag. "You must be upset, too."

"It's not actually my stuff, it's my friend's stuff. So yeah, I'm pissed. I've spent most of my adult life living in shared quarters and rarely had possessions, let alone formed attachments to them. But this place, this stuff, it was in my care."

Which not only made this an invasion, it was a damned insult. One that made him so angry, he had to shove his fists into the pockets of his jeans to keep from punching a wall. Seeing the shocked look on Lila's face, he covered the fury with a joking tone and smiled.

"Don't forget, replacing all this crap is going to seriously cut into my hammock time."

Her laugh was barely a puff of air, but it got her moving.

But even as she dived into the cleaning, Lila didn't know how he did it. She could see the fury and hints of grief in Travis's dark eyes, but he made jokes.

All the guy had been doing was napping on the beach and now, thanks to her, he was in the middle of a nightmare. Yet he didn't seem to blame her in the slightest.

Why didn't he blame her?

More to the point, why had he kissed her?

Memory of that kiss still tingled on her lips. She could taste him. Feel him pressed tight against her. God, the man could kiss.

Forget it, she ordered herself. It'd been a great kiss, sure. But he obviously regretted it. And she had no business wanting another one. Not with a SEAL.

In silence, the two of them moved through the handful of rooms, Lila surreptitiously studying him as they cleaned. By the time the trash was bagged, the irreparably broken furniture piled on the front porch, the clothes and towels stuffed in a laundry bag and foodstuff swept and washed away, she'd figured out one thing.

And only one thing.

She wanted him like crazy. In ways she'd never wanted another man—never even imagined wanting one.

There was a grace to his movements. Oh, they had that economical precision she'd always associated with the military. But they flowed without hesitation.

He made her smile; he made her think.

He made her feel safe, as if she never had to worry if he was nearby. At the same time, she felt as if he thought there was nothing she couldn't do.

Talk about empowering.

And, oh, that body.

Sweeping up the piles of sugar and powdered energy drink, Lila turned the broom in the opposite direction so she could watch Travis bent over the recliner, straightening a metal bar with a hammer. The view of his bicep bulging and stretching with each swing was drool-worthy. But the real treat was the sweet curve of his butt encased in well-worn denim. She had the strongest urge to run her hands over his tee where it stretched across his shoulders.

Nope.

No touching, she warned herself, tucking the broom away in the closet, now tidy because it was empty.

"So what do we do now?" she asked, more to distract

herself from wanting Travis's body than because she was ready to do anything.

"*We* don't do anything," he said, straightening to kick the chair upright, then into recline, then upright again before facing her. "You stay here. I'm heading out to ask a few questions."

Out? "Why?"

"Because answers probably aren't going to saunter up to the door and hand themselves to me."

"I'll go with you."

"No. You won't."

Lila scowled and grabbed herself a bottle of water. So much for being crazy about him.

"I'm not under your command, Mr. Badass SEAL. You don't get to tell me what to do."

"I've rescued you twice now, Blondie. And you said it yourself. Badass SEAL or Super SEAL. I'd say either one puts me in charge of this little situation we have here. Which means I do get to tell you what to do."

She wanted to tell him to shove his orders and his protocols and his hierarchy right up his butt. But she was afraid that the second she did, he'd shove her out the door and leave her to fend for herself.

"They'll come back," she said, sure of it.

"Not right away."

"Sooner or later, what difference does it make? I can't stay here. Especially not alone. It's not safe." She shot him a narrow look and pointed in the general direction of his very flat, very toned, very amazing belly. "Besides, you have a gun. That means you've got the protection."

"You want me to leave it with you?"

She could see it on his face, the condescending amusement at the idea of Lila willingly taking the gun, let alone wielding it with any efficiency.

She wished so hard that she could prove him wrong.

Instead, all she could do was cross her arms over her chest and give him a dirty look.

Instead of giving her threatening pose any attention, Travis pulled a device out of his pocket and keyed in something with his thumbs. After a few minutes, she couldn't stand it.

"What are you doing?"

"Mission report," he said absently, his attention still focused on what he was doing. "We're in a question-able situation with elements of danger. You're stuck here with no documentation. And someone jacked up my friend's place."

"So you're, what do they call it? Calling for backup?"

That got his attention and earned her a piercing stare that made her nervous enough to actually shuffle her feet.

"What? Is that the wrong military term?"

"No. It's the wrong assumption. This is not a situa-tion that calls for backup."

At her baffled look, he lifted one finger. "There's nothing that's happened that I can't handle."

He lifted another finger.

"In the event of any situation, reporting said situa-tion to one's superiors ensures that there is someone to take over if necessary."

Before Lila could ask what would make that neces-sary, the third finger went up.

"You can have cash wired, but what are you going

to do with it? Your chances of getting ID, or of leaving this country without a passport, are slim, none and zip. Once I clear up this mess, I'm going to want you out of my hair. That'll be easier if I pull strings now and get the ball rolling to replace your documents. You can leave all the sooner."

Oh.

Lila forced herself to ignore how much that hurt.

"How long before you get a response? Can I leave tomorrow?"

"Maybe the day after." His lips quirked in a half smile. "If we nail Montoya and close down whatever the hell is going, of course."

"Of course." Lila waited a beat. "And how were we doing that?"

Impatience coated her hurt feelings, making Lila throw up her hands in the air.

"Quit with the secret Super SEAL crap already. You're trained to work with a team, to trust the people you're in the trenches with. Well, here I am." She swept her hands down the sides of her body. "Right next to you in the trench. So let's work together."

"Sure. As soon as you can take a gun and cover my back, we'll work together."

Uh-huh. Lila pressed her lips together.

"What am I supposed to do while you're gone?"

"Keep the doors locked," he suggested, paying more attention to the small tablet than her. "You'll be fine."

She wanted to throw the water bottle at his head. But she'd already chugged all the liquid, and she had lousy aim so if she tried, the bottle would only fly a few inches and most likely in the wrong direction.

Instead, she sucked in a deep enough breath to drown the frustration in air. When that didn't work, she tried a couple more. The frustration was still there, but she was able to think clearly.

She wasn't proud, but dammit, she didn't want to stay here alone.

So she shifted her weight, thrusting one hip to the side and resting her hand on the other. A tiny tweak of her shoulders and a deep breath thrust her breasts high. She gave a little toss of her hair and smiled.

A slow, sexy smile.

"I'd rather not sit here. Alone. Waiting." She fluttered her lashes. "I feel so much safer with you. You Super SEAL, you."

She could see the heat flare in his eyes and knew he was remembering their kiss. Gratitude surged. He'd dismissed that kiss so easily, she'd been afraid he hadn't liked it. But now she could see that he'd liked it a *whole* lot.

"Are you flirting with me?"

Feeling power for the first time since she'd ran into him on the beach, Lila bit her bottom lip and gave him a teasing look through her lashes.

"Would that work?"

She held her breath, waiting for him to tell her to grab some pride and get over herself.

Instead, he jerked his head toward her pile of suitcases.

"Get casual. We leave in five."

Chapter 10

"Keep that hat on," Travis ordered the third time Lila tried to pull off the baseball cap he'd found in the pile of Paulo's trashed laundry.

It wasn't much of a disguise, but paired with his baggy jeans, cuffed and cinched tight with a skinny leather belt and a flowing peasant-style blouse she claimed she'd bought as a gift, she wasn't exactly a fashion plate.

She was still gorgeous, which was a distraction.

He could still taste her on his tongue, which was an irritation.

But the hat helped. He just had to keep telling himself that.

"Where are we going?" she asked, double stepping to keep up with his pace.

"We're up against an enemy combatant who knows the territory better than we do. They've already breached my quarters, so the first stage of this operation is alternate accommodations."

One hand on her arm to keep her by his side, Travis stepped up the pace. Weaving in and out of the sidewalk crowd, he kept a lookout for possible assailants. Or cops, which he now trusted just as much.

He didn't expect actual trouble on the street, but it paid to be cautious. He knew that he should have made Lila wait at the bungalow, but he could see her point. Sitting unprotected in a trashed house knowing bad guys were coming was hell on the nerves.

And then there was the flirting.

Every flutter of her lashes reminded him of that kiss and all it took was a saucy smile to get him hard.

He was glad he had a solid poker face. Otherwise the woman would know just how much power she had over him.

Mulling that, he stopped when they reached the small corner market. Still gripping her arm protectively, he pulled her down a side street lined with stores.

"What are we doing here?"

"You're going to do some shopping while I have a chat with my friend, Manny."

"Shopping?" Insult rang out, crystal clear. "Is that all you think I'm good at? Buying things? Spending money? Wasting it, more likely."

Before she could finish what was probably going to be quite an informative rant, Travis cut her off. They were too close to the market to do otherwise.

"Get food for two—no, three—days' camping. Stuff that can be eaten raw or cooked over a campfire."

He didn't wait for another protest, or more likely, for her to say she had no idea what to get. Instead, he pulled Lila into the small, open-front market and, making as if giving her a one-armed hug, he slipped some cash into her hand.

"I'll be right there—" he gestured with a jerk of his chin "—talking to that skinny guy wearing the bird shirt."

Before she could ask questions, Travis headed over to where Manny was arranging towers of plantains.

"Yo, Manny."

"Yo, it's the Hawk. You in disguise with that hat and sunglasses?"

"The sun is bright out there," was all Travis said.

"Dude, you be hungry?" Manny left the plantains half-stacked and looked around for his wife. Frowning when he saw her helping a line of customers. "Glory is busy, but she can make you a plate soon."

"I'm good." He and Lila had grabbed a few tacos from a cart on their way here. "But I have a favor."

"From me?" Manny's eyes looked like headlights. Round and shining bright. "You want my help? Is it SEAL business? No, no. You can't tell me. Still, anything you want, Hawk. I can get it for you."

Travis let him wind down, then outlined his plan. He had to grab the skinny man's arm to keep him from running off to get started before Travis had finished his instructions.

"You got all that?" he asked when he'd gone over it all twice.

"Got it," Manny promised, lifting one hand as if to swear to it. "I'll go now. I have brothers, cousins, they'll help. I'll take care of everything."

"Keep it on the down low," Travis reminded him. "Nobody knows why, nobody knows I'm involved. Right?"

"Right," Manny agreed, the word pretty much an echo since he was running as he said it.

Mission accomplished?

He watched his ace in the hole disappear around the corner of the shop as fast as his sandaled feet could carry him. He narrowly missed mowing down three pedestrians on his way and yelled a totally nonsubtle goodbye to his wife.

Travis rubbed two fingers between his brows and sighed. Damn, he missed his team.

A flash of blond hair caught his eye. He turned in time to see Lila tuck the hat into her back pocket, the move making the baggy jeans snuggle against her curves. Chatting easily with Manny's wife, Glory, she filled the mesh shopping bag slung over her arm with such impressive speed he could barely make out exactly what she was buying.

Her easy laughter filled the small market, garnering enough interested looks to tempt him to go over there and shove that hat back on her head himself.

Incognito, he thought, gritting his teeth. She was supposed to be incognito, dammit.

As if hearing his thoughts, Lila looked over. Her brilliant smile faded fast at the look on his face. At his arched brow, she combed her fingers through her hair as if in question. When Travis inclined his head, she shot him a guilty look, bundled her hair back under the hat and pulled the brim low.

Yeah. He missed his team, and he missed real missions.

It was pointless to regret things he had no control over. So he took that undeniable regret outside, as planned, leaning against the lamppost to wait for Lila to finish her shopping.

"I hate hats," was the first thing she said when she joined him. Hers was still firmly in place, as was the look of defiance on her pretty face.

"I hate people trashing other people's stuff. We're both going to have to get over it." He shrugged, heading down the wooden sidewalk toward the beach.

"Do you really think a hat is an effective disguise?"

Hell, no. But it, along with the baggy, nondescript outfit, wouldn't garner any extra attention, either. He was on keeping his eye out for Montoya or his men. It'd be easy enough to tuck Lila out of sight if a cop came into view, but that didn't stop the random shopkeeper or tourist from reporting their movements to the police.

But he didn't figure knowing that would help her fade into the woodwork.

"What'd you get?" he asked instead, gesturing to the pair of mesh bags hanging off her arm.

"Yogurt, bagels, diet soda and rice cakes."

She burst into laughter when Travis stopped midstep and stared in horror.

To hell with being discreet. He wasn't eating that crap.

"I'm kidding," she said, still laughing.

Thank God. Part of his instructions to Manny included food, but a man never relied on someone else for the basic necessities.

"I actually got fruit, veggies, bread, meat, chocolate and fresh-pressed juice." At his look, she shrugged. "Fresh pressed is healthier."

"And the chocolate?"

"Considering the amount of stress I'm under, you're lucky these bags are filled with only chocolate."

"Some go for chocolate to relieve stress. Some go for sex."

"What?" She stumbled, stepping on her own feet, then righting herself before he could grab her. "You want sex?"

Hell, yeah. Especially with her. Lila was turning out to be everything he hadn't realized he wanted in a woman, wrapped in everything he knew he desired.

But he'd learned the hard way that he didn't get everything he desired. Which meant sex and Lila were off the table. He just had to remind them both of that.

"I'm a man. Sex is always on the want list," he said, managing to keep a straight face when her mouth dropped open. "And it'd probably go well with chocolate, now that I think about it."

There, he decided. Her horror should do the trick.

"You are kidding," she said after a long moment, her relieved laugh belying the curious look in those mermaid eyes. "Right? That's a joke?"

Heat flared in him, tempting him to throw caution to the wind and show her just how serious he was.

Under his protection, he reminded himself. For good measure, he repeated it a few more times in his head until he was sure he had temptation back under control. Still, pushing a few of her buttons couldn't hurt.

"You flirted your way into coming along," he pointed out. "No worries, though. I'm not stressed."

"Well, that's a relief," she said, biting off the words and spitting them out.

He leaned sideways, just enough so his arm brushed her shoulder, then he gave her a long, slow smile.

"Tell you what. I get stressed, you'll be the first to know. I promise."

He waited for that alarm to flash in her eyes again. He liked it. It was as effective as a shotgun-toting monk.

Instead of alarmed, though, she looked interested. Those pretty eyes roamed his body before she offered a smile. The kind of smile that assured him she very much liked what she saw.

Damn.

Before he could decide just exactly what he wanted to do about it, the beach came into view. The rolling dunes and golden sand. The glittering waves of the ocean beyond.

As always, the water called out, its siren song an enticing invitation.

How the hell was he going to live without that? he wondered. Here he was, fooling himself into believing he was still qualified to lead a mission.

To save a life.

"Where is it that we're going?" Lila asked hesitantly, whether because she was worried he'd mention sex again or if she simply sensed the emotional roller coaster riding through his system, he didn't know.

"First, we stash the food. Then we hit the restaurant."

"Casa de Rico?" Even over the ocean's call and chatting shoppers, he could hear Lila swallow. "Okay. I'm ready."

He gave her a long, careful look to be sure. The mission didn't depend on her. He would never charge a civilian with that much power. But she could seriously screw things up if she had a meltdown.

She didn't look like she'd freak out, but she didn't look ready to kick butt, either. Still, he was glad to see the worry in her eyes. Worry would make her careful, and carefulness would help keep her alive.

"Look, we can camp out at the bungalow, wait a few days until my contacts come through. Play it safe until you have ID. Then you can get out of here. No muss, no fuss."

"Do you think I'm that much of a wimp?"

"I guess we'll find out."

With that, he led her into Manny's nephew's surf shop. After pulling the dreadlocked man aside to ensure that Manny had been by, then he tucked the groceries, their hats and glasses behind the counter. Shrugging out of the long-sleeved cotton shirt he wore over his tee, Travis gestured for her to use the tiny backroom.

"Change it up," he instructed. "And make it fast."

An order he regretted five minutes later when Lila walked out looking like the sexy siren of earlier. She'd stripped off the jeans and loosened the neckline of the peasant blouse so it draped off one shoulder. Untucked, the shirt hit her midthigh, leaving the long length of her golden legs gleaming. She wore the belt again, angled so it lay on her hips while still emphasizing her slender waist.

Damn.

"Okay?" she asked, scooping her hands through her hair so it fell in a cloud of glinting curls over her shoulders, the long strands teasing the vividly embroidered flowers covering her breasts.

"Yeah. Okay." More than okay. And totally not okay. She was off-limits, he reminded himself. "You remember the plan, right?"

"Follow your lead, keep my mouth shut. Study everyone in the restaurant, keep my mouth shut. Look for clues or hints or more dead bodies. And keep my mouth shut." She gave him a stiff smile. "Did I miss anything?"

"Maybe keep your mouth shut?"

"Ha." She clenched and unclenched her fists a few times. At his questioning look, she shrugged. "I feel a little naked without my cell phone or purse."

"Do you want to pick up a purse at one of the markets?" he offered, figuring she needed the distraction as he led her from the shop and through a side street, so they could approach the restaurant from the opposite direction.

"You're offering to take me shopping?" Before he could point out that he wouldn't be doing it himself, she continued, "You'd have to go with me, since you've decided I'm not safe on my own. You'd have to lend me the money, since we both know I'm broke. What's the—I mean, what would I even put in a purse? All of my purse-type stuff was stolen."

What was the catch? What kind of people was Lila used to dealing with that a simple offer like that would come with tight enough strings to make her hesitate?

Something to add to his interrogation list of questions, he decided.

"We'll get you a cell phone," he told her. "You can stick that in there, along with whatever else you women carry in those bags of yours."

"Chocolate," she stated with a hesitant smile. "A hairbrush, techie toys, world secrets and a bottle of scotch."

"It's tequila around here. If you're willing to make that minor adjustment, I think we can handle the rest."

Her laughter wrapped around and tickled him as they walked into the bar. Over the course of his career, Travis had been in some tight situations. There was no counting the number of times he'd put his life on the line. Every single time he'd felt a small thrill deep inside.

So he recognized that thrill now.

His training—as extensive and exclusive as it was—had never covered defending against irrational thoughts or stealth emotions. But his training was solid enough to know better than to enter any battle without a winning plan.

So instead of giving into the impulse to grab ahold of Lila, press her between his body and a wall and take her mouth in a hot, wet kiss that'd serve prelude to even hotter, wetter sex, he'd wait.

And plan.

The restaurant was hopping, so Travis did wrap Lila's hand in his. But only to keep her close. A quick survey had him aiming for the bar. He waited for her to scoot onto a stool, making a show of checking out her legs as the filmy fabric offered teasing hints of smooth thighs.

"Hey. It's the Hawk," the bartender greeted, her smile shifting to include Lila. "And a guest?"

"Hey, Dory." He nodded at the redhead. "Two beers and a table if you've got one open."

"It's a little early in the day for date night, but I think we can accommodate you." Her smile didn't shift, but there was something in the narrow look she gave Lila that bothered him. "You want something in the bar or would you prefer the restaurant?"

"In here's good." It'd throw off anyone watching for Lila to revisit the scene of the crime. And it'd give him a chance to watch the bartender a little longer.

Maybe Montoya had just tipped her to watch them. Or maybe it was something more. He'd watch. He'd see.

"Why are we here, exactly?" Lila asked quietly once they were seated at a rickety table with a bowl of roasted pepitas, warm tap water and menus.

"We're watching. We're waiting."

"For what?"

"For someone to get nervous." Travis made a viable show of looking around the room, noting Dory whispering to one of the waiters. "Rodriguez was killed for a reason. From the intel I've gathered, he spent all his time here. So the reason is here."

He watched Dory for a few more seconds. Other than whispering and sending a couple of glances their way, she didn't do anything suspicious. Still, it might be worth doing a little digging.

"I have two questions." Propping her forearms on the table, Lila leaned closer and pulled his attention her way again. Especially when the move made the fabric of her blouse flutter, showing tempting hints of silky skin. "First, what intel?"

Travis forced his gaze to stay on her face. But he had damned good peripheral vision, so her breasts were still a temptation.

"I accessed covert informants, interrogating and extracting key details." At her arch look, he shrugged. "I tapped a few gossips and asked the right questions."

There was that laugh again. It lit her face and reached in to wrap around his heart. Not wanting to analyze why, Travis gestured with one hand.

"What's the second question?"

"How will our sitting here, eating pumpkin seeds and sipping what I hope will be bottled drinks, help us find the reason?"

"First, in here they're called pepitas," he corrected. "It's easier to blend in if you align yourself to the local customs and verbiage."

"I stand corrected."

Those mermaid eyes shimmered with appreciation as she smiled. Travis couldn't help but smile back. He leaned closer, as much to breathe in the scent of her hair as to keep his words just between the two of them.

"Did Rodriguez give you anything? A message, some code, anything they might be looking for?"

"Nothing," she insisted. "Believe me, if I had anything, I'd have given it to that jerk, Montoya."

That's what he'd figured.

"Okay then. So, we know whoever shot Rodriguez realizes that you're a witness. They grabbed you, they trashed my place, both in an attempt to scare you away."

"You think that abduction was an intimidation tactic?" she asked in a wondering tone that had him narrowing his eyes.

"What did you think it was?"

"I don't know?"

When Travis hardened his stare, she shrugged.

"Kidnapping, maybe," she muttered.

From the disconcerted look on her face and the embarrassment in her tone, he knew he'd tapped into something major. The same something, he was pretty sure, that'd put that look in her eyes earlier. Not the time to look into that. Not here, not now. Instead, he'd use it to interrogate her later.

"If we go with the belief that those were scare tactics, our being here sends a signal. That you're not scared. That you're watching. And that you're not going to back down."

He waited for her protest over being murder bait. Instead, Lila gave an admiring nod.

"So basically you want to make them nervous," she said with dawning comprehension, looking around the bar with an evaluating stare.

"Nerves are like a recognizable flare, signaling guilt. As soon as I see it, I'll know where to push to get the answers you need."

"Then these are pumpkin seeds," she said, popping a few into her mouth. "Because blending in would defeat that purpose."

Grinning, Travis leaned back in his chair and signaled for two beers. He'd never have pegged the woman he'd deemed a total pain in the butt to be so interesting.

Oh, she was still a pain in the butt, he silently acknowledged. But she was also providing more fun than he'd ever had with a woman fully clothed.

Something he'd be changing, he decided then and there.

They'd finish this stakeout.

They'd get somewhere safe.

He'd get the answers he wanted from her.

And then they'd get naked.

Lila wasn't sure what to make of the look in Travis's eyes. It sent a needy little tingle through her, yet made her nervous at the same time. It was as if he knew what she'd look like naked and had already figured out exactly where to touch to give her the most pleasure, but was holding out until he'd decided she was worthy.

She hated that feeling.

Oh, not the pleasure feeling. She was pretty sure she'd love that if he ever gave in and showed her what he was thinking.

But the unworthy part? That made her want to scream. And not with pleasure.

"Am I supposed to be doing anything?" she asked, more to say something to distract her thoughts than in search of instructions.

"Look around. See if you recognize anyone. Even if you don't, it wouldn't hurt to hand out a few assessing stares. Pretend you recognize someone, then lean over and whisper to me."

"What should I whisper?"

"Doesn't matter. It's just for show."

"Well, I want to make it good. You know, really make an impression."

Thinking fast, she put on her most sincere smile and gave him a wide-eyed look. She leaned in just a little and tiptoed her fingers up his bare arm, then slid them back down to caress the back of his hand.

She only wished she could feel his pulse to better

gauge his reaction. Since she couldn't, she amped it up. Just in case.

She wet her lips, waited for his eyes to lock on her mouth, then shifted even closer. She breathed in his scent—morning at the ocean—as her mouth brushed his ear.

"Are you sure there isn't something special you'd like to hear?" she whispered breathily. "Something specific? Or would you like me to just make it up as I go? I'm really, really good at making things up."

Lila waited a beat, just long enough for that to take hold of his imagination, before leaning back in her chair again. She watched Travis. The man was a SEAL, trained to hide his reactions, gifted at hiding emotions.

But she was a woman.

And she knew when she'd turned a guy on.

Resisting the urge to pump one fist in the air, she gave him an easy smile instead.

"So?" she asked innocently. "How was that?"

"Good." He cleared his throat, then tried again. "That was just fine."

"I'm so glad," she purred. "I want to make sure I do it just right. You know, for the strongest impact. Get the most bang for your buck, and all that."

She added a flutter of her lashes for good measure.

And was furiously pleased to see his eyes blur.

Riding on triumph, Lila shifted to give the waitress room to set down a pair of coasters and their beers. She kept that flirty little smile in place and her eyes locked on Travis's the whole time.

Unworthy, her ass.

Chapter 11

"So this is interesting."

Lila's expressions was as doubtful as her tone as she looked around the cabin cruiser. She'd started the day in a decrepit excuse for a boat, and it looked like she was ending her day in the same.

"Smarter to mix up our locale instead of sitting in the same place," Travis explained offhandedly, his attention on motoring the boat away from the small dock hiding in the weeds behind a two-story adobe house he claimed belonged to the second cousin of his friend Manny's wife.

"Other than keeping the bad guys away and enjoying these luxury sleeping arrangements, is there a reason we're on this boat? Heading out to sea. At night?"

She clutched the single tote bag Travis had allowed her against her chest, wondering if she should have skipped the hydrating facial mask and laptop, and packed a flotation device, instead. But when Travis said to grab what she needed for the night, she'd figured on a nice hotel room.

Not a hotel room, like the two of them rolling around

naked on a rented bed, exploring each other's bodies and moaning with pleasure. No, she hadn't thought that's what Travis meant. Not at all.

But she hadn't thought he meant they'd be spending the night camped out on a smelly, dilapidated boat with no running water and, most likely, no sheets.

"You should sit, get comfortable. We won't be stopping for a while."

"Where, exactly, are we going?" she asked, gingerly sitting on a bench, shifting when the ripped plastic scratched her thigh through her baggy jeans.

When the coordinates he reeled off meant nothing to her, Lila asked again, "Where are we going?"

"A cove I know. It's secluded enough that we can rest comfortably. Nobody is following us, nobody will find us."

Catching her nervous look at the big black emptiness that was the sea at night, Travis reached into his pocket, pulled out a small device and handed it to her.

"A cell phone?" Lila said, turning it over in her hand.

He'd gotten her a cell phone. Why did that make her feel like her heart was in danger?

"Something to put in your purse," Travis said, flashing her a smile before turning his attention back to the ocean so black that it was impossible to tell where the water ended and the night sky began. "There's no international calling. But my number is programmed in, as is the *policia*'s, for all the good it'll do. Use it if something goes bad."

Lila pressed her lips together to resist asking for examples. Instead, she looked out over the water. It was so dark, it looked like it could swallow them whole. She shivered.

"There's a cabin below. Why don't you stow your bag, wrap yourself in a jacket or something?" With a flip of a switch, he turned on a dim, sad lightbulb that barely lit the way belowdecks. "It's a chilly night, you're bound to be cold."

Yeah. Cold was good. Cold sounded way better than scared. She didn't want Travis thinking she couldn't handle things.

"The steps are solid, but the lighting is crap. Better for stealth, so that's good. But take it easy going down. No point losing your footing and smashing that pretty face up."

He thought she was pretty.

Hugging that to her as tightly as her tote bag, she picked her way down the steps. Unlike the last boat she'd been on, this one held no hint of mustiness. Just the fresh scent of the sea.

Belowdecks consisted of a two-burner stove and compact refrigerator, which she supposed was the galley. The bathroom was so small, if she lifted both arms she'd bump her elbows from any angle. The rest was what she supposed was the bedroom, or cabin, since this was a boat.

A very cozy cabin, she realized. Her belly tightened at the sight of the single bed, wide enough to span the aft wall and comfortably sleep three strangers without touching.

Or for two lovers to easily roll around in any variety of adventurous positions. She'd just bet Travis had all sorts of adventurous ideas. She'd heard stories of those sailor guys. A ménage à trois in every port, a skill for under-sheet maneuvers. And with hands like Travis's— wide palmed, long fingered, oh so skilled—she'd bet he knew just how to do all those adventurous things he'd learned on his travels.

The only thing she wondered was if his tongue was as talented as his hands.

Nope, she told herself with a little shake. Not thinking about it. She was going to put all thoughts of Travis, sex and pleasure out of her mind.

Instead, she found a corner to claim as her own and dug into her tote bag. She hadn't packed much in the way of cool weather wear, but she managed to layer a tank, a tee and her favorite oversize bat-wing sweater with jeans and felt the chill dissipate a little.

Then, even though she knew it was stupid, she took her toiletries into the tiny excuse for a bathroom. Checking her reflection in the tarnished mirror, she added a hint of smudgy gray to her eyes, a dash of bronzer to her cheeks and a slick of color to her lips.

She brushed and tousled her hair, bending at the waist to give it a good shake. There, she decided. It looked artfully tousled. Natural, yet seductive.

Bad idea, she realized, giving herself a horrified look before tossing her makeup bag into her tote and dropping onto the bed. She shoved her fingers through her hair, taking satisfaction in mussing away the allure.

What was she doing?

Yes, she was attracted to Travis.

Who wouldn't be? The man was gorgeous. Sexy, strong, funny and protective.

But not in an arrogant, take over her life way that she'd come to associate that with a guy looking out for her.

And his kiss?

Oh, God. That kiss. Lila hummed as the memory worked its way through her body.

He gave her the tingles.

The kind that promised all sorts of delights and orgasms galore. These sort of tingles were almost a guarantee to amazing climaxes, if only because the tingles themselves were a turn on. Because she knew, after tasting his lips on hers, that all it'd take was a single kiss, one sweeping caress, to send her careening into a puddle of delight.

Oh, she knew better than to believe promises and guarantees when it came to sex. She wasn't that naive.

But it would be pretty cynical to dismiss them out of hand. Without even giving them a chance? That just seemed rude.

And none of this was helping, she lectured herself, pushing off the rough mattress to pace the room until she got herself under control.

Or at least until she'd shook off the allure of those tingles.

Because Travis had done enough for her already. The last thing she was going to ask after the guy had his place trashed and his vacation ruined was that he do her right.

A guy like Travis? One with all those heroic qualities, grumpiness and rocking body? He was the kind of guy she could fall hard for.

Which would be the stupidest thing she'd ever done in her life, she reminded herself firmly. He was too much like her father, too much like her brother, for feelings like that to be anything but heartache in the end.

By the time she joined Travis on the deck, she had a firm handle on her emotions, even if a few thoughts still careened around her head. The sight of him, shadowed in the moonlight with one hand on the wheel as he stared out at infinity, stirred a few other thoughts—most of them naked.

But she firmly squashed them.

"Hungry?" he asked as soon as he saw her.

"Sure," she said as she realized she was. "The groceries I got this afternoon are below. I'll put something together."

Awesome. A distraction that'd keep her away from him a little longer.

"No need. The boat came with dinner." He gestured to what looked like a small lockbox. "Go ahead and get it set up. I'm going to drop the anchor."

Crossing to the lockbox, Lila noted that instead of open sea, he'd tucked them into a quiet cove, with trees blanketing three sides of the bottleneck.

It was fairy-tale pretty and, more importantly, it felt safe. Some of the tension that'd threaded tight across her shoulders easing, she smiled as she opened the silver box. It was an insulated food warmer, she realized. Stacked on top of three covered dishes were paper plates and plastic utensils, a roll of paper towels and a foil-wrapped cylinder that she figured contained tortillas.

"Drinks? Dessert?"

"Small cooler."

She found it behind the bench, set a pair of ice-cold beers next to the food then, priorities being priorities, went back to see what was for dessert.

"Cupcakes?"

"You said you liked chocolate," Travis said over her shoulder.

Lila started. She hadn't heard him move, and yowza, the shadow was even huger than the man. And that was saying something.

"There's bottled water, too," she said after clearing the surprise from her throat. She wasn't going to touch that chocolate comment with a ten-foot pole. "In case you don't drink on duty."

"I don't." He snagged both beers in one hand, twisting off their caps in a single move, then handed one back to her. "But we're not on duty tonight."

Not sure what that meant they were on, Lila looked around to find somewhere to set up dinner. She didn't want to eat belowdecks. Safety reasons aside, she didn't think eating on a bed was going to help keep her mind off of sex with Travis.

As if reading at least part of her mind, he reached between two benches to pull out a three foot square of plywood. After dropping it flat on the benches to create a table, he began unloading the food warmer.

Lila had to take a second to acclimate to the fact that he didn't expect her—the little woman—to handle setting the table and putting out food, before she dived in to help.

Ten minutes later, they were cozied up around the impromptu table enjoying a surprisingly delicious meal. Seated cross-legged between the table and the bulkhead, Lila was impressed at how comfortable Travis was to be with.

In the short time since sitting, they'd discussed world politics, the latest blockbuster film and the spiritual merits of the Rolling Stones.

Finally, as much because it was driving her crazy not to know as because she thought all this common ground was getting just a little too intimate, she returned to their reason for being together.

"Could you fill me in again on this mission plan of yours?" she asked, swirling designs in the verde sauce with her fork. "Everything this time. After all, I'm trusting you with my life."

She added a flutter of her lashes to that last part.

"Trust well placed." With a half laugh, he shot a finger her way before scooping out a second helping of chili verde. "So, the plan. We're in a holding pattern until your documents arrive. I've called in a few favors, but I don't know when they'll pay off. So until they do, we spend our days being visible, scoping Casa de Rico and making people nervous."

"Nervous people tend to get nasty," Lila pointed out.

"They make mistakes, too. If they figure we know what they're doing, they're either going to screw up or they're going to confront. Either one gives us answers."

Lila shuddered. She'd already experienced confrontation and wasn't eager for another round.

"Did you get anything out of that little recon?" Despite her feelings about her brother, she was loving using military terms. There was something strong and sexy about them.

"Other than the fact that Montoya is anti-tourist and feels threatened by your presence in Puerto Viejo, that Garcia is unquestionably dirty and that whatever the crime, Casa de Rico is the hub?" Travis shrugged, scooping up another helping of rice. "Nope. I didn't get anything."

"Slacker," she teased before digging into her beans and rice. The food was delicious. "Who cooked you dinner? Let me guess. Manny's wife's second cousin, right?"

"Nah. Alberto doesn't cook. From the taste of it, this is Glory's doing. You met her. Manny's wife," he added at her questioning look. "We'll have a variety of boats, and meals, available over the next week. After that, we might have to make new arrangements."

"Do you think it will take that long?" Unable to swallow, Lila switched her fork for her beer, then traded that for a napkin. Shredding the paper into tiny, even strips, she tried to think it through. Clients, bills, Corinne's worries, bills. They kept circling.

"We'll touch base with the States first thing in the morning," he said, his words coated in reassurance. "You can check in, offer assurances, make arrangements."

"I emailed Corinne from the hotel this afternoon after our visit with Montoya." Had it been only that afternoon that she'd been kidnapped, rescued and walked into a trashed house? "She does work for my company, At Your Service, and she's my roommate."

"Did you fill her in?"

"About all of this?" Wide-eyed, Lila waved her hand to encompass the boat, the cove, the island and the countryside. "No way. Look, I'd already told her about the murder, so I gave her Montoya's name and yours. That's enough for now. If you think I'm a drama queen, you should see her crown."

She barely resisted rolling her eyes at his impatient look. She wasn't about to explain that her father already knew where she was. One hint that she was in trouble, he'd sweep in and handle everything. From the cops to her documents to ending her career and hauling her away from Travis with nary a goodbye.

It wasn't that she wanted to be in trouble.

It was just that she didn't want her father getting her out of it.

"You must have other people. Don't you want to contact them?"

"People?"

"Family. Friends." He waited a beat. "Lover."

Oh.

Lila wet her lips with another sip of beer and tried to be smart. To remember all of the reasons getting involved with Travis would be a bad idea.

But looking across the dimly lit table at the man, his shoulders so broad they seemed to fade into the darkness, his face scruffy from a couple of days of not shaving and those eyes—oh, those eyes—filled with concern, she couldn't recall a single one.

"I'm not with someone. I mean, nobody is waiting for me. That way, that is." God, she sounded like an idiot. Lila blew out a long breath, reminded herself that she'd had sex before and dug up a flirtatious smile. "I don't have a lover."

And after that show of grace, she wouldn't. Especially not when he pushed his plate away and leaned back with his beer, giving her that look of amused interest.

"And family?"

Lila rolled her eyes. He was like a dog with a bone. Here she was thinking about getting naked with him and all he wanted was intel.

"The email I sent my friend, Corinne, is enough for the next day or so. If she doesn't hear from me then, she'll contact my family."

"Wouldn't they prefer to hear from you directly?"

"So when you touch base in the morning, is that with your SEAL friends?" she asked, desperate to change the subject. "How long are you on leave? Do you have to report back soon?"

It was too dark to see Travis's expression in any detail, but Lila felt a sudden chill. She swallowed the last of her beer to wet her suddenly dry throat.

Okay. So like her family, Travis's SEAL career was an off-limits topic. Only his off-limits sign was surrounded by barbed wire. And landmines.

"Cupcakes?" she offered, desperately pushing to her feet to grab dessert. Since the sum total of doing dishes was to dump all the containers in a trash bag, she cleared the table and put down the chocolate-frosted chocolate answer to peace in a single move.

"Are half of those cupcakes going to be enough chocolate to bring your stress levels down, or are you going to need them all?"

Was he interested in her or not? Starting to feel like an emotional yo-yo wondering, Lila decided it was time to find out once and for all.

"Well, it has been a rough day." She swiped a finger through one frosting swirl. Her eyes locked on his, she licked it clean, then swiped again.

"How's it taste?"

"Mmm, delicious."

Her grin faded as he slowly stood until he loomed over her. The man was huge.

"You shouldn't be stressed." He moved around the table.

"Is that an order?" She took an unobtrusive step toward the wheelhouse.

"Are you under my command?"

"I've been told I'm too insubordinate to command."

"The trick to being a good commander is knowing how to motivate."

Eyes wide, Lila stared up into the dark depths of his teasing eyes. How had he gotten so close? Why did he smell so good? She cleared her throat.

"So what's your favorite motivation technique?"

He looked at her mouth for a long moment. Her heart jumped a couple beats, then started beating faster. He shifted his gaze to hers again. Then, damn him, he smiled. And sent her stomach diving into her toes.

"I prefer to tailor the motivation to the individual."

"Is that so?"

"It is. Interested in the knowing what I'd do to motivate you?"

Oh, God, yes.

But Lila wasn't sure she could handle finding out. That the man was out of her league was glaringly obvious.

"I think I might be pretty good at motivating myself," she confessed.

"Everybody should know how to motivate themselves," he agreed with a wicked smile. "Aren't you going to ask about my stress levels?"

"Are you stressed?" she asked, taking one step backward.

"That depends."

"Depends on what?"

"On if you're interested in doing something about it." His smile sexy enough to make her light-headed, he moved forward one step.

Since his legs were longer than hers, his step brought him close enough to touch. To feel. To taste.

She held her breath when he reached out. He shifted his gaze to his fingers as they combed through her hair, swirling one long strand around and around. His gaze met hers again and he gave a tug.

"So?" he asked quietly. "Interested?"

"I shouldn't be. This would probably be a mistake," she murmured, her eyes locked on his mouth. His lips looked so soft, a contrast against those dark whiskers. Were they soft, too? How would they feel against her skin?

Desire wrapped around her like a silk ribbon, pretty and tight.

"Let's see what it feels like making a mistake together."

With that, his mouth took hers.

The kiss was whisper soft. The lightest teasing touch of his lips to hers. Pressing, sliding, enticing. Then his tongue slid along her bottom lip in a way that made Lila want to purr. She straight up melted, the trembling in her knees spreading through her entire body.

Unable to resist, desperate for more, she opened for his tongue, welcoming it with a sweep of her own. He tasted like chocolate and something headier. Something Lila was deathly afraid she could easily be addicted to. He pushed her sweater down her arms, the fabric a whisper as it hit the deck. Before she could acknowledge the cold, his hands were there, warming.

When she hummed her appreciation, Travis pulled his mouth away and took a small step away.

Wanting more, not ready to stop, she gave a tiny sound of protest. But when he took her hand, pulling her along toward the stairs, she realized he wasn't ending this. He was moving to somewhere more comfortable.

"We can't leave the boat unguarded," he said, grabbing a sleeping bag from one of the topside bulkhead cabinets. With a quick jerk of his wrist, unrolling it so it floated, a flat fluffy pillow, on the deck.

In the same economical move, he dropped down and pulled her with him, acting as a cushion so she didn't hit the deck. Their bodies aligned, hard against soft. Anticipation tightened in her belly like a wound rubber band, ready to snap at any second.

"Is this one of those adrenaline things?" she asked, watching her hand as she caressed small circles over his chest. "You know, coming down off a danger rush with physical intimacy."

"Physical intimacy" sounded so much classier than hot sex.

"I've served on a lot of missions and been in dozens of dangerous situations. None of them ended in physical intimacy," he promised with a half laugh. "But we can talk about what's going on here between the two of us if you want."

He slid her hair over her shoulder, baring her throat for kisses while waiting for her answer.

"Okay." Lila shivered as his words danced like a warm caress over the bare skin of her throat, teasing her breasts. Her nipples tightened, budding with need.

"Okay," she agreed as she skimmed her hands along the waistband of his jeans, then under the denim to get ahold of that sweet butt. Rigid muscles under satin skin warmed her palms. "Do you mean like dirty talk? Or safe sex talk?"

His laugh rumbled through her, the vibration as much a turn on as his hands cruising down her back to tease the gentle slope where her back met her butt.

"The is-this-a-smart-move talk."

"How can I say it's smart if I haven't seen your moves?" But Lila knew he was right, so she rested her hands on his waist and leaned back just enough to focus on his face.

As soon as she did, he took her mouth with a hot sweep of his tongue. Thrusting, teasing, swirling. Her smile disappeared in the explosion of passion. It was like being plugged into an electrical circuit powered by a desire so intense it could light up a country.

It might have been a few seconds that passed, or it might have been a few decades when, with the brush of one more kiss over her swollen lips, Travis lifted his head. His eyes were slumberous and heavy, the expression in them hot enough to melt Lila's insides.

"There," he said. "That's my smart move. Now let's talk."

"It's a very persuasive move," Lila acknowledged, swiping her tongue over her lower lip in hopes of tasting him again. Even as the need grabbed at her, reason whispered that this was a mistake.

Then he skimmed his knuckles over her jawline. And that little voice drowned in a heavy wave of desire.

"Persuasive enough?"

Instead of answering, Lila leaned in to kiss him.

A slow, soft kiss that teased and tempted.

His answer was to skim his hands under her shirt, teasing a fiery trail up her torso to cup her breasts. The heat singed her nipples into aching peaks through the satin of her bra.

He shifted the angle of his mouth so he was above her and took the kiss to another level. Their tongues danced, teeth scraped, lips slid together in an intense mating heat.

Lila's hands raced over his body, scraping, squeezing. Reveling. The man was a work of art. She felt like she could spend a lifetime appreciating it.

His fingers skimmed under her bra, knuckles teasing her nipples. When Lila moaned her approval, he stripped the fabric away, his hands slid up her waist until his pinkies teased the sides of her breasts, making her yearn. Need curled in her belly as he released her mouth long enough to pull her shirt over her head.

In the spirit of fair play, she shoved at his tee, wanting nothing between her hands and that flesh but air. She had to stop a second and catch her breath at the sight of that chest because it was so freaking amazing.

Cupping both breasts in his hands, Travis leaned down to suck one aching nipple into his mouth. She arched her back when he swirled his tongue, wanting more. Needing all of him.

With the same intense concentration he showed everything else, his teeth scraped one turgid bud, fingers working the other until she was squirming, panting and ready to beg for more.

He made quick work of her pants, freeing her legs. Before she could wrap them around his waist, he shifted to kick off his own pants, stopping only long enough to pull a condom from his wallet.

Then he was back. Excitement arced between their bodies like electricity, zapping, energizing and teasing all at the same time. Lila rubbed her hands over his chest, gripped his biceps, scraped her nails down his rock hard abs until she reached the straining satin of his erection.

Oh, God. He was so big.

So hard.

So beautiful.

And for right now, so hers.

He wanted her.

He needed her.

"Up," he growled.

"So gallant," she breathed, shifting to straddle him. The moonlight kissed her naked body with a delicate glow, forming a glinting halo on the gold of her hair.

Gallant?

If he had any breath, he would have laughed. He was good enough to avoid that and make sure they still had the ride of their lives.

No, it wasn't gallantry.

He just didn't want his knee going out midthrust.

With that in mind, he eased into her, his eyes locked on her face as her wet heat surrounded him.

Heaven.

Sliding into Lila was like finding his own personal heaven. So good. So damned good.

He grabbed her hips, easing her up, then down.

In, almost out of her wet heat.

It took only two thrusts before she caught onto and took over his rhythm. Sliding, slow and easy. Twisting with a little grind.

Oh yeah. Travis was damned sure this was heaven.

Each thrust into the welcoming pleasure of Lila's body took him higher, closer.

Wanting more, he reached up to cup those silken breasts, reveling in their weight. Moonlight glinted off that golden skin as he rubbed cherry-red nipples between his fingers.

She stiffened, arching her back to press her breasts harder into his hands. Travis cupped them. Squeezed, the nipples stabbing his palms.

Lila let out a mewling cry, her moves jerky now, her breath coming in hard, hot pants.

He released her breasts, grabbing her hips to keep her moving. Up. Down. In. Out. His vision blurred. His breath shortened.

She came with a scream. Her body clenched his erection, gripping so tight he followed her over the cliff with a grunt of his own. The orgasm went on and on as her body milked him for all he was worth.

Amazing.

The woman was so damned amazing.

Travis's head hit the deck with a thunk, his blurred gaze staring at the starry sky as he tried to catch his breath. He was still inside her. Still felt the aftershocks of her orgasm trembling through her delicate body.

And he already wanted her again.

Bracing himself in case the aftershocks sent him falling somewhere he didn't want to go, Travis gripped Lila's waist and firmly lifted her off his still throbbing body. He started to set her aside, but she gave a low purr and just curled into his side. She angled one knee across his thighs and tucked her head under his chin so all that silky hair floated like a soft blanket over his chest.

His heart rate smoothed out as he breathed in Lila's perfume. It mixed with his favorite scent, the fresh balminess of the sea.

It'd been good. She'd been good.

That's why he already wanted her again.

Because it'd been a long time—maybe a lifetime—since he'd had sex like that. It had nothing to do with messy emotions that screwed with a guy's head.

A few more bouts, and he'd burn her out of his system.

Except the way he felt right now, he'd want her in the morning, and tomorrow, and every day after that.

Travis closed his eyes and grimaced as reality set in.

Damn.

He was in trouble.

Chapter 12

Day four of Operation Stakeout, as Lila had laughingly dubbed it, and Travis was going quietly insane.

Sure, three days plus this morning of mind-blowing sex had him feeling pretty damned awesome. Thank God Lila had a stash of condoms in her suitcase. She very well might be one of the most entertaining women he'd ever known out of—and in—bed. The hints of danger and intrigue were more intense than he was used to in a relationship, but there was plenty of fun conversation, interesting communication and great sex to distract him from that.

"So what are you in the mood for next?"

After a long, intense look that brought a gratifying wash of color to Lila's cheeks, Travis tapped his beer bottle.

"I'm thinking another drink," he said. "How about you?"

As was their habit, they'd switched stakeout locations and sat in the restaurant today. Instead of across the table like a few days back, Lila sat next to him. Close enough that her scent teased out a reminder of whispered pleasure every time she turned her head.

They'd spent every minute of the last five days together, but he was still fascinated. They'd spent hours in each other's arms, but he still couldn't get enough of her. They'd explored every inch of each other's bodies, but he still craved her with a hunger he didn't think would ever abate.

"Another round?" the waitress asked, frowning as she gave them both the once-over.

"A beer and a water," Travis said.

"More food?" The question wasn't unreasonable since they tended to take a table for a few hours at a time. And it made Travis happy, since it meant people were noticing.

Might as well keep their attention. "Nope. We'll take our time finishing what we've got here."

"The ceviche was a lot better last week," Lila told the waitress with a challenging smile. "Too bad Chef Rodriguez isn't still working the kitchen."

"Right. Too bad he quit," the woman said, biting off that last word before turning on her heel and heading to share a whispered discussion with the bartender. Dory Parker glared their way, jaw clenched tight enough that it had to hurt, and she grabbed the phone.

"Do you think it's her? Dory?" Lila asked, leaning close enough to whisper the question in his ear. When she straightened she gave him an impatient look. "We should talk to her. Push a little."

Watching Dory flay a rag over the bar with enough force to lift varnish, Travis considered that.

"Well?" Lila asked.

"Risky," was all he said before biting into his last taco.

"Maybe it's time for risks? We're not seeing much progress with the eating and drinking the truth out of them plan."

He didn't blame her for pushing. They were making people nervous. That was clear from the sidelong looks and sudden silences sent their way. A few more weeks of this and someone would break. But it wasn't enough.

He'd do better on his own, he knew. He could meet with more people—the kind of people he didn't want Lila around. He could ask questions that'd get reactions—the kind of reactions he didn't want Lila subjected to. Without Lila, he could push buttons, kick asses.

But he couldn't risk her.

Despite her assurance that she could take care of herself, he wouldn't leave her on her own. He'd assigned himself as her protective detail first and foremost, and he never shirked a duty.

Still, this could go on for only so long. As soon as her papers came through, they had to break this open. Lila had a life to get back to. A career, an apartment. People who cared about her. He had a hammock.

Life was simpler there.

No future. No wishes. No heart-wrenching desire for an amazing woman. Nope. In the hammock, he had regrets and doubts and loss.

Somehow, that was easier to handle.

He watched Lila do another of her deliberately obviously looks around the room, her sea-green eyes blatantly narrowed and those full lips pursed in consideration.

And knew he'd have plenty more loss to contemplate just as soon as she was gone from his life. Unlike his career, which'd left him with no choices when it'd been ripped from him with one bad jump, he might have options here.

"What?" Lila asked with a laugh, pushing her hair behind her ears and giving him a look of curious demand. "Why are you staring?"

"Just thinking."

"About the operation?"

It was risky. But he lived for risks. So Travis leaned closer, rubbed his thumb along her jawline and smiled. "No. About you."

"Oh," Lila said, exhaling a puff of breath.

He liked seeing her like this. Those wide eyes drenched with desire and her pulse beating in her throat. His gaze dropped to her full, glossy lips. Pursed in consideration, they were worth a second and third look.

Before he could see if they tasted as good as they looked, there was a commotion at the door.

Like a minispecter, in walked Montoya with Garcia, his ghostly deputy a gray shadow. Not even bothering to hide why they were there, they made a beeline for the table.

"Senor Hawkins, senorita," he greeted in that quiet voice just this side of menacing. His dark eyes shifted between them before settling on Travis. "What are you doing?"

"Eating." Travis leaned back, wrapping one arm

around the back of the chair as he gave the policeman a direct look. "How about you? Found any murdered chefs lately?"

He reached under the table to pat Lila on the knee when she gave a choking sort of laugh, then left his hand there. Because it felt good.

"You're stirring up trouble," Garcia said, his furious whisper giving color to a man who otherwise faded into the woodwork. "You *are* trouble. The both of you."

Travis didn't catch enough of Montoya's mutter to know more than it was said in Spanish. But whatever he said put a plug in Garcia's complaints. It didn't shut the guy down, though. Travis watched with interest as the stick pole of a man gritted his teeth and clenched his fists like he wanted to take a swing.

Interesting.

"What, may I ask, do you think to accomplish by this harassment?"

"Harassment?"

"No laws broken here," Travis said at the same time as Lila's exclamation. "We're patronizing a public establishment, paying for our meals and drinks. What's the problem?"

"You're upsetting people. You're asking questions. You're pushing your nose in where it doesn't belong," Garcia snapped, leaning down to get in Travis's face. "That's the problem."

"Good," Travis said with a slow smile, satisfaction filling him as he stared into the deputy's eyes. "That's exactly what I want to be doing."

"Enough," Montoya said quietly, laying one hand on

his deputy's shoulder and squeezing with enough pressure that Travis could see the indentations. He had to credit Garcia. For a long second, it looked like the guy was going to ignore the order—and the pain.

Finally, the skinny man straightened. He still crossed his arms over his chest and tried an intimidating glare. But Travis had cut his teeth on terrorists. One skinny deputy was child's play.

"Did you track down that dead chef yet?" Travis asked, directing his question at Garcia. "How about that guy who abducted Ms. Adrian? Do you have any details or are you still pretending none of this exists?"

"You're questioning us? We're the police in this town. We don't need some hotshot jerk who couldn't hack the SEALs trying to tell us how to do our job."

Other than giving Lila's hand a squeeze when she gasped, Travis ignored Garcia's taunt. No, he decided, ignoring was too good for the guy.

So he tilted his chair back. And smiled.

Garcia's face turned tomato red, and those watery eyes bulged. Travis's smile widened.

"You're all washed up, you cocky son of a bitch. A has-been," Garcia ground out through clenched teeth. "You don't know jack about police work. Or any work. All you're good at is lying on the beach."

This time Travis laughed out loud. Because, damn, the guy was reaching.

"Actually, he doesn't lie on the beach, he swings in a hammock," Lila corrected in cheerful tone. "It's a tiny difference, but I think it counts, don't you?"

God. He might be falling in love.

Before he could decide, Garcia lunged. Montoya grabbed him before he made contact.

"That's enough," Montoya snapped, finally losing his cool. Going toe to toe with Garcia, he issued a sharp order.

Enjoying himself now, Travis wrapped his fingers over Lila's to stop her from nervously flexing them and settled back to watch the show.

"What's going on?" she asked, leaning into him close enough that the whispered question tickled his ear and her breast warmed his arm.

"Montoya's ordering Garcia to go back to the station house, shuffle some papers and get out of our faces," Travis told her, not bothering to keep his voice down as Garcia started to argue. He liked watching the cop's reaction. It was telling enough to give him a solid handle on where to focus next.

"My apologies," Montoya said when his deputy finally turned heel and stormed from the restaurant, shoving and cussing the whole way. "May I sit?"

Travis gestured to the empty chair.

"Your deputy has some issues."

"The internal workings of my department are my responsibility, and I'll handle them, thank you." The unspoken *back off* was clear in Montoya's voice as he took a seat and tidily folded his hands on the table. "What concerns me right now is your actions."

"Lunch is concerning?" Travis crunched down on a salsa loaded tortilla chip.

After a long, cold stare, Montoya turned his attention—and his body—toward Lila.

"Senorita, you have a family who must be concerned about you."

Instead of tossing around more attitude, Travis held his breath and waited for her reaction. She'd used her laptop and Paulo's satellite server to send one email, two days ago. Letting her roommate know not to worry, she'd explained. She'd blown him off when he'd told her that Paulo wouldn't mind her using it a little longer, to let her family know she was okay.

They'd talked about plenty of things over the last few days. But her family and his career had both been off-limits. He knew his reasons, but the more time he spent with her, the more he really wanted to know hers.

But it looked like his curiosity—and Montoya's—were going to go unanswered, because Lila only offered a disinterested shrug.

"You are a career woman, which means you have re-sponsibilities," the cop said, taking a different tack now. "Those responsibilities cannot be met here in Puerto Viejo. You'd do well to let this go and return to your home. To your life there."

"You're the one who told me to stick around," Lila said, outrage clear on her face.

"Perhaps that was my mistake. To rectify it, I will help you acquire the necessary documents to leave our town and return to your own country."

"Sounds like a bribe to me." Travis arched one brow at Lila. "Sound like a bribe to you?"

Unlike Garcia, Montoya had a solid handle on his reactions. So he just smiled.

"No bribery intended, senor. I'm simply doing my

duty as an officer of the law to help an unfortunate victim. My superiors would agree."

Uh-huh. So it might be a bribe, but it wouldn't get Montoya into any trouble.

"Just out of curiosity, did you bother looking for Rodriguez?"

Montoya drummed his fingers on the table a few times before inclining his head.

"It is not my habit to inform civilians, especially non-residents, of the status of anything to do with the *policia*. But in this particular case, I will make the exception." He looked around carefully, as if making sure nobody knew he was making an exception. "In the process of looking into Señorita Adrian's accusations, I have confirmed that Señor Rodriguez is missing."

"Missing?" Lila prodded.

"He has not been home to his apartment. He has not reported in to work. Nobody, it appears, has spoken with him since the evening of your call."

"Would that be the call I made telling you that I'd witnessed a murder? The one that you didn't bother to investigate?"

"It was through my investigation that I was able to confirm that Señor Rodriguez is missing." Montoya paused a beat, whether because the guy had a sense of humor or just for impact, he couldn't tell. "I can tell you that the investigation is ongoing. Which is why I'd prefer that you stay away from Casa de Rico. Your presence here is causing stress to the proprietor and staff. We will resolve this matter as quickly as possible so that you can leave Puerto Viejo."

Travis had a gut-deep urge to punch the man in the face. But since a night in jail would leave Lila unprotected, he decided to settle for viciously shredding the man with only his words. This time it was Lila squeezing his knee before he snapped.

"How about Mr. Hawkins? Are you planning to push him around? To order him to stay away from local businesses or celebrate when he leaves town?"

"Senor Hawkins is the guest of Senor Constantine. A man who owns property in Puerto Viejo and, as such, contributes taxes. As a resident, it's my responsibility to offer protection to Senor Constantine and his guest."

Damn, Travis shook his head. The man really did have a serious issue with tourists. That, and he obviously had an easier time trying to intimidate visiting women.

Enough was enough.

"Let's go," Travis ordered, getting to his feet and tossing enough cash on the table to cover lunch and a tip. As soon as Lila joined him, he smiled at Montoya. "You have a good day now."

Not wanting to lead anyone to their hideaway, he headed for Paulo's instead. He and Lila maintained silence all the way to the beach path that led to the bungalow. He felt her shaking against his arm.

Shit.

She'd been handling everything so well, he forgot just what that everything was. No wonder she was getting shaky.

"Hey—" he wrapped an arm around her, shifting so he could gauge her stress level. He was pretty sure there wasn't any chocolate at Paulo's place, but maybe he could distract her with sex.

Then he got a good look at her face.

"Why are you laughing?"

"The look on Montoya's face," she said, still giggling. "He looked like he was sucking a lemon when he claimed that you're under his protection."

"I don't think he's capable of protecting me. Or anyone," Travis replied, ushering her into the bungalow. Once inside, his initial plan to settle her somewhere safe so he could follow Garcia faded in the knowledge that they were alone, with a bed right there in the next room. They'd done it in a lot of places so far, but they'd yet to make love in an actual bed.

Maybe it was time.

So instead of laying out his plan, Travis pulled her into his arms and took her mouth in a hot, wet kiss.

Oh, how she wanted him.

So much.

Too much, Lila acknowledged, pulling away before she lost the ability to think.

"So did we learn anything new?" Lila asked when she'd caught her breath. Wow, the man had a way with his lips. She was pretty sure every time he kissed her, a dozen brain cells melted from the heat.

"Enough that you're going to hang out in a safe place while I track Garcia tonight."

Ignoring the idea of being stashed somewhere like a child—or worse, a pretty toy he didn't have time to play with—Lila focused on the rest of his plan.

"You think Garcia is the one?" Lila shook her head. "I didn't see much of the shooter, but that arm had a little color and meat on it. So he might be behind it, but he didn't pull the trigger."

"He's involved. I'm going to find out how deeply."

"Are you going to wear camo and paint your face, skulk around in the bushes and do that serpentine thing?"

"I'm blown away at your knowledge and respect of all things SEAL," he said with an amused smirk.

She opened her mouth to reel off facts, figures and details of the SEALs, from missions to training to team structure. Then snapped her teeth closed before the words could escape.

"You shouldn't go alone," she said instead.

"That's not your call." Pulling open the false front on a cabinet to reveal a safe, he spared her a glance. "Don't worry. I'll make sure you're covered."

Covered?

"Is that military speak for getting me a babysitter?"

"What's the problem?" he asked, straightening with a wince.

"The problem is, I don't want to be tucked away like a good girl and told to follow orders."

"Have I tucked or ordered? Or, for that matter, even once indicated that I think you're a good girl?"

"No."

"Then what's with the attitude?"

Lila hesitated. She'd bared her body to the man, and now she was afraid to be honest?

"I grew up with that attitude," she finally confessed,

walking over to stand close enough to him so she could see the minute gold flecks in his dark eyes. "All my life, I've been expected to be a pretty accessory. To sit silently where someone else decided I belonged until it was time for me to come out as decoration."

"All your life? So it's a family issue?" Seeing the acknowledgment in her eyes, he shook his head. "You're all grown up now. Why are you still carrying it?"

"Some things don't change with age. My father's expectations being one of them."

"Are you meeting those expectations?"

"Not a single one," she said with a bitter laugh, crossing over to drop onto the couch. "I tried when I was younger, but finally I realized that who my father wanted me to be wasn't who I wanted me to be. So I made a choice."

At his questioning look, she said, "I chose me."

She waited for him to ask how her father had taken that, what his thoughts were. So she was surprised when he said, "That's the best choice."

"Not according to my father. He's still trying to control my life. That's probably why so often I go out of my way to do the opposite of whatever I'm told."

"Is that a warning?"

"More like a heads-up," she laughed. "I always try to do what someone asks, but the minute it's an order, I go in the other direction."

"I'll keep that in mind."

She watched him shift his leg, bend his knee, then straighten it again. Nothing showed on his face, but he had to be in pain. She'd spent enough time exploring his body to know that the scars were recent, pink and slightly puffy.

He'd obviously been injured.

On duty?

He crossed over to drop onto the couch next to her. It was only because she was watching for it that she saw the infinitesimal flash of pain.

"Are you okay?" she asked quietly.

"Fine."

He didn't snap the word but it was close. Message received. He didn't want to talk about it.

Even though she knew every centimeter of his body, Lila gave him a thorough once-over. The man was gorgeous. So fit, even his muscles had muscles. Even after months on leave, swinging in a hammock, his body was a machine.

Fitting, she supposed, since he'd made a career out of using it as a weapon. And he wasn't the type to be careless with a military weapon.

Which meant that he'd been injured on duty.

Which, she realized with a tiny pang, was probably why he wasn't on duty. Why he wasn't talking about reporting in or needing to be back on base.

"Are you still on active duty?" she heard herself.

"Doubting my ability to take care of you?" This time he did snap the words.

"No. But I can see that you're hurting. Maybe it'd help to talk about it," she suggested quietly.

"Maybe we should talk about your family first. You know, you fill me in on all of the details you've skipped over. Who your father is, what you've done to rebel, why you refuse to ask for help."

Lila blinked back her hurt at the ferocious tone, but couldn't say it wasn't fair. She supposed they both had their secrets. Even if none were really secrets any longer, that didn't mean they wanted to bare their hearts.

But she couldn't let him keep hurting like that.

Lila jumped up and grabbed a pair of bundled socks off the pile of laundry someone had left on the couch, then went to the kitchen to search the pantry for the bag of beans she remembered putting there last week. She poured the beans into a sock, executed a quick knot and put it in the microwave.

While it heated, she dampened a dish towel, wrapping it around the hot sock and carrying that back to where Travis sat.

"What are you doing?"

"Making a hot compress for your knee. You've been pushing it pretty hard. This should ease the swelling." Kneeling, she laid the compress on his leg, taking care to tuck it under the joint to keep a slight bend in the knee. "There. That should help."

Risking a glance at his face, she hid her wince behind a wide smile. She didn't know if that was anger or embarrassment, but whichever it was, his face was like ice. Cold, sharp and deadly.

"Anything else you want while I'm down here?" she joked, hoping a little naughty humor would break some of that ice.

When it didn't, she let out a breath and pushed to her feet. Looked around, desperate for something to do. The broken furniture had been hauled away, and the air was scented with lemon as if someone had polished what was left. So cleaning was out. A single glance dismissed the kitchen. They'd just had lunch.

"Where's your face paint? I can get it for you while that works its magic."

His expression didn't change.

Lila knew that look. The, you failed so I'm punishing you with icy disapproval, look.

Give him a break, she told herself. He'd spent four days protecting her, keeping her company, making her moan with pleasure. He didn't deserve to pay for her years and decades of father issues.

But she couldn't help it.

"Okay, *Hawkins*," she snapped, emphasizing his last name. "Don't give me that look. You were in pain, I'm helping. I'm not mothering you, I'm not babying you. So don't go all manly on me."

His expression didn't change, but he did arch one eyebrow.

"You know what I mean. All offended like I'm impugning your manhood or dissing the size and skill of your talent." A wave of her hand toward his crotch confirmed which talent she was talking about. That got her a lip twitch.

"We've spent the last couple of days doing naked gymnastics together. Do you really think that I am so self-absorbed that I didn't notice the scars on your knee or that you limp sometimes?"

"I never thought of you as self-absorbed. I did, however, believe I was so damned good at sex that you didn't notice anything beyond the pleasure I was pouring over your body."

"Well you did pour on an amazing amount of pleasure," she teased, curling up on the sofa beside him. "But yeah. I noticed everything about you."

His dark eyes sparked with something she didn't recognize. She knew what the answering heat flaming in her belly meant, though.

Ignoring it, she rubbed her hand over his arm and gave him a beseeching smile.

"Please. Will you tell me what happened?"

She wasn't surprised when he shrugged, but she was when he told her, "I blew out my knee."

Well, that wasn't much in the way of details, but that he'd actually opened up enough to share that much melted her heart.

Then she noticed the pain in his eyes. Pain beyond his physical injury.

"That kind of injury isn't going to go away quickly, is it?"

"Already did months of physical therapy. This is about as good as it's going to get."

Lila's heart sank into her toes.

"Which undoubtedly affects your ability to perform your regular duties as a SEAL."

"Undoubtedly."

"What's your rating?" At his frown, she quickly added, "Special Ops, I know. But what else?"

"EOD."

"Ahh." She didn't have years of Special Ops training, but decades of socializing in the vicious jungles of high society had taught her plenty. So she kept her smile easy, her expression upbeat and her tone light.

But her heart broke for him.

She knew what his words meant to his career. There was no way he could perform the required duties given his injury.

He wasn't on leave.

He'd been discharged.

Lila couldn't imagine the devastation he must feel. She wanted to wrap her arms around him, cuddle him tight and promise to do anything to help him feel better.

But she could see the pain in his eyes, and knew that there was nothing that'd make it better. Not hugs. Not talking it out. Not even hot, wild sex.

A part of her wanted to curl up and cry. Her father was right. When push came to shove, she couldn't hack it. She didn't have what it took to help the man she...

Liked. Liked a lot. More than she'd ever liked anyone else. Liked, teetering on loved. Which terrified her more than men with guns, dirty cops and her father all rolled into one.

"Don't look so freaked out," he said, clearly reading her expression but not the reason. "I'm alive. My brain is solid and my body, while not up to SEAL standards, is still working. I can keep you safe."

"Who's questioning your abilities?"

"You are. You're acting like you figure I can't handle simple recon because I'm a cripple."

It took Lila three seconds to haul her chin off her chest. As soon as she did, she threw her hands in the air.

"What is your problem? Who the hell thinks you're a cripple?"

"The US Navy, for one."

"Ooh, the perfect Navy. Don't get me started on what I think of the military and their idea of perfection."

"You have issues with the military?"

Oh, let her count the ways.

"Explosive ordnance disposal means you have nerves of steel and specialize in electronics. That's in addition to all the other training you'd have had. Nobody reaches the rating of chief petty officer without leadership skills. And then there's all that SEAL tech training. Did you store all that in your knee?" She gave him a frustrated stare. "You have everything to offer. So why would I doubt that you'd keep me perfectly safe?"

"You have an interesting grasp on navy terminology, heavy on understanding how the SEALs work. Why?"

"Maybe I read a lot."

"Or?"

She wanted to brush aside the question with some innocuous response. She had one right there, on the tip of her tongue. But she couldn't do it.

He'd cared enough to open up and share with her. How could she do any less?

"Actually, my father is tight with a Navy SEAL and talks about him all the time." Incessantly, as a matter of fact. "I've picked up some things over the years."

There, she thought with a smile. She bared one of her secrets. Okay, so she'd more danced around the edges of it, but she'd still shared.

"Yeah? What team?"

Nope. She'd share her body, she'd tell him her every secret fantasy. But explaining that her brother, *the most perfect man in the world*, was a SEAL and had served on the same team as Travis? That was simply TMI.

"I'm pretty sure the guy retired," she said, sidestepping, swallowing the bitterness coating her tongue at the memory of the party her father had thrown for that event. Despite his fury at losing bragging rights to a SEAL offspring, he'd made sure to wring every drop of notoriety out of it while he could with a huge retirement party for her brother.

"So is all of this your way of saying you don't think I can handle going after Garcia alone?"

Lila blinked, a little amazed at how much poison was dripping from that voice.

"I think Garcia and his ilk are small potatoes for you. They don't stand a chance against someone with your skills and talents. Unless you keep up this pity party you've got going on." She shoved to her feet and crossed the room, needing to pace off the anger. "You're a freaking Super SEAL, aren't you? Just because you aren't on active duty doesn't mean that superpower goes away. A SEAL is a SEAL forever, Hawkins. That brotherhood, it's forever. So contact one of your team. Some of them must have retired. See what they're doing. Better yet, do whatever you want. Find another military option. Work in the private sector. Security or police or, hell, keep swinging in a hammock."

She had to throw her hands in the air to keep from throwing them around his body and holding tight in hopes of easing his pain.

But there was only one way she could think of that would matter. She didn't want to do it for a million reasons, not the least of which was being put in a safe corner to wait while the qualified grownups did the job. But she could see that Travis needed this.

"Let's go," she said, sweeping her hand toward the door. "You need to fill me in before you drop me off wherever I'm going. I don't supposed it's a spa or salon? I could really use a little pampering."

Chapter 13

As dives went, Desperados was about average: dirty, rank and full of lowlifes. The perfect place to meet a potential snitch.

Considering himself on duty, Travis sauntered into the rickety building with only one thing on his mind. Completing the mission at hand.

Everything else—everyone else—was locked away in a separate compartment in his mind.

He examined the bar, noting the exits first, threats second.

Front door, six windows, walls flimsy enough to walk through. Check.

Four refrigerator-sized goons, twelve armed thugs and a couple dozen drunks with attitudes. The bartender's hand twitched under the bar for just a second, so he was likely hiding a small arsenal.

Travis had a Glock and a pocketknife.

Seemed fair.

For just one second, he let the thought of Lila into his head and gave silent thanks for her little pep talk. She was right. He could handle anything.

He threaded through the bodies until he reached the bar.

"What you want to drink?" the stocky man behind the bar asked after giving him an assessing once-over.

"Beer." Resting one elbow on the bar, Travis turned to face the crowd. Dregs, losers and scum sprawled on barstools and in the rickety chairs.

It wasn't hard to pick out his target in the crowd. A short, round guy with pockmarked skin and a head like a peanut, he sat alone in a corner nursing a whiskey.

Travis waited for his beer before weaving through the bodies, hooked one foot around the leg of the chair opposite the guy and sat.

"You're gonna want to find somewhere else to sit," the peanut-headed guy said.

"I like it here just fine."

With the flip of his wrist, Peanut had a knife in his hand. With a flick of his hand, Travis had it in his.

"What you—"

"Pulling a knife on me is not only a mistake, it's downright rude."

"Who are you?"

Travis leaned back in the creaking chair and waited for the guy to figure that out for himself. The little man's eyes dashed from one side of the room to the other as if searching for clues. Brow creased, he gave Travis a long look.

"You're that bird guy? The Hawk, right?"

"Manny told you I'd be around." And had paid a hefty advance for the information this guy was supposed to be skilled at gathering. Other than teammates, Travis didn't like relying on anyone else to be his eyes. But his first duty had been to protect Lila, which meant using rats instead of reliable recon.

"You're a friend of Manny's, yes? One of the American SEALs?"

Travis shrugged. Former, ex. Semantics. Either way, he wasn't serving as a SEAL now. Which meant he wasn't hindered by any team ethics, if things got ugly.

"Rodriguez, Garcia, Montoya, Parker." Travis reeled off the names of the people involved, the ones he'd been observing, and watched the little man's eyes. "What've you got?"

"Lots of names. Not much reason." The guy tapped one finger on the table.

Travis tapped his own fingers on the table, a twenty tucked between them.

"Details," he said. "Details on each and every one."

"Rodriguez is roadkill, all gone splat. Montoya is square. No jive there."

"And before he was roadkill?"

"Snitches get stitches. Word is, Rodriguez was over his head. He got nervous and twitchy."

Travis was conversant in three languages, but that statement took him two run-throughs to translate.

"So someone shot Rodriguez because he ratted out his dirty pals? Who'd he rat to? What was he into? And who else is involved?"

The peanut-head guy tapped his finger on the bill and slid it out of Travis's hand. Apparently, that's all twenty would buy. Travis debated pulling out more, but he didn't like paying for intel. Especially not when he'd already paid in advance.

So he smiled instead.

The guy's finger stopped tapping.

"You know what I like? I like being able to depend on the people hired to work for me. Is my intel wrong? Were you not hired?"

Grinding his teeth Peanut just shrugged. Smart man. Because Travis wasn't finished talking.

"Now, what I don't like is being dicked around. Dicking me around would include doing things like withholding agreed upon information in the hopes of extorting more money." He tipped back the beer, finishing the tepid liquid in a couple of swallows. "So what's the deal? You dicking me around?"

"Maybe I just think we should renegotiate, you know what I mean?"

"You're sure you want to do that'?"

Triumph flashed stupidly in the guy's beady eyes, and he gave an eager nod.

All it took was a twist of a wrist, a thumb against a pressure point, and the dude went down with a scream. He panted from the floor, clawing at his chair in an attempt to gain traction. Bent at the waist, still gripping the guy and breathing through his teeth, since proximity proved the man didn't believe in regular bathing, Travis waited.

Peanut's cussing threats were a keening whine over the noise of the crowd. A few people looked, but nobody bothered coming over.

"Now," Travis continued as if they hadn't been interrupted by a poor attempt at renegotiating. "Who is dirty? And how are Garcia and Parker involved?"

The Peanut sucked air through his teeth for a few seconds, then seemed to realize he was out of options.

"Garcia, he's got his fingers in every pie worth tasting. Girls, games, blow. He runs them all. Has for years," Peanut said, the words falling over themselves as his eyes darted around the room in case someone was listening. Both hands wrapped around his empty glass, he leaned closer. "Word on the street is he's got something new, now. Something big."

Prostitution, gambling and drugs. Nice sidelines for a cop. What about the bartender? From what Travis had seen and heard, she was a woman who liked calling the shots and if gossip was to be believed, she and Garcia had hit the sheets a few times.

"And Parker's involvement?"

"I dunno." The man shrugged, his eyes darting nervously around the room. "Garcia is bad. He's the one you should be worrying about."

Uh-huh.

"Is he behind Rodriguez's demise?"

"Yeah. Yeah, he's the one."

For a lowlife criminal, Peanut was a lousy liar. And from the way his nose was twitching, he was working for Ms. Dory Parker.

Since a lousy liar didn't mean stupidity, Travis put a little covert into the rest of this op, leading Peanut through a series of innocuous questions ranging from his fishing habits to his favorite brand of beer to how many times he'd tried to bang Dory. It took buying the guy a couple more beers and three more scary smiles until he felt he got to the meat of it.

"Why is Garcia stalking the blonde?" he asked, his words absent of any interest.

"Do—I mean, Garcia, he thinks Rodriguez gave her something. It's no biggie, but he's kinda paranoid, you know."

"Word is she only ate his food. Did he slip secrets into the shrimp sauce?"

It took a solid heartbeat for that to sink into Peanut's head. As soon as it did, the guy burst out laughing, complete with a few snorts and a knee slap.

"Not the shrimp sauce, man. I hear she ate ceviche."

Well, there it was. Another checkmark in the Dory column.

"Still, it's not like he passed her info along with the bill. So why the suspicion?"

"Dunno. Just know Do—I mean, Garcia is sure she's got something. He's making sure she sticks around until he gets it back."

"And then?"

"And then he don't need her no more."

The finality in those words sent a frisson of fear shooting down Travis's spine.

What was taking him so long?

Lila paced from a cozy recliner to a rattan rocker and back again, each time peeking through the crack in the curtains. Nothing, nada, no one.

The enclosed courtyard was filled with colorful plants in vivid pots, an artfully rusted metal table and chair, and a two-wheeled tricycle falling into a begonia.

But no Travis.

"Can I get you a different chair, senorita? Or maybe something else to eat? Chocolate, maybe?"

"No. Thanks. I'm full and the chair is great." And she couldn't even think about chocolate without getting hot for Travis.

"Would you like the television? We have videos. Or a book? Glory has stories you could read. Something to help pass the time."

"No. Thanks, Manny." She shot the man an absent smile and kept pacing. "I'm fine. Just fine."

"The Hawk, he'll be back soon. You shouldn't worry. He's a big hero. His reputation, it's huge, you know. He has medals and awards and those, what do you call them? Commendations? He has lots of them. You're lucky to have a hero like the Hawk looking out for you."

He started reeling off facts, mission details—most of which sounded pretty made up—and career information—most of which was straight up impressive—all starring Chief Petty Officer Travis Hawkins, Navy SEAL.

"You know a lot about him," Lila said, slowing enough to give Manny a real smile this time. "Have you known him long?"

"A few months, yeah. I've known his teammate, Senor Paulo, since I was a little boy." With that, Manny launched into more stories, these all starring Senor Paulo.

Lila let the words roll right over her as she peeked out the window, checked her watch, then peeked again.

Where the hell was Travis?

And how damned typical of the man.

Sure, she'd asked for it. She'd practically insisted on it. Which made her even more angry.

She'd been the one to insist he go it alone. But he hadn't given her any information. Not even the courtesy of explaining his grand plan. Just, hey, this is my friend. A pat on the back, an absent, you stay here, I've got things to do and a warning that she keep her ass where he put her.

She flexed and unflexed her fists.

Her ass.

Where he put her.

"You sure you don't want something to eat?" Manny asked, his tone just this side of worried. "Glory, she's out with her sisters but she left food. Good food, if you're hungry."

"No, but thank you again." Then it clicked. "Glory has been cooking all the delicious meals we've enjoyed, hasn't she?"

"Some of them. Not all." He listed every meal they'd had, assigning the cook to each one.

"Glory cooked all of my favorites," Lila said, realization dawning. "Please thank her. Everyone's gone to a lot of trouble and I appreciate it."

"The Hawk asked," Manny said simply. "My family, we do anything he asks."

The man had pulled strings, used his connections and arranged for a different place for them to stay each night, complete with delicious meals. Just because Travis had asked him to.

Now he was offering her his home, keeping guard so she was safe. Just because Travis had asked him to.

Why?

Before Lila could ask, Manny went into a long recital of all the things Travis had done to make the world a better place, including getting Glory a better job at the hotel, kicking the butt of some guy who'd hit on Manny's sister and generous payments for every little thing. By the time the man got to a highly imaginative list of Travis's military missions and accomplishments, Lila was ready to scream.

Then she looked over and saw the hero worship on Manny's face and realized that she was being rude. Rude and ungrateful.

Lila took a cleansing breath, stepped away from the window and sat. She shoved her hair back, folded her hands in her lap and this time offered a real smile.

"So Manny, do you and Glory have children?"

Within a half hour, Lila knew Manny's entire family tree, had a solid handle on which relative had cooked which meal and was looking through the third photo album. There was so much love packed in those pages.

Lila had never felt that kind of affection. The family kind, where everyone smiled. Real smiles, as if they liked each other. Not social smiles that made for a good photo op. A family tree with branches that crossed and intersected instead of a single trunk with a couple of stunted sticks it tried to control.

Intellectually, she knew family could be loving and fun and happy. But she'd never actually seen it. But here it was, right between the pages. Her eyes were too blurred to even blink when Travis surprised them by walking in through the back of the house.

"Everything five by five?" he asked.

Manny leaped to his feet, jumping into a minute by minute rundown of the last hour and a half. Lila simply flipped, unseeingly, through the rest of the photos.

"Yo, Blondie? You ready to head out?"

She thought she'd been a poor guest once already tonight. So instead of responding, she carefully closed the album, set it aside and stood to give Manny her thanks.

"You want a ride to the boat?"

"We're good."

"Here's dinner. Glory made it for you before she left." Manny handed Travis a soft-sided thermal bag. "There's dessert, too. Chocolate, just like you asked, Hawk."

A tiny part of Lila's heart melted at hearing that Travis had asked for chocolate. She knew he'd asked because of her. To treat her.

But she'd learned long ago that no amount of chocolate could make up for patronizing dismissal. Nor could jewelry, shopping trips or sternly voiced disapproval. Now she was adding sex to that no-go list. Not even great sex.

So she offered Manny another thank-you, checked that her cell phone was still in her pocket, then silently followed Travis to the door.

She maintained that silence when he strapped the bag across his body and gestured to a moped she'd never seen before. Lila didn't question where the hell the stunted red wannabe motorcycle had come from. She just climbed on behind Travis, and watched for landmarks on their way to wherever the hell he'd decided they were staying tonight.

He'd decided, she realized, clenching her teeth again.

Just like he'd decided every damned other thing since she'd met him. The man was her father all over again.

She stewed and chewed on that during the bike ride.

By the time they reached the boat, she'd added her perfect brother to the mix.

"You okay?" Travis asked as he reached out to help her onto the deck.

Lila shrugged.

Apparently, he took that as her answer.

Typical.

Lila continued to chew and stew, her thoughts taking on a little extra bitterness as Travis expertly piloted the boat off to wherever he'd decided they were going.

When he moored in yet another little cove, she checked the GPS on that handy dandy phone to see where they were this time. And stood, arms crossed, until he got around to paying attention to her.

It took a few minutes.

"Okay, spill it."

"Spill it?" Lila wasn't being passive aggressive, although that was something she excelled at. She was simply buying time until she had a solid grip on her temper.

She liked this guy.

Most of the time.

Which meant, according to the rules of her father, the last thing she should do was show her bitchy side. So she tried for reason instead.

"I know I said you should handle the *mission* alone, but I still didn't appreciate the choices you made this evening," she said in her most reasonable tone. "Instead of conferring with me and discussing choices and options, you stuffed me in some guy's house and told me to stay. Like a freaking well-trained dog."

"Are you indicating that you have a problem with the manner in which I'm performing my duty?"

Could he sound any colder?

"Are you indicating that you don't believe I'm capable of understanding the basics of your mission? Like how long it would last, when to expect you back, where you were going and what to possibly expect if something happened while you were gone?"

"Sorry." He threw himself onto the hammock with an ease that Lila might envy if she didn't want to hit him. "I thought you were bitching about my decision to do recon on your behalf in order to keep you safe, to ascertain the people involved and to nail down the exact nature of the crime."

"No," Lila corrected. "I was bitching about your decision to stuff me in a stranger's house, then put that stranger on guard duty to keep me locked up while you went off and played hero without any input from me."

Furious that there wasn't enough room in the boat to pace, she shoved his hip so the hammock went swinging.

"You didn't explain what you would be doing while I was being babysat by your Manny." Whom she was pretty sure she could take down if things got ugly. "You simply took over."

"My job is to protect you."

In other words, he'd done it for her own good. Lila held her breath until the urge to scream passed. One more breath to cool her burning throat, and she shook her head.

"No," she corrected coldly. "You were not hired to

protect me. You were not even asked to protect me. You chose this little task."

She didn't know how he stopped the hammock from swinging by just flexing his leg, but it stopped a half second before he sat upright.

"You brought this task to me." In one easy move, he planted his feet on the deck and straightened. All the better to loom, threateningly, over her.

"No," she snapped, jabbing a finger at his chest to show she wasn't going to be intimidated. "You not only chose this protective detail, you orchestrated it. You engineered every element of it without asking me a damned thing. Not even if I wanted to be protected."

"You're being targeted by a crime ring with law-enforcement connections and no scruples about murder. And you're complaining about government-trained protection?"

Targeted? All the air whooshed out of Lila's lungs in one fast puff.

"You found that out? That I'm an actual target?"

"I found out a lot of things. If you're finished being pissed, I can fill you in."

"Go ahead and fill me in on what you found out. Maybe by the time you're done, I'll be finished."

Lila leaned against the side of the boat and waited for a barrage of placating bullshit.

"I haven't pinpointed the exact criminal activity being run out of Casa de Rico, but given everything I'm seeing so far, I lean toward money laundering. The bartender, Dory Parker, runs the show, but Garcia is a part of it and in the crosshairs himself."

"You think they're going to kill a policeman?" Why did that shock her?

"I think he screwed up killing Rodriguez, and as soon as he takes care of the fallout, Parker will have him taken out."

"And that's why they're after me? Because they think I can identify Garcia as the killer?"

"Maybe. Possibly. But I think it's more than that." Travis frowned and scrubbed one hand through his hair. "No, they're targeting you because they believe Rodriguez passed you something."

"Me?" Now Lila frowned, too. She thought back to her only meeting with the chef while he was alive and finally shook her head. "He didn't give me anything."

"Notes? A card? An autographed menu? Nothing?"

Lila rubbed two fingers over her temple in hopes of massaging out the information. But all she came up with was, "I paid for the meal with my credit card and he brought me the receipt."

Travis's eyes lit in the moonlight.

"Do you still have it?"

Of course she did. It was a business expense.

"It'd be in my laptop case, which is wherever you stashed my luggage." She couldn't remember there being anything written on the slip of paper. "Do you really think that's why they're after me?"

"I think that's what they're after," he said precisely before furrowing his brow in frustration. "The only thing I didn't get was a handle on the man who hit your hotel."

Nope, Lila didn't want to go there. She was sure even mentioning her father would ruin what they had.

"Look, why don't you just focus on the guys who are trying to grab me?" she suggested. Afraid he'd ask why she didn't think that particular guy was in on the grabbing, she lifted her chin and returned to her earlier attack. "And this time, keep me filled in on the plan ahead of time."

"My goal is to do whatever is necessary to get you home, while keeping you safe in the process. But if you don't like how I'm handling this, just say so."

For the first time, Lila saw the expression in his eyes and realized she'd insulted him. His comment about being a cripple flashed through her mind, and sent her stomach careening into her toes.

Not only insulted, but quite possibly hurt.

"You're handling it all fine," she heard herself say as she moved close enough to slide her hands up the delicious expanse of his chest. "I don't know what I'd do without you. You make me feel safe and protected and sure that everything will be okay."

Every bit of that was definitely true. And because it was, she took a deep breath and forced herself to add, "My father is pretty overbearing. He tries to take over everything, to call all the shots. So I guess I just have a few issues with the idea of someone controlling my life."

He gave her another one of those long looks. Nerves knotted in Lila's stomach as she waited for his reaction. For his dismissal of her feelings.

"I'm not looking for control over anyone except myself," he finally said, tucking her hair behind her ear in a gesture so tender that her eyes burned. "But my training—and I suppose, my personality—demand that when I'm faced with a threat, I do what I can to mitigate danger and safeguard lives. That's all I'm doing here."

Oh.

Lila wet her lips and tried to figure out why she suddenly felt let down. Of course she didn't want him controlling her life. But being a responsibility wasn't a whole lot better.

"You want to tell me what got you so twisted, exactly? It's not the recon, is it?"

Lila opened her mouth to explain, but couldn't think of any way to describe her family issues without sounding like a spoiled-brat society princess. Besides, she told herself, she'd already used up her quota of hot-guy-repelling bitchiness for one day. So she smiled instead and caressed her palms down Travis's biceps. With a soft hum of appreciation, she tilted her head toward the hammock.

"You ever make love in one of those before?"

"Given that most of my time in one was while I was in the service, that would have required a major change," he teased, his eyes just a little too watchful for her comfort.

He always looked as if he could see all the way into her soul, into that corner where her doubts and fears and secrets hid. So Lila did the only reasonable thing.

She distracted him with sex.

"Me, either," she said, fluttering her lashes. "Why don't we lose our hammock virginity together?"

Chapter 14

He didn't like leaving Lila again.

Travis remembered the look on her face the night before. Anger and frustration looked good on her. So good that a part of him didn't mind her pitching another fit. The makeup sex had been stellar. But it was that bone-deep hurt beneath her tantrum that'd warned him that he was treading on the ground of painful emotions.

Emotions she wasn't willing to share.

His own emotions a turmoil, Travis watched her sleep. Dressed in a silk shirt—the woman was class all the way—her body curled into the blankets like they were a long lost lover. Her hair was like spun gold threaded with silver, rich and tempting as it splayed across the pillow. If those mermaid eyes opened, she'd give him a look of blurry confusion before blinking it away to pleasure.

She always looked so damned happy to see him. Even now, after he'd confessed that he wasn't the Super SEAL she'd dubbed him.

Travis couldn't remember anyone, ever, looking at him like that. Welcome and joy and trust. He didn't know what to do with it.

So he'd do what he did know.

He'd make her and the world safer by ending the threat Parker and Garcia posed.

Still…

Travis gave Lila one last look and grimaced.

He really didn't like leaving her.

She was going to be seriously pissed.

That her father was an overbearing, arrogant ass was irrelevant when it came to Lila's safety.

So he did the only thing possible.

He yanked on his pants, turned his back on the woman who'd captured his heart and left to do his duty.

He'd make it up to her, he promised himself. He'd already started tugging the strings. All he had to do was wrap up this threat, see her to safety, then…

Well, then they'd see.

Even as he pulled himself up the stairs to the deck, he could hear her berating him for going. Like all things that stood in his way, he ignored it.

It wasn't like he didn't know how to be a team player, he silently defended when he came on deck and saw the crew he'd called in. There was nothing he valued more than teamwork. But that was with a team that knew what it was doing, one armed and trained and capable.

But as capable as Lila might be, she wasn't trained or armed. And he worked alone now.

"You good here?" he asked Manny quietly.

"*Sí.* Me and Raul and Hank, we'll anchor just offshore and make like we're fishing. Senorita Lila, she'll stay below," Manny said, his skin so dark it was blue in the morning sunlight as he repeated Travis's instructions back at him. "If anybody comes near the boat, we leave."

Ignoring the foreboding itching its way down his spine, Travis nodded. That was the plan.

"You have my cell number, right?"

"*Sí.* Your number, and that other one you gave me for just in case."

Yeah.

"That number is for emergencies," Travis reminded him. "Only to be used if I don't return."

"By noon, right?"

Travis glanced at the sun making its slow climb over the ocean and gauged the time at half-past six. "Yeah. Noon should do it."

With that and one last concerned look toward the cabin where Lila slept, Travis went off to get the job done.

Lila didn't need to check above deck to know Travis had done it again. The moment she opened her eyes, she knew he was gone. After everything she'd said, he was gone.

She'd thought he might be different.

That his good qualities—and yes, he had a million of them—outweighed the overbearing ones.

She was an idiot.

After a quick trip to the bathroom and time with the hair and toothbrush, Lila yanked on jeans and a dark tee, shoved her feet into flats and stuffed all of her belongings into her tote. She didn't have an actual plan, but damned if she was going to stay here, under orders, being ignored.

"*Buenos días*, senorita," Manny greeted as soon as she'd climbed the stairs. "Breakfast?"

Her fury intensified when she recognized the two other men, who were fishing, from Manny's photo album and realized that Travis had called in the troops for this little babysitting venture.

She wanted to toss the breakfast—and the men—over the side of the boat. But since she had twelve dollars and no credit cards to her name, Lila wasn't stupid enough to refuse food when it was offered. She popped fruit into her mouth, grabbed a tortilla full of eggs and chorizo, then stuffed three muffins in her bag for good measure. A swig of orange juice and she was ready.

She knew she shouldn't be mad at them; they were only doing what Travis asked. But Manny and his friends weren't going to just let her leave.

No problem, Lila decided. She had a lifetime of getting around arrogant men's agendas.

Manny must have noticed something in her expression because he took a step away from his pals to give her a commiserating look.

"The Hawk, he's only looking out for your protection, senorita," he whispered.

"Of course he is," she said in a saccharine tone. Noting that the dingy tied to the side had a motor, she finished her plan by amping up her smile. "And I'm lucky to have you gentlemen here to look after me."

That got a preening look from the two pals, but Manny's suspicious stare didn't dim. So she made a show of eating a muffin and pouring more juice. She spent a few minutes offering food all around, asking about families and generally bullshitting Manny into complacency.

As soon as she saw his shoulders relax, she went for it.

"I noticed a small leak in the cabin below. I don't know a lot about boats, but it kind of worries me. Do you think you gentlemen could take a look?" She countered Manny's narrow glance with a flutter of her lashes. Her dingy tone got a suspicious look out of Manny, but the other two just nodded. "Just a quick look. I know you're on guard duty and you can't all leave your post."

And just like that, the suspicion faded from Manny's face. He nodded, gestured to one of the guys.

"Hank can keep watch. Raul and I will go look for the leak."

It wasn't easy, but Lila managed to smother her triumphant smile. She felt a little bad since Manny had spent the previous evening filling her in on all the many household skills he had, including plumbing, and now she was using it against him.

But girls had to do what girls had to do.

With that in mind, she waited until the two men were belowdecks, then made a show of spilling the pitcher of juice. While the third man went to get something to clean it up, she went over the side and into freedom.

Now Travis would realize once and for all that she didn't take orders from anyone.

No matter how much she cared about him.

Travis slipped into the small outbuilding at the rear of Paulo's property, built to look like a shack on the outside, with reinforced steel walls in the inside. He had to admit that Paulo might have danced over the cautious line into paranoid land with a setup like this.

But his friend's paranoia worked in this case, since one look through the bungalow's window showed that the dwelling had been searched again. He'd taken that as a sign to get his ass in gear, get the intel and get back to Lila.

Lining one wall of the bunker was an arsenal. Rifles, shotguns, three pistols and enough ammo to withstand a zombie apocalypse. The other held food, because Paulo figured he might starve fighting off those zombies. A satellite communications center, electronics and a strongbox that Travis suspected held cash took up the far wall.

And there, tidily stacked in the center where he'd left it, was Lila's luggage. After a dozen years with a duffel serving his needs, he wasn't savvy on the names of each particular bag, couldn't tell an overnight case from a weekender. But process of elimination, and a look inside a slender leather shoulder bag, netted him the laptop case.

Unsurprisingly, everything inside was tidily organized, making it easy to find the leather portfolio filled with notes and receipts. Embossed with Lila's name in gold, the folder had pockets and sections, each carefully labeled. It took only a second to find the Casa de Rico receipt.

Frowning, Travis noted that Lila was right. There wasn't anything there. No handwriting, no special message, not even a thank you. Then he noticed the series of numbers across the bottom of the small slip of paper.

A transaction number?

Or, a slow smile spread over his face, a bank account number?

He glanced at his watch, calculated the time and figured he had plenty enough to check this out. He debated for all of ten seconds going back and grabbing Lila, taking her with him. She was awake by now, and if he knew her, she was spitting flames. Taking her with him for the rest of this part of the op would go a long way to calming that fury.

It would be a simple op without much threat of danger. Make a few phone calls. Hit the bank, the cop shop and the restaurant. If he knew Lila, she'd get a kick out of being part of it.

Besides, he wanted her with him.

Travis glanced at the receipt again. This was it, the key piece that'd break this ring and end the threat. With that, and Paulo's string pulling, Lila's docs should be here today. Which meant she could leave.

Get back to her own life.

It was a damned good one, from what he'd gathered from their chats over the last few days. She had a kick-ass career, one she was skilled at. She had good friends who went back a ways, a killer apartment in one of his favorite cities.

Maybe she'd be interested in adding a lover to the mix. Being protective, out of work and homeless probably didn't work in his favor, but he could change two of those three.

If she was interested.

To hell with *if*, he decided, shoving the receipt into his pocket and his hand through his hair. He'd make sure she was interested.

He took risks for a living—or had.

How hard could it be to dive into one emotionally?

Feeling like he'd finally figured out at least part of what he wanted to do with the rest of his life, Travis walked out of the bunker with a grin.

And his cell phone began to ring.

Scurrying around town, looking over her shoulder and jumping at the slightest sound was definitely on her top ten least favorite things to do, Lila decided as she approached the hotel's front desk.

"Hola," greeted the same dark-eyed brunette Lila had seen before. "How can I help you?"

"I'd like to get a room." Amping up equal parts charm and confidence into her smile, Lila leaned against the counter and gave her name. "You can just use the same credit card I left on file."

"Of course." The girl flipped open a ledger and ran her finger down the entries, then tapped a few keys on her computer keyboard. "The same room is available if you'd prefer it?"

"Actually, I'd rather try something on the other side of the hotel. A jungle view instead of the ocean this time." Lila added an innocuous giggle for good measure. "I have a ton of work to do, too, so I'd like to make sure I'm not disturbed."

"Sí, senorita," the desk clerk said agreeably, handing

over a key card before arching to look over the counter. "No luggage?"

"It's being delivered."

Lila held her breath for the entire elevator ride and fast-walked down the hall. It wasn't until she'd closed the door and flipped the security lock that she exhaled. It took another few seconds before her knees quit their wonky dance, but as soon as they did, she crossed the room, tossed her bag on the bed and checked the balcony. There was a handy fire escape for running if she needed it. Since it doubled as a way for the bad guys to get in, she made sure the door was locked, then wedged a half-dozen of the wooden hangers in the slider so it couldn't be forced.

Travis would roll his eyes and point out the many ways that wasn't an efficient defense, but she figured it'd do for now. Since she planned on being out of here before dark, now was all she had to worry about.

Well, that and doing what came next.

Figuring getting this far deserved a break, Lila unpacked, then used the hotel's amenities to take a long, hot bubble bath. Feeling clean, fresh and a little more relaxed, she debated room service but figured it was safer to stick with her muffin.

Then, knowing that it was time to pull up her big girl panties and do the right thing, she reached for the phone.

Travis wanted to rant. He wanted to curse and demand and blame. He really wanted to punch something. Instead, he buried the urges along with his fear and gave Manny a calming look.

"Quit beating yourself up, man. Just tell me again what happened."

"Senorita Lila, she was angry. She tricked me into lowering my guard, into making mistakes. She snuck away in the dinghy." The words were a little muffled since Manny had his head between his legs trying to keep from passing out, but Travis got the gist. "I tried to call you. Tried and tried and tried. I was afraid something happened, so I called the other number."

Dammit.

Pissing her off enough that she bailed was, possibly, salvageable. But calling her father's number?

He was so screwed.

Okay, he thought. The op's gone south and things looked dire. He'd been here, done this plenty of times. Extricating himself and his men—or in this case, his woman—from precarious situations was his specialty.

First, assess the damage.

"You called that number. Did you make contact?"

"It took seven tries but I didn't give up. You gave me an assignment. I'd never fail you, Hawk," Manny said with self-righteous fervor.

"And the response?"

"Response?" Manny looked blank for a second, then he shook his head. "You mean, like a message? There wasn't anything like that. I said what you told me. I said that Senorita Lila was here and she needed help. The man, he said Puerto Viejo and I told him yes. Then he hung up."

Seriously?

Travis scraped his hand through his hair and tried to process that.

He wasn't sure what he'd expected but abject indifference wasn't it.

"No ETA, no directions, nothing else?" he confirmed.

"Nada."

"Then it looks like we're on our own. Rally the troops, Manny. Step one, find Lila."

"And step two?"

"Step two? In step two, I'm going to kick some ass."

Lila drew in a long, slow breath. She wasn't ready, but that didn't matter.

It was time to pay the piper.

She needed Travis if she was going to get the rest of her luggage. But given a choice between leaving a message and hoping he'd ship it or facing him, she figured she'd be fine without it.

Or maybe he'd deliver it in person.

Maybe she mattered that much.

Even as the thought occurred, Lila flicked it away. They'd had a fling. One she'd blown to bits by ignoring his command and sneaking away.

There was no way in hell he'd ever want to see her again.

Lila had to blink hard to clear the tears from her eyes when the elevator reached the lobby. No point crying over something that was never meant to be.

As soon as she stepped out, she recognized the hulking bear in a suit as one of her father's staff, standing by the glass doors. Lila hitched her bag higher on her shoulder and lifted one hand to get his attention. Before she could wave, someone clamped a fist over her mouth.

Lila screamed anyway.

She kicked and squirmed and tried to bite. A quick jab of her elbow got a grunt, but the abductor kept dragging her toward a narrow hallway. Not sure if anyone had saw them and knowing her chances of escaping a second time if he got her out of here were slim and none, Lila fought harder.

"Calm down or we'll shoot Hawkins in the head," the man growled.

Lila stopped her struggles for a brief second. As much faith as she had in Travis's skill, she wasn't about to go quietly while someone took shots at him.

She kicked, twisting and turning until she could hip butt the guy in the groin. He cussed, loosening his hold enough that she could get her teeth around one meaty finger.

Lila chomped down.

He cursed, but not quite loud enough to catch the bear's attention. So Lila bit again, then let her legs buckle so her feet slid out from underneath the rest of her. Her deadweight pulled the guy off balance. As soon as his hold loosened, she gave a quick wrench and yanked free. As soon as her butt hit the floor with a loud thud she screamed.

"Travis!"

Travis walked into an impressive Charlie Foxtrot, his mind automatically using the military acronym for one hell of a mess.

Cops and suits—very expensive suits—milled around the hotel lobby with expressions of frustrated indignation. The reason why was obvious. What wasn't obvious was why the guy holding court next to the elevators was standing on a table. It sure gave him a good view of his minions, though.

Catching sight of Montoya's rigid face, Travis pushed through the minions.

"What happened?" he asked when he reached the cop.

"Senorita—excuse me, Ms.—Adrian is missing."

Missing?

Travis's gut clenched, fear gripping his body in an icy fist. There was a roaring in his head that made it hard to get past the single fact that Lila was in danger.

As soon as the roaring faded, his body kicked into rescue mode. Gather intel, pinpoint target, execute plan and release hostage—all while ensuring that not one single hair on said hostage's head was hurt.

But all he let show was an arch of one brow at that corrected form of address. "She was abducted last week and you blew it off. Why is this time different?"

"Please, senor. Last week the abduction was reported after the fact. It was not, as you say, blown off. This time, however, there are witnesses. And then there is that." Montoya inclined his head to indicate the man on the table. Middle aged with gilt hair and a chiseled jaw, the guy directed his minions like he was conducting an orchestra.

Cops to the streets, suits to the phones, hotel staff to the dungeon.

Who the hell was this guy?

Travis watched him toss off a few final orders, then jump gracefully from the table to stride his way. The man spoke with a few people here and there crossing the room, but his gaze stayed locked on Travis.

Interesting.

Once Travis got past the arrogant tilt of the head and the way the guy looked down his nose at everyone and everything in view, it was easy to see his resemblance to Lila.

"Mr. Adrian?"

"Mr. Hawkins, I presume. Perhaps you could do what these people seem incapable of, and tell me where my daughter is."

Travis was impressed. The guy managed to pack a ton of supercilious disdain and familial disinterest into that single sentence. He wasn't big on arrogant jerks, but he was pretty sure that level of asshattery took talent.

"I'm Hawkins. What's the situation with Lila?"

"The situation, such as it is, will be rectified soon enough. In the meantime, I think it would be best if you give whatever information you have available to the police before returning to your home."

Oh. Really.

Travis's lips twitched with barely concealed amusement that this guy thought he could give him orders.

"According to the police, Lila is missing. Do you have the details of her abduction?"

"Weren't you in charge of protecting my daughter? Given the current situation, what makes you believe that those details are any of your business?"

"Charged by what authority? Am I to take it that

you're the person in command of ensuring Lila's safety and issue such protective orders? Given that this is the first time we've spoken, sir, I believe there has been a dereliction of duty."

The man blinked. Frowned. Blinked again.

"Yes. Dereliction of duty on your part," he finally said, jabbing a finger in the direction of Travis's chest.

"Not possible, given that I was never given those orders," Travis countered. He'd enjoy this if it wasn't for the worry over Lila knotted in his gut. "But I'm happy to accept them now. Give me the details you have and I'll get her back."

Actually, he'd get her back regardless of what this ass did. But he figured he should give the guy a chance.

"Actually, my son will facilitate the situation from here on out."

Travis had been dismissed plenty of times in his career. So he recognized the tone. And ignored it.

"Details, sir."

The man's face flashed with surprise before anger screwed it tight. Before he could explode with more orders and abuse, a shadow moved between them.

"Hawk?"

Frowning, Travis looked over. His eyes widened in shock.

"Frosty?"

Holy hell, it was Frosty the Snowman, otherwise known as Lieutenant Lucas Adrian.

Lucas Adrian, Travis silently repeated, his head dropping back a little with the weight of the realization.

"You're Lila's brother?"

"She didn't tell you?"

"That'd be a negative."

"I want this man out of here. Now," the elder Adrian snapped. "He's disrespectful and insolent, and I will not tolerate his presence."

"Isn't the priority getting Lila back?" Lucas asked, giving a tilt of his head toward a handful of men milling between cops and suits. It took only a second for Travis to recognize them as fellow SEALs. Some of his tension eased at the realization that the best were on hand to rescue Lila.

So while Lucas reeled in his father's drama, Travis processed the new intel. Lila hadn't talked much about her family. Just enough for him to know she had issues with her father. There had been no indication that she had a sibling, let alone one who served in the Navy as a SEAL.

He could see why she'd kept all mention of her father on the down low. The guy was a nightmare. But they'd talked SEALs. They'd discussed Travis's career. Why hadn't she ever mentioned her brother?

He'd add it to the list of things to ask her as soon as he got her back. Right after *why the hell had she left*?

Before he could ask, though, he had to get her back.

"This man is not qualified to be in charge of anything, let alone the rescue of my daughter," the old man snapped, his expression cold enough to freeze a penguin.

"This man is as qualified as I am. Which means the two of us are a hundred times more qualified than you are," Lucas snapped, launching into an icy barrage of reasons that his father wasn't worthy of leading a sing-along, among other things.

Travis appreciated the support, but didn't need anyone taking a punch for him.

"Excuse me, Mr. Adrian," he said, stepping between the two of them to get right in the man's face. "But I think that's enough."

"Hawk—"

Travis lifted one hand.

"No. Right now the priority is Lila. I want every piece of intel, and I want it now. Because one way or the other, I'm going to get her in T minus thirty seconds."

Chapter 15

Okay, this sucked.

Lila told herself to focus on that, to count the many ways she was irritated and put out. As long as she thought about her grumbling stomach, the fact that her hair was a tangled mess that she had to keep blowing out of her face, and how bad her butt hurt from the fall, she was able to keep the panic at bay.

She knew where she was. This time, she knew the face of the guy who'd grabbed her and recognized the voice talking in the other room as the bartender from the restaurant, so she was sure that Dory Parker was involved. She'd been grabbed in a more populated place than before, which meant chances were higher that someone had seen something. Had heard her scream. Anything.

Her arms were tied behind her back to a table leg, but her ankles were free so she used her heels to scoot to one side. The table moved with her, scraping like nails attacking a chalkboard.

Lila froze.

She bit her lip, waited for the sound of her heart roaring in her ears to quiet, then listened intently. Had they heard her?

She still heard the murmur of conversation in the room beyond, but when the voices didn't come any closer, she slowly, carefully let out a long breath.

Lila scanned the room serving as her prison again, desperately mapping out possible escape routes. From the elaborate cooking supplies stocked in the greasy kitchen, she assumed it was Rodriguez's apartment. The grabby guy and the bartender were in the living room, cutting off access to the only door.

But there was a window above the stove. Lila squirmed around, trying not to pull at the table as she angled her head to gauge the size. Long and narrow, it had a flip lock and appeared to be painted shut, but if she could get untied, she was pretty sure she could fit through it.

Instead of a rope, her hands were anchored to the table with what felt like a plastic zip tie. It had no give, but maybe she could lift the table somehow and set her wrists free.

She froze, all the saliva disappearing from her mouth when the voices grew louder. They moved away again, but she waited.

Just in case.

That she'd essentially been kidnapped right in front of her father's head of security held a nasty taste of irony, offset only by the bitterness of knowing she'd walked right into a trap.

She should have trusted Travis.

Yes, he'd been high-handed and domineering.

But he'd also been honest with her. His only goal had been to keep her safe. Okay, she admitted to herself, he'd been a little bossy with it, but he'd never made her feel incapable or inadequate. Instead, he'd made her feel like he valued her. Not just for hot sex—although he'd been pretty darned appreciative of that. But over the last week, he'd show her that he valued her input, he'd listened to her advice. He'd made her feel special.

He'd made sure she had chocolate.

Oh, God.

Lila wiped a tear off her chin with her shoulder, not caring that the move scraped the table against the floor again.

She was such an idiot.

She let her head drop against the table leg and breathed deep to keep the tears at bay.

She'd spent her life crashing up against someone else's pride and arrogance. She couldn't believe she'd learned so little that she didn't recognize the difference between protective caring and megalomaniacal disrespect. All Travis had done was try to safeguard her. Instead of appreciating his skill, his time and effort, she'd thrown it in his face like the spoiled brat her father had so often accused her of being.

Lila vowed if she got out of here, she'd apologize to Travis and tell him the whole story, every single thing, right down to the fact that he probably knew her brother.

She stiffened when the bartender sauntered into the kitchen. The tiny brunette didn't look anything like a criminal mastermind as she pulled open the fridge and grabbed a beer.

"Want one?" Dory laughed and rolled her eyes. "Sorry, obviously you can't drink in that position."

"Maybe you could free me, then."

"That'd be a no," Dory chided, still using that friendly tone. "I can't risk you doing something stupid."

Lila debated promising she wouldn't try anything, but knew she wasn't a good enough liar to be convincing. Instead, she tried toughing it out.

"You won't get away with this, you know. The police, my family, the Navy SEALs, they'll be looking for me."

"Nah." Dory grabbed a bag of tortilla chips off a shelf and popped one into her mouth. "The cops are in my pocket, so they won't bother us. Your family is in another country. And if you're thinking that Hawk guy is the SEAL coming to your rescue, you really need to get a clue."

Lila's glare was for show, but her mind was racing. Dory obviously didn't realize who she was, and had no clue that her father already had people in place. And dismissing Travis like that? That was going to be what brought this whole thing down.

Travis would stop at nothing until he'd rescued her. Holding on to that belief with all of her heart, Lila realized all she had to do was stall until he found her.

"Why are you doing this?" she asked. "What'd I ever do to you?"

"That's crazy thinking." The brunette shook her head. "Life isn't all fair and tidy like that. It's not about what you deserve or payback. It's just one of those wrong place, wrong time things, you know?"

This philosophical cheerleader was in charge? Trying to wrap her mind around that, Lila could only shake her head.

"Still, I don't mind filling you in," Dory said, straddling a wooden chair and resting her chin on the back to give Lila a friendly look. "This has really screwed up your life, so while I'm not into that whole fair thing, I suppose it could be called fair to tell you why."

"I don't have anything, if that's what you're thinking. I barely spoke with Chef Rodriguez."

"I wondered. Garcia, he's my partner—" she put a little wink-wink-nudge-nudge into that word, as if she considered her partner a joke "—he's sure Rodriguez passed something to you."

"But you don't believe that?"

"Nah. Rodriguez was a dumbass. He thought he could steal from me, hide the money in a U.S. bank and then skip the country. But I don't figure he was stupid enough to put anything in writing." She tossed back a handful of chips. Speaking with her mouth full, she added, "I figure it was a verbal thing. Like, he told you what was going on."

"He didn't tell me anything," Lila insisted, leaning forward to give intensity to her denial.

"Then why were you and the hottie hanging out in the bar all week? Intimidation tactics?"

Well, yeah.

"They worked, sure. But we were pretty much done here anyway. The restaurant, it served its purpose and let us wash a lot of money. Enough that we were already winding things up, closing up shop and all that. Just a few loose ends to tie before we're done. You're one of them."

She pointed her beer bottle at Lila. "We can't have anyone linking us to criminal activity, if you know what I mean. Garcia, he's not big on moving so he'll stick around here. Which means we can't just pick up and go. Not until we squeeze every detail out of you that you know."

"Squeeze?"

"Garcia, he's got a weak stomach. You should have seen his face when I made him help me clean up the mess my guys left after hauling Rodriguez's dead ass out of that office. But me? I'm good at the torture thing. Knives are my specialty, but I'm not adverse to using fire."

For the first time, the woman's evil showed through her bubbly cheer.

Terror coated Lila's vision with a greasy black film. She had to blink a few times before she could focus past it to Dory's cheerful face.

"And then?" she finally asked.

"You mean after we get that info from you and finish everything?" Dory shrugged. "Then Garcia wants to kill you."

"Recon reports that Lila is being held in an apartment building across from the Apartamentos Blancos. Body heat monitors indicate two hostiles in the apartment with Lila being held in the kitchen."

"Weapons?" Travis asked, checking his own handgun before adding another two magazines to his belt.

"Both hostiles are armed. Two pistols and an automatic rifle, with knives on the premises."

"Accessibility to the apartment, specifically the kitchen?"

Lucas pulled a sketch out of his pocket and handed it to Travis. One side of the paper indicating the building, the block and streets with access points and sniper nests clearly marked. The other side was a detailed drawing of the apartment, Lila's location designated with a star. The op was outlined in the margins, along with two backup plans.

"The local cops have been apprised?" Travis asked, gesturing with the sketch.

"They won't be integral to this operation, but they've been informed."

"Montoya must have loved that," he said with a derisive shake of his head.

"His focus, his priority, was on breaking the money laundering ring," Lucas mused. "Protect the locals, to hell with the tourists."

"He used Lila as bait to break that ring," Travis pointed out.

From the look on Lucas's face, that was news to him. Not good news, either. The man's nod made it clear he'd be dealing with that issue at a later date. Travis wanted to be there when it happened. Hell, he wanted to eat popcorn and watch.

"Let's get this started." Was all he said, though. Adrenaline sparked and sizzled in his system, fueled by fear and fury.

Once they were in place in the apartment directly above Rodriguez's and the men had synchronized their watches, Lucas leaned against the wall, his forearm resting above his head, and watched from above while Travis used the laser drill to cut a small hole in the floor.

He waited until Travis had threaded the optical wire through the hole, then attached their end to a handheld computer. They did it again toward the back of the apartment above what was supposed to be Rodriguez's kitchen. As soon as the wire was fed, Travis ran the electrical. Within three minutes of stepping into the upstairs apartment, they had eyes below.

Each taking a cell-phone-sized monitor, they silently studied the layout. Parker had two goons with her in the living area. One of them cleaned a hunting knife, and the other sat on the couch watching TV while the bartender talked on her cell phone. Since they hadn't drilled for sound, Travis couldn't tell what she was saying. But she didn't look happy about it.

A slide of his thumb over the monitor brought up the kitchen view. Lila was tied to a table weighted down with a tube TV, an ancient microwave and a stack of cast iron pans. Plenty heavy enough that she couldn't lift it enough to slide her hands free.

Gripping the monitor so hard his knuckles showed white, Travis watched Lila struggle to free her hands from behind her back. Every few seconds she angled a look toward the door and stopped as if to listen. Then she'd resume her struggle.

The black wave of fury surged, coating his vision and burning his gut. He gritted his teeth and forced himself to move past it. To focus on the goal: get Lila out and get her out safely.

He could be as pissed as he wanted once she was free.

He wanted to dive into that room and get her out of there. Now. But the orders were to wait until all of Parker's associates had been rounded up. So after tamping down the fury and impatience, Travis adjusted the feed. He checked it again, then gave Lucas a satisfied nod and they both left the room.

They were halfway down the hallway toward the stairs when Lucas spoke again. "I'd heard you were good. Nice to know I heard right."

Travis wasn't surprised that the lieutenant had ran his credentials. It'd be stupid to bring a man onto his team without a thorough vetting.

"After I checked your service record, I talked to your former teammates. Looked at the details of your medical discharge."

Travis frowned.

"Some would say going that deep was pretty damned invasive."

"Would you say that?"

Travis took the time to dig beneath the remark and remember that the guy was looking out for his sister. The insult was still there, but understanding made him shrug.

"Family comes first, man," was all he said.

"I heard that somewhere," Lucas muttered as they reached the end of Rodriguez's hallway. Travis held his silence until they shut the door of the apartment Montoya had commandeered for them across from Rodriguez's. "But this was for something else."

"If not out of concern for your sister, why'd you run me?" he asked as soon as the door closed. He figured that was a more relevant question than asking what the hell was wrong with their family.

"I'm interested in plans now that you're out of the military."

"I've got a hammock on the beach waiting." Travis checked his watch. Montoya's wishes or not, he was going after Lila in three minutes.

"You're going to get bored swinging on a hammock," Lucas stated, his green eyes narrowed in concentration. "You need a challenge. Something that will maximize your skills and talents."

"Medical discharge," Travis reminded him. No point in expanding, since those words said it all.

"Irrelevant," Lucas dismissed.

That got his attention. "What are you talking about?"

"We'll discuss it after," Lucas said, glancing at his monitor. For a brief second, worry as intense as Travis's showed in his eyes. Then, in a blink, it was gone. "But I've got another question."

"About the op?"

"Nope. I figure you've got that covered. I'm just along for the ride."

Another test? Travis added punching Lucas in the face to his list of things to do after Lila was safe.

"Fine. What's the question?"

His hands hooked in the pockets of his jeans, Lucas arched one brow and rocked back on his heels.

"I've got a pretty good handle on your prospects. But let's just clarify what your intentions are regarding my little sister."

Sure he hadn't heard that correctly, Travis asked, "I beg your pardon?"

"You and my sister. What're your plans there?"

Shit. He had heard Lucas right. Travis blew out a long breath and gave serous thought to jumping in front of the bad guys. It'd be easier to take a bullet than face that particular question. Mostly because he had no idea what the answer was.

"What's this?" he asked, hedging. "Are you standing in for your father?"

"Hell, no." Lucas sneered. "If he actually deigned to show interest in Lila's personal life, he wouldn't even give you a glance. You're not worthy."

"You say that like it's a good thing."

"If he thought you were worthy, I'd be doing my damnedest to run you off." Lucas angled his head to check out the window. "No way I want some uptight, pretentious ass with more money than skills for a brother-in-law."

A frisson of terror did a greasy dance down Travis's spine. Brother-in-law? Was the guy crazy?

First, no matter what Lucas thought, he had no prospects. He was a destitute-by-Adrian-standards, broken-down former SEAL.

Second, he had no career, no home, no actual clue what to do with his future. And as much as he appreciated Lila's career and independence, he'd never go into a relationship unless it was as an equal.

And third, people getting married should be in love. He wasn't...

Travis rubbed both hands over his face, realizing he

couldn't deny his feelings for the sexy little blonde. But that didn't mean she felt the same. And even if she did, love didn't make up for the rest of it.

No. No matter how appealing the idea might be somewhere in his heart, he would never be Lieutenant Lucas Adrian's brother-in-law.

But he couldn't tell the guy that.

So he did the only thing possible.

He focused on the op.

And on getting Lila out alive.

Nothing else mattered.

"Well, well." Dory shut off her cell phone as she stepped into the kitchen and gave Lila a look that sparked with fury. "Looks like you really are trouble."

Her heart shaking so hard in her chest, she was surprised it didn't just fall out. Lila tried to bluff.

"How is that possible?" She shook her hands, the table rattling against the grimy linoleum tiles. "I've been right here."

"Turns out you're a big deal," Dory said, scowling. She checked her phone again, thumb scrolling fast before she gave Lila an assessing look. "Or should I say, your family is."

Lila's heart jumped. They knew who she was now. Was that good? Ransom meant they'd keep her alive. Alive and listening to her father crow *I told you so* was better than dead.

"So you're going to ask for ransom?"

"Garcia is. He's all sorts of excited." Dory rolled her eyes. "He actually thinks he can hold you here without anyone figuring it out, extort a whole pile of money from your family without them tracking down who's behind it, and then make the switch without getting caught."

Relief surged through Lila in such a rush it left her dizzy. She'd face a lifetime of her father saying *I told you so* if it meant getting out of this alive.

Then she got a good look at Dory's face.

"You don't seem to have much confidence in Garcia's plan."

"The guy is an idiot. There's no way he's not going to get caught."

Her mind racing, Lila waited for more. But Dory was focused on whatever she was typing on her phone. She typed, swiped, muttered and typed some more. Finally, she tucked it into the front pocket of her jeans and gave Lila a smile.

"Sorry about that," the bartender said with that way-too-friendly-for-a-criminal smile. "I had a few arrangements to make."

"Arrangements for me?"

"Nope. I have everything I need to deal with you here already."

"What were you arranging, then?" Lila's eyes shot around the room, desperately searching for answers.

"I had to book a flight, transfer funds, stuff like that. I'm actually going to clear out a little early." Yanking open a drawer, Dory grabbed a slim notebook and shoved it into her back pocket, then pulled out a gun. Lila wasn't a weapons expert, but she knew enough to be sure that one could kill her really fast.

"But first, I need to deal with you."

Her eyes burning with unshed tears, Lila watched as Dory checked the gun for bullets. Her gaze locked on Lila, and with a nasty half smile on her face, Dory started to aim the gun.

A scream tickling Lila's throat, she wrenched her arms as hard as she could. Her heart exploded with terror so loud it sounded like a crash.

It wasn't until Dory's expression changed that Lila realized something actually had crashed in the apartment.

"What the—" Dory spun, running into the other room. Travis?

Lila sagged, her head falling back against the table as relief poured through her with the intensity of a waterfall.

Travis was here to save her.

Suddenly, a gunshot rang out in a loud blast that echoed through the room, making her ears ring. Dizzy with fear, Lila pulled with all her might against the table leg until she heard it crack, then shoved to her feet, yanking as hard as she could. The table leg splintered, the top crashing under the impetus of everything weighing it down.

She jerked her hands free of the table leg, then stepped one foot at a time through her arms so her hands were in front instead of behind her. They were still bound, but at least she had a tiny chance to defend herself this way.

She started for the door when more crashes boomed out, like someone hit a wall, then came the sound of furniture breaking. She looked around for a weapon, grabbing one of the big, sharp professional knives off the magnetic strip on the wall. Hefting it in both hands, she held the knife, point out, in front of her and angled herself against the wall next to the door.

"Everybody down."

That was Travis's voice.

Lila sagged with relief, but didn't lower the knife.

Not yet.

"C'mon, Lila," Lucas said, wrapping an arm around his sister and half carrying her as they headed out the splintered kitchen door. "Let's get you away from this."

"Travis—"

"He'll be fine. I swear," Lucas promised when she tried to yank away and go to see for herself. "He's fine."

Lucas guided her out of the kitchen, blocking her from the view of the still cussing Dory and her goon, a lump of a guy with a contusion on his forehead and a bruised jaw.

And Travis.

Lila strained in her brother's arms, trying to look around his broad shoulders to see Travis. Why wasn't he escorting her?

"I want to talk with Travis," she insisted.

"He's handling the takedown. Let him have this, Lila. He deserves it."

Okay.

He did.

For so many reasons.

But she still wanted to touch him. To feel him.

To thank him.

But Lucas wouldn't let go; he kept murmuring that she was safe. It took a couple minutes of that before Lila realized he was saying it to himself as much as to her.

By the time they reached the hotel, she was saying

it, too. And, for the first time since her teens, she was laughing with her brother.

Her giddy joy faded the second they walked into the hotel lobby and she saw the suit-clad security detail. And her father.

At the sound of the doors closing, Wayne Adrian stopped midpace and turned. She felt Lucas stiffen at the same time she did.

"Hello, Father," Lila said from the protective security of her brother's arms. "Is this where you say, 'I told you so'?"

His face gray, his expression more haggard than she'd ever seen, her father only shook his head.

She barely bit back a scream when he lunged. Then had to lock her knees to keep her legs from buckling from shock when he wrapped his arms around her.

It'd been a pretty crappy day, so Lila would be the first to admit that her brains might be a little scrambled. But as far as she could remember, this was the first hug her father had ever given her. After a couple of hesitant tries, she managed to give him a half hug, half pat on the back in return.

"I really am fine," she assured soothingly. "Everything's okay."

"You could have died. You would have died. If not for Lucas and the team he put together, those criminals would have killed you."

Her spine automatically stiffening at the praise for Lucas—because of course, he was so perfect and always did everything right—Lila gritted her teeth to keep from snapping an apology for getting herself kidnapped.

Then she remembered that she had, indeed, got herself kidnapped. And that without Travis—and, of course, Lucas—she probably would be dead. So instead of putting on her bitch face—the one she always wore around her family—she rested her cheek against her father's chest and, in another first, simply fell apart.

Saying nothing, he led her away. Lila was vaguely aware of the elevator, even more shakily aware of a large hotel room. But mostly all she knew was her father's scent and the unfamiliar feel of his arms.

She didn't know how long she cried, she just knew she couldn't stop. Her breath came in jagged bursts, pain tying greasy knots in her stomach. She bawled with the abandon of a two-year-old and the ripping pain of a newly widowed bride.

She didn't know how long she purged the fear, but by the time she'd stopped, her brother was missing and the security team was on the doors instead of huddled around her.

"Go wash your face," her father ordered in a gruff tone, patting her on the back. "I'll call up for some tea and crackers. That'll settle your stomach. And your favorite meal is waiting on the plane."

Lila gave a shaky smile of thanks before stumbling into the well-appointed bathroom. She looked at the array of toiletries laid out on the marble counter through swollen eyes, not surprised to see that he'd thought of everything. That he knew her favorite brands both soothed and amazed as Lila wet a cloth with cold water and held it over her face. It took a good twenty minutes before she was satisfied that she'd released all evidence of her meltdown, and looked good enough to apologize to Travis.

She frowned in the mirror, then added a hint of gloss to her lips. She had a feeling she was going to need all the appeal she could garner just to get him to listen.

It wasn't until she returned to the room that she realized exactly what her father had said.

First. "My favorite meal?"

"Roast chicken with baby potatoes, carrots and asparagus."

Lila's lips twitched. She was allergic to asparagus. But her heart sighed because he had all the rest right.

"Thanks, Dad," she said with a grateful smile. She didn't expect it to last, but this fatherly attention was pretty amazing. But second, "What do you mean, the food is waiting on the plane? We're not leaving yet."

"We are. The helicopter is waiting to take us to the airport. You'll be home by nightfall. Your home or my home, whichever you'd prefer."

He was giving her a choice?

"I want to speak to Travis before we leave. Please, I need to thank him."

"I'm sorry, Lila, but that's not possible." Her father looked like he wanted to grant her anything. There was even regret in his eyes when he shook his head and led her down to the lobby.

"Of course it's possible. He did so much for me this week. He saved me today. Besides, I have to get my luggage he stored." And tell him she was in love with him.

"I can get myself home later this week." Seeing his frown, she quickly added, "Or if you don't mind waiting, I can be ready tomorrow."

"We're going now," her father stated, gesturing for his

security team as they entered the lobby. "You can send a thank-you note. I'll make sure it's delivered."

"No." Lila dug in her feet for the second time in the same lobby today, and let her deadweight drag him to a stop. The security circle stopped, too, surrounding them. "I'm going to see Travis."

"He's gone."

"What? No." Lila shook her head, still shifting from side to side in an attempt to see past her father's security guards. "He wouldn't leave without telling me goodbye."

"Apparently, he would," her father corrected. "He'll handle the police report, and then he's returning to the States with Lucas."

Lila shook her head, refusing to believe the man she loved would choose her brother over her. A part of her wanted to think this was one of her father's power games. But the look on his face was too honest, too sad, for her to believe that.

"Did he have a message for me?"

"He said goodbye."

The onslaught of emotions was so heavy, Lila felt as if she were simply caving in on herself. She was too empty to even cry. She could only stare.

"It's time to go, Lila." He wrapped an arm around her waist to move her along. Lila didn't have the energy to resist. "This is over. So let's get you out of here."

Chapter 16

Two weeks later, Travis stared at the wonder that was the Golden Gate Bridge, watching the clouds gently hug the dull, red towers. Even in the shadows of the redwoods, the sunshine was just warm enough for comfort. A light wind danced a shimmer of whitecaps over his beloved Pacific.

It wasn't a hammock on the beach, but a perfect San Francisco day was a pretty good place to figure out what the hell to do with the rest of his life.

No, he corrected. He'd already figured out what he wanted to do. Now he would find out if he could do it.

With that in mind and one last look at the ocean beyond the grassy knoll, he headed out to see the woman who held his future in her hands.

It hadn't been easy, but he'd been prepared to let Lila go. She'd made her feelings clear when she'd ditched him, so the least he could do was respect her choice.

Before he could change his mind, before he could beg for a chance to hold her and assure himself that she was okay, her old man had hauled her away. Smart, getting her away from the scene. Smarter, even, getting her away from him.

Even without seeing the world she'd come from, without Lucas's questioning his intentions, he knew they had no future.

He'd done the right thing, leaving.

But maybe it'd been a jerk move, leaving without saying goodbye.

All things considered, he'd have stood by the jerk choice. Until he'd received Lila's thank-you note.

A freaking thank-you note.

He pulled the heavy parchment note card from his pocket. The crease was worn from opening and closing it so many times, and the corners a little crushed from time in his pocket. He traced his fingers along the simple floral design and Lila's name before flipping it open. Not to read. He'd memorized it a dozen reads ago. But to stare at Lila's handwriting. The loopy scrawl made him ache for her.

If that'd been her purpose, she'd tucked it safely between the lines of the friendly and slightly generic words. *Thank you, appreciate your time, grateful for all you did.* Blah blah, freaking blah.

Did everything they'd been to each other come down to gratitude? Yeah, he'd protected her. And yeah, dammit, he might have been a little overbearing. But he'd thought there was more to their relationship than security and sex.

That's what he was here to find out, he decided as he parked his rental on the steep hill in front of a brilliant blue house. The white wraparound porch gleamed like a tidy apron, flowerpots overflowing with colorful blooms lining the railing.

He walked up the renovated Victorian's short staircase. The wide porch framed two doors, one a vivid purple, the other glossy maple.

He knew Lila, so he went for the glossy maple. With a single deep breath, he steeled his shoulders and knocked.

Someone else answered.

"Hi, there," a redhead said, giving him a thorough once-over. "What can I do for you?"

"I'm looking for Lila Adrian."

The redhead gave him a longer study now, the interest in her eyes shifting to suspicion. Given the evident mistrust, she surprised him by stepping back and pulling the door open wide.

"Please, come in." She gestured with the grace of a queen welcoming a peasant to her castle. And never took her eyes off him as she led the way down a narrow hallway.

"You're the Super SEAL, aren't you?"

"I'm Travis Hawkins," he corrected, looking around the living area.

"She's due back any minute now." The redhead pushed her long swing of hair behind her ear and sent him a flirty look. "Want a glass of wine while you wait?"

"No. Thanks."

That didn't stop red. She poured and she talked. By the time she'd filled a goblet-size wineglass, he knew her name was Corinne, that she'd lived with Lila off and on for the last two years, eight months. Her father was a banker and her mother a distant relation to the Dutch royal family. She liked sunsets, baby roses and U2, and thought Lila should give him a chance because he was obviously a nice guy.

How she figured that last part was baffling, since he hadn't said more than ten words since they'd met. He had the feeling her explanation could take hours.

Thankfully, the sound of the front door stopped him from asking.

Lila on the phone; her voice ricocheted around the hallway so that her chatter entered the room before she did. She said her goodbye as she stepped into the living room, but stopped with her phone halfway into her bag to stare.

Dressed more formally than he'd seen before, her chocolate-hued skirt hugged from hip to knee. Paired with a fitted jacket in the same shade, the austere look was softened by the creamy lace blouse that dipped just low enough to hint at cleavage. From the top of her hair, slicked back in a glossy roll, to the pointed tips of her five-inch pumps, her appearance screamed kick-ass professional.

This must be the Lila-does-business look, he realized. Confident, assured and proficient. It suited her. She was so damned beautiful. Even wearing a shuttered expression and looking like she wanted to turn around and head right back out the door, she was the most beautiful sight he'd ever seen.

"Hello, Lila," he greeted when she was silent.

"Look who stopped by. He just, you know, came to the door. I offered him wine but he said no. I'll put together a cheese plate. Maybe he'd want that?"

"Corinne." A quick look sent her friend into silence as the woman scurried out with her wine sloshing dangerously close to the top of the glass. Lila stood just inside the room, watching him without expression until they heard a door slam. Then she strode over to the couch. She didn't sit, but she did set her leather bag—he recognized it as her laptop case—on the couch before crossing her arms over her chest.

"This is a surprise," she finally said. "I didn't expect to see you again. Ever."

"I had to take care of a few things—" he started to say. Before he finished, though, she waved a hand in the air as if erasing his words.

"No explanations necessary. I ran out on you against your express orders. Doing so not only put me in danger, but also endangered numerous others in the rescue." She said it all so matter-of-factly, as if reading a cost report. "It's only fair that you walked out on me in return."

"It wasn't like I was keeping score and walked out as payback," he snapped. The look in her eyes told him she'd thought he'd done just that.

Anger burned away some of the guilt he'd been carrying as Travis strode forward. She angled behind the couch before he could touch her, telling him just how deep her mistrust for him went. Seeing firsthand how badly he'd hurt her, Travis clenched his fists, focusing all his frustration in his fingers. Squeezed it away. It wasn't until he saw Lila doing the same on the back of the couch that he realized that he'd picked up the habit from her.

"I found my new career," he heard himself say as if it were a confession. "It'll offer the same challenges I excelled at in the navy. But other than the occasional assignment, I'll live stateside instead of being deployed all over the world. And it pays a hell of a lot better than the military."

"What'll you be doing?"

"As of yesterday, I'm an operative for Aegis Global Security."

He tensed, waiting for her reaction.

"What's that?"

Travis frowned. That definitely wasn't the reaction he'd expected.

"A firm that offers protection in every form. Global, cyber, physical security, all provided by elite former Special Forces personnel. It's an impressive setup. Military protection for prominent civilians in jeopardy."

"It sounds like the perfect job for you." Shrugging off her jacket, Lila folded it over the back of the couch. "The company must consider itself lucky."

"Actually, the company belongs to Lucas. I thought you'd know that."

"Lucas, my brother?" She shook off the surprise with a roll of her eyes. "Why would I know that? Other than the occasional family dinner, I've had minimal contact with him in the last five years. Like you, he's Mr. Super SEAL. Out saving the world and ignoring the people who lo—" She bit her lip, then finished, "Know you."

She cleared her throat and started over.

"You're going to work with my brother?"

Since she said it in the same tone someone would use to ask if he was going to work in a puppy-killing factory, he hesitated.

"Work for," he finally corrected. "He's launching this security firm and wants me on board."

"And you came here to tell me that?"

Damn, the woman could be a hard-ass when she wanted to. He had to admire that.

"That's part of it. But mostly I came here to ask you to give us a chance," he confessed with about as much charm as a shy schoolboy. "What we have, it's special. I want to see how far we can take it."

For a second, hope lit in those mermaid eyes. Then she pressed her lips together and found her attitude again.

"What we had was sex."

"We had incredible sex," he agreed. "But that's not all there is between us. I think we owe it to each other to see where those feelings take us. See what we can build out of them."

"You don't mean that." She looked scared. More scared than she'd looked when that whack job bartender had pointed a gun at her head. Then she blinked as if an idea had suddenly occurred to her. "If you feel that way, why'd you wait so long to tell me?"

"First, because I had to finish the mission. I took down Garcia, closed down the money laundering ring and nailed the coffin shut on the criminals. Second, I figured you'd had enough stress—and you were pretty pissed at me—so I thought I'd give you some space to decompress."

"And third?" she asked when he hesitated.

"Third, I wanted to be able to offer you more than a beach-bum lifestyle. Hence, the new career." He studied her expression, but for the first time since they'd met, he couldn't read her. "What do you say?"

"What if I said yes, I'd like to see what kind of future we can build together? That I'm very interested and have strong feelings for you? But that I can't feel right being with you if you take this job or, better yet, if you have anything to do with my brother?"

It was like taking a hard, swift kick to the nuts. Mind-numbingly painful in a way that had stars exploding in his head and left him feeling bruised and nauseous.

But like any pain, Travis took one long breath and pushed right through it. And considered. It took only a few seconds.

An incredible career, one that not only fulfilled him but one that utilized the skills he was so proud of. A chance to live the rest of his life with a sense of accomplishment, to help keep others safe and to excel in his chosen field.

Or Lila.

He stepped around the couch and took her hand, grateful that she didn't try to get away again. His gaze roamed the face he'd spent every night for the last two weeks dreaming about. Those lush, full lips and sea witch eyes tempted, and his fingers itched to skim the ivory of her cheek before diving into the rich silver-gold of her hair to loosen that severe hairstyle.

Her scent filled his lungs, a teasing reminder of watching her in the moonlight. Of holding her close as they slept, her hair wrapping around him like silk. Of making love with her, watching her eyes blur with passion as she went over the edge of pleasure.

They'd laughed together. They'd talked for hours, about everything under the sun. They'd discovered hundreds of things they agreed on and had enjoyed the ones they'd debated.

They fit.

And most of all, she made him feel whole.

"You say the word," he told her, lifting her fingers to his lips. "And I'll quit."

Damn the man.

Lila pulled her hand free.

"If Lucas is engineering it, it'll be a huge success. You'd be crazy not to take his offer."

"I'd be crazy not to do anything and everything possible to make things work between you and I," he countered. "That's my priority."

Lila wanted to believe him. She wanted to reach out and grab ahold of everything he meant to her, whether he was offering it or not.

But she'd tried that once already.

And when he'd done nothing more than be true to who he was, she'd run away. Because despite her oh-so-wise advice and heartfelt encouragement, she hadn't let herself see who he really was.

Then he'd left.

Just left her with the aftermath of her own stupid mistake.

She wouldn't—couldn't—make that same mistake a second time.

"You have to make yourself happy first," she said aloud. "You have to find that something—whether it's with the military again, this job with Lucas, or even if it's just swinging in another hammock."

She couldn't be responsible for his happiness. Just like he couldn't carry the weight of hers.

"I'm not going to settle for anything less than being as happy with my work as you are with yours." He tapped his fingers on the strap of her laptop case. "For a while on that beach, I thought I could. But you reminded me of how important it is to love what you do."

"And you'll love working with my brother?"

"It'll require travel and irregular hours, dedication and training. Your brother is a demanding kind of guy, and he's damned ambitious with this plan to make Aegis kick ass. He respects my skills, and while he acknowledges my injury, he doesn't see it as an issue. Aegis is based in San Diego, but their operatives live wherever they want. Which means I could move anywhere. Even San Francisco. So, yeah. It's a job I'm going to really get into."

"I'm happy for you," she said truthfully, giving his hand a squeeze before saying again, "It really does sound like the perfect job for you."

"It is. But our relationship is still my priority."

Lila bit her lip, wanting to believe him. He read her doubts as easily as if they were written on her face.

"I know I should say that I'll never issue orders again, but I'd be lying. It's too deeply ingrained for me to not take charge when I see a situation going south."

Watching her face intently, he slowly reached out to take her hand. Everything inside her seemed to sigh at his touch.

"But I can promise that any orders I issue are never because I don't respect or doubt you. And I promise to listen better, and to always factor in your opinion, your wants and your needs."

Seeing the doubt in her eyes, he lifted her hand to his lips again and brushed a heart-meltingly soft kiss over her knuckles. His gaze locked on hers, he murmured again, "I promise."

Lila had spent a lifetime surrounded by powerful alpha men. She'd thought she knew what to expect from one. But Travis's words were like an explosion, blowing away all of her preconceived concepts and leaving the world wide open.

All she had to do was step into the possibilities.

She was terrified.

Not that he was lying. But that he really meant it.

She wanted Travis. She loved him with depths she'd never thought possible. She admired him and respected him. But she was so scared of being with him. Of losing herself to him. She'd spent her life trying to be independent, but Travis was so forceful, lived life so huge. How could she withstand that and still be her own person?

Slowly, carefully, Lila slipped her hand free of his and took an infinitesimal step away. Because she was watching so closely, she saw his wince. Saw the pain flash in his eyes just before his expression cleared.

It was that pain that made her realize what a jerk she was being. But she couldn't help it.

Trying to find the right words, Lila folded her fingers together, straightened then folded them again. Travis laid his hand over hers, stilling the nervous gesture and warming her so much, the fear melted.

"I'm afraid," she admitted.

"Of what? I'm in security, remember. I can protect you from damn near anything."

Lips twitching, she couldn't resist rubbing her hand over his chest in appreciation. For the words, and because she'd forgotten just how amazing his chest was.

"Of losing myself." She wet her lips and tried to explain. "I've struggled my entire life to stand up for myself against strong men. And even though I am finally able to, I'm lousy at it." She remembered how hurt her father and brother had been that she hadn't contacted either of them to help her when she'd first gotten in trouble in Puerto Viejo. "I get pretty insistent on being independent. So insistent that I was recently told that I hurt people who care about me."

"Like when you skipped out on me in Puerto Viejo?"

Ouch. "Yes. Like that."

"And you think I can't handle that?"

"I think it wouldn't be right to expect you to handle that."

He rocked back on his heels and nodded, his expression mulling as he considered her.

"I actually get that attitude," he finally said. "And I used pretty much the same argument with myself before coming here."

"You did?" It was her own argument, but Lila still felt offended.

"Well, you did ditch me, blow off my protection and needed to be rescued. So the independence thing isn't news to me. But here's the thing. As willing as I am to protect you, it's not because I think you need me for that. I have complete faith that you can take care of yourself."

"Costa Rican crime rings aside."

"Crime rings are the exception, not the rule. So I have to say in that case, I'd snap into protection mode," he agreed, his smile flashing. "But for life in general, I'm more interested in a partner than a subordinate."

Lila's heart simply melted. She wanted him so much, and this was it, her chance to have him. She opened her mouth to agree, her body tensing in preparation for jumping into his arms.

Before she could, he took both of her hands in his and pulled her close again.

"You might not believe it, but I need you just as much as you need me."

No. Big strong alpha men didn't need anyone. She was already shaking her head before he finished his sentence.

"I do. Seriously. Lila, you pulled me out of a crappy place I don't think I could have gotten out of myself. You not only reminded me of my purpose in life, you made me believe I could handle it. If it wasn't for you, I'd still be swinging in that damned hammock."

"My advice made that much of a difference?" Suddenly, she felt invincible. Like she could be as important to him as he would be to her. Her imagination soared, picturing everything she could do to make a good life with him.

She could spend forever making sure he never forgot how special he was. And, she realized as the last of her fears fell away, she would actually believe him when he showed her the same.

"I want that," she told him. "I want us. A future together. A life together. I want to see if we can make it work."

"I know we can," he vowed, releasing one of her hands to rub his knuckles over her jaw. "But I'm willing to give it as long as you need until you're just as sure."

"You're perfect," she said with a soft laugh, her heart finally settling into a happy place. And just like that, she had all the confidence in the world—which meant she had as much as Travis—that they'd spend the rest of their lives making each other happy. "We'll be perfect."

"I promise I'll respect your independence and value your choices," he said, brushing a whisper of a kiss over her lips.

"Then I promise to let you know when I'm feeling overwhelmed, and to always tell you what I want and need, instead of assuming you should know."

"Never assume," he said, the words a cadence she knew he'd repeated hundreds of times. "With one exception."

Using the hand he held, he pulled her to him until their bodies were pressed close. He wrapped one hand around her waist, his fingers cupping her butt and holding her tight against him.

"You can always assume that I love you."

Lila's breath caught painfully in her chest, but her pounding heart finally pushed it free.

"You love me?"

"Yeah. I love you."

"You know that I love you, too, right?"

"I'd hoped," he said just before taking her mouth in a hot, wild kiss that sealed their future.

And just like that, the final piece fell into place and her life was perfect.

* * * * *

COMING SOON!

We really hope you enjoyed reading this book. If you're looking for more romance, be sure to head to the shops when new books are available on

Thursday 7th February

To see which titles are coming soon, please visit

millsandboon.co.uk/nextmonth

MILLS & BOON

Want even more ROMANCE?

Join our bookclub today!

'Mills & Boon books, the perfect way to escape for an hour or so.'

Miss W. Dyer

'Excellent service, promptly delivered and very good subscription choices.'

Miss A. Pearson

'You get fantastic special offers and the chance to get books before they hit the shops'

Mrs V. Hall

Visit millsandbook.co.uk/Bookclub

and save on brand new books.

MILLS & BOON

LET'S TALK
Romance

For exclusive extracts, competitions
and special offers, find us online:

f facebook.com/millsandboon

🐦 @MillsandBoon

📷 @MillsandBoonUK

Get in touch on 01413 063232

For all the latest titles coming soon, visit
millsandboon.co.uk/nextmonth